Oh Susanna

Enjoy!
Love,
Karen Peeples Walker

Oh Susanna

An Old-Fashioned Love Story

by Karen T. Walker

Bonneville Books
Springville, Utah

ISBN: 1-55517-822-7
v.1

Published by Bonneville Books,
an imprint of Cedar Fort, Inc.
925 N. Main Springville, Utah, 84663
www.cedarfort.com

Distributed by:

Cover design by Nicole Williams

Printed in the United States of America
10 9 8 7 6 5 4 3 2 1

Printed on acid-free paper

Dedication

In memory of my mother—
whose story this is;
and of my father—
whose love sustained her.

Acknowledgments

A special thank you to family and friends who have continually encouraged me in my writing. Candy, you have amazing patience, great tenderness, and a gentle humor. I could not have written this story without your assistance. You know I love you. And Joker, thank you for being my Morris!

Chapter 1

Early June 1925

What in the world am I doing, lying on this scratchy, dirty ground? I asked myself for the thousandth time. *This is not the way I expected my day to go! Older brothers can be such a gigantic pain.*

For months I had been anticipating summer. Summer—my favorite season of the year. Summer—days of lying in the hammock, reading library books, swimming in the lukewarm canal, and riding Maebell, our fifteen-year-old sorrel mare, through the sand dunes. Summer—catching catfish in the Snake River, building bonfires on the shore, and racing barefoot through the spiky green grass. *Summer.* The word made my eyes light up with unrestrained yearning, my skin glow in anticipation of the delectable sun, and my mouth pucker in its longing for fresh-squeezed lemonade.

Unfortunately, I had ten brothers and sisters. Somehow, that just didn't leave much time for being alone. At eighteen, I had hoped to be able to choose what I wanted to do. Instead, there was always some necessary chore awaiting me.

Take this early summer day, for instance: a perfect day for finishing *Anne of Green Gables.* The earth lay warm and vibrant, freshened by a night's rain that had rinsed the cloudless, azure sky clean as fresh laundry hanging on the line. Best of all, there was no perceptible wind. Few things are more gratifying to me than the absence of wind, with the warm sun beating down on my back. In my mind, I have always equated wind with cold, and I crave the warmth.

From over by the front porch, the smell of peonies and lily of the valley filled the air with sweet fragrance, and the gently swaying hammock in the backyard was calling my name. Idyllic! Instead, here I was, lying on the uneven chickweed under Ol' Sal, Rudolf's 1920 Model T, trying to twist off a bolt up by the oil pan.

It seemed that I always got rooked into such tasks because my fingers were slender and able to slip into spaces the boys' more muscular hands just couldn't reach. I had been concentrating hard on the job at hand. The heavy metal wrench had slipped out of place twice already, causing me to cuss mildly as it hit my shoulder with a thud and bounced onto the packed earthen driveway. Each time, I was forced to fumble around to locate it again before carefully repositioning it. As I was trying the third frustrating time to get the wrench properly in place, I subconsciously became aware of a new and interesting conversation taking place above me.

"Rudolf, Fred, this is Morris. He's working up on the water canal for ol' man James."

"Morris, these are my brothers, Rudolf, Fred, Walt, and Sam." John, four years my senior, was busy with introductions, pointing out each sibling hunched over the engine or puttering around the car.

The boys loved Rudolf's car and spent many of their free hours tuning up the engine, washing and polishing the shiny, black paint, and working oil into the black leather top to keep it soft and supple. Working hard in the fields and doing chores together was a necessity. Still, when it came to their free time, the boys continued to spend it together. Rudolf was married but spent as much time at our place as his own. My brothers were best friends, as is often the case with farm families. Their school friends were busy on their own farms and with their own siblings.

"Glad to meet you," came the new, very deep male voice, rich with vibrato and warmth.

And then John muttered, totally as an afterthought, "Oh,

yeah, and that's Susie." He pointed to my skinny legs, bulky gray anklets, and sturdy brown farm shoes sticking out from underneath the car body. "My sister."

After mumbling hi's all around, John and Morris moved leisurely toward the white brick farmhouse. The house had undergone many changes over the years. What had started out as a two-room log cabin had blossomed with a large lean-to on the east, which became the kitchen, and a second-story addition for more bedrooms to accommodate our large family. Later, when the parlor was finished, the wide front porch was added, and the outside was bricked, the sprawling house took on a semblance of respectability.

Another stray. No doubt John will invite him to stay for dinner, I thought briefly and then returned mind and energies to the wrench and bolt problem.

John often brought home some stray for a meal or a visit. It just seemed to be his nature to befriend anyone or anything looking lonely or fascinating. John was my sensitive brother. He seemed to have that innate ability to discern almost instantly a person's character. Although he was pleasant to everyone, he easily spotted those with greater depth and gravitated toward them, usually making them into fast friends. John was probably my most handsome brother too, but if anyone looked closely they could see burn scarring covering his left hand and snaking high on his neck, especially on the left side. John always wore long-sleeved shirts, though, and between that and his congenial personality, many people never noticed the scars.

With a family the size of ours, it wasn't a big deal to set another plate on the table or even make up a bed on the divan when needed. Within a few short days, it became evident that Morris, John's latest acquisition, was going to become a rather permanent fixture. He'd show up for meals mostly, but John had latched onto a good thing this time. Morris wasn't above helping with chores or working on Ol' Sal. What's more, he actually understood finicky motors, and his tinkering, much to Rudolf's delight, brought some results.

Not that it was hard to look at Morris as he moved around the place. His not quite six-foot frame was both slender and muscular, with broad, slightly rounding shoulders, narrow hips, and strong, capable arms and hands. His skin was smooth and already well-tanned, bespeaking the many hours he worked outside in the sun. He was clean-shaven and sported a head of thick, dark hair. His smile, though, was his most arresting feature. It appeared easily and often during any conversation, with the top lip on the left side lifting slightly higher than the other in a crooked sort of grin. With sapphire-blue eyes sparkling and his deep laugh rumbling, Morris was not hard to like.

"What's ol' man James gotcha doin', Morris?" Dad inquired as we sat down at the long-plank dinner table. He and the boys had made the table years ago, and it seated fourteen people comfortably.

"Actually, sir, I'm his new water master on East Sand Creek."

"Hey, well, that's good," Dad exclaimed. "How old are you, son?"

"I'm twenty-three, sir. I just got home from a mission to the Southern states—the Tennessee-Kentucky area."

"Never been there. What's it like?"

"Green, lush land. People live in big, sprawling cabins to accommodate big, sprawling families. Great people! Friendly but pretty set in their ways. Old family traditions are strong there. Great food too—especially the fried chicken and dumplings—except when dogs are allowed to snatch a bun off the table, or a cat decides to take a taste off your plate. Occasionally, a pig would wander in during meals and root around by our feet. I definitely had a problem with that."

My family softly chuckled as they pictured the raucous dinner scene, but Dad was nodding vehemently at the suggestion that such a situation would be a problem. Inspired by his Swiss background, Dad insisted on cleanliness and wouldn't have stood for any such shenanigans happening at his dinner table. To Dad, eating was serious business. We ate on time, and we ate well. Growing up in Europe in the late 1800s, he had seldom been full. As he had established his own home and family, he vowed that neither he nor his would ever go hungry.

I should have guessed Morris was somewhat interested in me that very first night when he offered to help with the supper dishes. But then, Morris seemed like that kind of a guy—good-natured, well-mannered, and wanting to do his part. So it sort of washed over my head that there might be an ulterior motive. We had just finished eating rich beef stew and warm corn bread slathered with fresh-churned butter and creamy, golden honey. Morris had commented several times on the taste of the honey. His dad's tutoring had made him a connoisseur of that delicious delight.

Ruth and Rachel, my two younger sisters, quickly cleared the long, fully burdened table, totally expecting to be stuck in the over-warm kitchen for the next hour or so.

"Could I wash the dishes while you dry them, Susanna?" Morris volunteered.

What male guest would be so foolish? flashed through my mind as I graciously, if somewhat reluctantly, agreed. "Why? I mean, why would you do that? You don't have to do that—it's actually Ruth and Rachel's job tonight."

"Oh, let's give them a break, Susanna." His voice was musical with laughter as if it were ready to break into song. "If I wash and you dry and put things away, I won't have everything in the wrong place when we're finished," he said. Then with that perpetual twinkle in his eye, he added, "Don't you know that's a sure way to have the girls ask me back again?"

"Oh, there's no doubt about that," I agreed. "They'll love you forever."

To my delight, I quickly found out that to have Morris help me with the dishes was no sacrifice on my part.

"You know, when I was on my mission, there was this one family who . . ." and off he'd go relating a story or joke full of laughter and charm. He was easy to be around. In fact, even though the younger girls were off the hook, they hung around for a while straightening chairs and wiping off the table just to hear him talk. Even my brothers weren't above listening in for a few minutes, and then they drifted off as the dish washing actually began.

After the dishes were finished, the conversation waned, and Morris also wandered off, looking for John and the rest of the boys. Eventually, in the deepening twilight, he headed down the lane toward his bunkhouse.

Another activity that I took real pleasure in was dancing. Since the moment I had turned sixteen, I attended the dances fifteen miles away at the red brick church in Coltman. Waiting to attend the dances until I was old enough had seemed incessantly long, but there was no use arguing. My folks didn't allow their children to attend social functions with other teenagers until they were sixteen, and that was that. The long-awaited birthday finally arrived, and I was allowed to go. And oh, how I did love to dance!

Dancing was in my blood and in my bones. I could feel the movement in my soul. Even though I was normally shy around schoolmates, when the music began, my heart swelled with the love of it, and my toes began to tap to the rhythm, no matter who was near.

My older brothers were pretty agreeable to my tagging along with them to the dances, as long as I didn't hang around them after we arrived at the church. That was fine with me. I just needed the ride.

Actually, Fred, the brother just older than I, would occasionally come and find me, sweeping me onto the dance floor with him. Fred! Such a great guy! He was a short, vivacious version of a swinging twenties hoofer with his hair parted in the middle and slicked down on the sides. And Fred was a hot dancer. He liked to show off, so all the attractive, popular girls would flock around him. Because I could follow a dance lead well, and we kind of knew how the other worked, I was a good floor-show partner. Then when things were perking well for Fred, I was left behind for older, prettier girls. But by that time, some of the guys were asking me to dance, so the ploy worked well for both of us.

Soon after Morris met the family, he began to attend the church dances, meeting the family there with a clap on the back, a full-bodied handshake, and a wide grin. Because he claimed he had a bad back, he didn't get into the swing and grind of the fast songs, but occasionally he would ask me to dance on the slow numbers.

Mostly, though, Morris just sat visiting with and entertaining those around him. He could embellish any story with enough humor to make it interesting, if not hilarious. Not that he had to be doing all the talking. He listened as well as he talked and seemed to bring out the verboseness in people. They would tell him about situations and incidents they hadn't even thought about for a long time. Morris would listen with eyes twinkling before asking a question or adding an anecdote of his own.

I was also aware that he often watched me as I danced. To be shy is a hard thing. Often people think you are stuck-up or unfriendly, when really you are half afraid of what they think of you. Talking to people had always been hard for me, but how I loved being on the dance floor, spinning and whirling. At the very back of my conscious brain was the acknowledgment of Morris's ever-watchful eye, allowing me the opportunity to impress him without having to feel tongue-tied and inadequate. Often he would seem deep in conversation with a sideline companion, when he would glance toward the dance floor, identifying me immediately with his laughing eyes, and then go back to his animated conversation. Subtly, I knew he was interested in me, and I could inadvertently flirt with him without having to commit myself to a deeper relationship. After all, I had only barely turned eighteen, and a whole world of boys was still ahead of me.

Truth be known, I really didn't have a lot of time for

Morris or any other guy. I was the oldest girl still at home. Mary and Sarah, my two older sisters, were married and had small children of their own. My older brothers, Rudolf—also married—Walt, John, and Fred were great guys and hard workers, but I had shouldered the full responsibility of caring for one younger brother and three younger sisters ever since my mother had died the September of my sixteenth year.

What a devastating shock that had been! Mama was every girl's dream mom. Besides being beautiful and kind, she was so understanding and available. She loved me even when I was less than loveable, and she let me know that she loved me in all the little kindnesses she showered upon me.

Sometimes I was so jealous of Ruth, my twelve-year-old sister, when she would wangle her way to get whatever she wanted. Ruth couldn't even gather chicken eggs in the morning because the setting hens scared her with their squawking and pecking. In my mind, gathering eggs before breakfast didn't count as work. That job was a regular chore, which took no more thought than eating fried ham and eggs for breakfast. Ruth couldn't weed the tomatoes or the broccoli because she abhorred the tiny spiders on the tomatoes and the fat squishy caterpillars sometimes found on the broccoli. I often felt overworked and underloved when I was assigned those chores, and my jealousy for Ruth grew when she got out of them.

"Never mind, sweetheart. You must remember that Ruth is four years younger than you are and quite high-strung," Mama would say, smoothing things over with her gentle manner. She didn't make me like my younger sister any more than I had before, but I loved my mother tremendously, so I would try to control my complaining spirit.

Even when Mama took someone else's side, you just couldn't get angry with her because she was always there for you as well. There wasn't anything I wouldn't do for Mama—given a little persuasion. I was a girl who suffered from a large dose of poor self-esteem, but Mama helped me feel both needed and wanted in a world that made girls feel unimportant or even valueless. Dad often seemed to exude the opinion that "boys are of value because they carry the family name, but girls marry and move away, not adding anything to the family coffers or progeny."

I will always remember the time when I was very young and Dad was holding me on his lap. Mama and Daddy were discussing the possibility of breaking more new farmland. My secure feeling in his arms disappeared as I heard him say, "Girls aren't worth anything. They grow up, take their husband's name, and move away. It's only the boys that count." I can only imagine the hurt that cutting remark caused my mother, though I don't think it even registered with Dad. Dad sometimes made us feel like that, but Mama always exhibited loving acceptance in her every act and tone.

The haze of an unseasonably hot, muggy September day hung low on the horizon. The kitchen windows were open to allow for a little cross-circulation of air. But for the most part, the sheer lace curtains hung limp on the thick, brown window casings. The kitchen door was open wide. Ruth and Rachel were contentedly playing just outside the heavy screen door on the shady porch with their homemade rag dolls. It was a tiny bit cooler there than in the house. Seven-year-old Irene was sprawled on Mama's bed napping, her hair wet with perspiration as it curled around her tiny ears.

Dad and Mama were making preparations to drive into Idaho Falls, where Mama was leaving by train the next day to travel to California. They would be staying overnight with Aunt Anna, Mama's youngest married sister. Then Mama would board the train the following morning to continue her journey. Mama would never think of paying a visit to either Aunt Anna or Aunt Rosa, another younger sister who lived in California, without taking a bottle of apricot preserves and a couple of loaves of light-brown wheat bread fresh out of the oven. These special treats were sitting on the cooling tray by the oven, ready to accompany her.

Earlier, Mama had suffered a small stroke, from which it had taken her nine long months to recover. What with raising eleven active children, helping with the farm, planting and caring for a huge garden, and keeping a clean, comfortable house, her body was tired and weak. She hadn't been feeling well again for some time. Aunt Rosa had been encouraging Mama to come to the mild, balmy climate of Northern California for a much-needed visit and rest. Finally, Mama had persuaded Dad that she should visit Rosa, who was a registered nurse, for a couple of weeks to convalesce and regain her strength. That discussion had been ongoing for some time and had not been well received on Dad's part, but finally even he could see the wisdom in it and had reluctantly agreed to her California visit. It wasn't that Dad didn't want Mama to get well. It wasn't even that he didn't want her to visit Aunt Rosa. He had just never had to cope for any length of time without her steadying influence close by. He loved her dearly, and he was loath to see her go even for a short time.

Mama was sitting in her underskirt and corset at the dressing table in the corner of the kitchen after her bath, arranging her hair. I was standing at the ironing board, pressing her pretty, pleated blouse with the pert white ruffle around the high jewel neckline. One heavy flatiron was heating on the stove while I used the other one on the blouse. When the first one cooled down, I would rush back to the stove, exchange irons, and go on with my work. The ironing board was traditionally placed across the room from the stove where the irons were heating. After wash day, each blouse, shirt, or dress needing ironing was sprinkled lightly with water and rolled into a tight individual bundle. After being packed overnight in an oilcloth-lined basket so the moisture could be evenly distributed throughout the cloth, each article of clothing was ready to be ironed. If the ironing board was positioned too close to the stove, the stove heat dried out the material too quickly before the heat of the iron could press the fabric smooth.

Mother's hair, long to her waist, was thick as fresh-churned buttermilk. She would brush it with long, firm strokes until the brunette strands gleamed like shining cherry wood. Then, while holding one end of a dark brown shoelace in her teeth, she would secure the other end around her hair, ponytail fashion, allowing the hair by her scalp to loosen slightly to soften her facial features. With a quick twist of her wrist, the long mane would be wound into a bun and secured with the shoelace and some hairpins. With fascination, I had watched her do this dozens of times.

"Susie, I want you to promise me something. You're getting old enough to date now, and soon you'll be going out with boys. I want you to promise me you'll never do anything you can't come home, crawl into bed with your little sisters, and tell them about."

"Oh, Mama, honestly! Why would I want to tell Ruth or Rachel about my dates? They are way too nosy as it is."

"It's not that you have to tell them; it's that you can tell them and not be embarrassed. If you could crawl into bed with them and tell them everything you did that evening, then your conscience would be free and clean. It's the being able to tell them because you haven't done anything wrong that's important."

My look of exasperation changed to one of understanding. "Don't worry, Mama. I won't do anything I can't tell my little sisters about."

The promise was heartfelt, but I was also pretty naive about dating relationships. Of course I was slightly aware of the boys at school and church, but my thoughts were pretty innocent because I was only beginning to appreciate the opposite sex. Mostly, boys seemed like a darned nuisance. But I was so eager for her to get well again that at that point, I would have promised my dear mother anything.

Mama smiled slightly in understanding and went on, "And another thing, Susie. I know Ruth teases you sometimes, but she is just a child. Remember, she is four years younger than you. You are older, and I want you to promise not to quarrel with her while I'm gone."

"But Mama!"

"The quarrelling doesn't solve anything. It just makes Ruth more obstinate and harder to reason with . . ."

"I know, but . . ."

"If you give in easily, it will probably surprise her so much that you'll be able to get her to mind you without a fight."

I hadn't ever really thought about that before. So after a long moment's pause, some reflection on what had just been said, and a huge sigh, I said, "Oh, I promise, Mother. I won't quarrel with Ruth, even when she deserves it. She just makes me so mad sometimes. But . . . I . . . I promise," I said, puffing out my cheeks in exasperation. Then almost without thinking, I made another significant promise of my own.

"Don't worry, Mama. I'll take care of the family while you're gone. As long as they need me, I'll take care of them. You just go and get well." I had taken care of my younger brother, Sam, and my three younger sisters many times before. The promise didn't seem all that hard to make. After all, Mama would be gone to California only for two weeks.

"Now, Susie, when you are . . ."

One minute Mama was giving me instructions to carry out during her absence, the next she was slumping forward as her beautiful hair cascaded from her suddenly limp hands and the moist end of the shoelace slowly slid from her mouth. The entire scene seemed to be playing out before my astonished vision in slow motion.

"Oh, Mama," I cried as I quickly ran across the room, putting the iron back on the stove, a lifetime of training clicking in. I would have never thought to drop the heavy iron on the floor or leave it on the ironing board. Then I rushed to her side and caught her weight against me as she gently slid to the floor, a limp pool of white starched petticoat and dark shining mahogany hair.

"Oh, Mama, Mama," I moaned as I stroked her soft, lovely hair, gently lifting it back from her deathly white face.

Time was suspended for an instant, then I screamed, "Ruth, come into the house! Ruth, come in and hurry!" My voice was choking with fear and urgency. Ruth heard me through the screen door and immediately rushed inside, the heavy door banging behind her. When she saw Mama lying there, her face clouded over with shock and confusion, and she started to cry, the tears streaking down her flushed cheeks.

"Go get Dad, right now!" My voice was harsh with the command. "He's down at the ditch, bathing. Tell him something's wrong with Mama. Tell him to come quick! Run, Ruth!" Ruth slammed the screen door open and was running hard even before I finished the last harsh edict.

Chapter 2

Dad arrived on the run—face flushed, short of breath, dark hair still dripping, striped coverall suspenders flapping. The screen door banged as he rushed into the room. He hesitated for only half a second as he took in the scene before him. A few moments earlier, I had gently laid Mama on the floor, a pillow under her head, and straightened out her body as best I could.

Gathering her up in his strong, farmer's arms, Dad cried brokenheartedly, "Marie, Marie," as he buried his big-brush mustache in her soft, flowing hair. "My sweet, wonderful Marie." Gently, tenderly, rocking her back and forth as one would a beloved child, he turned slightly toward me. His clean, shiny face was stricken with bewilderment and sorrow as he softly intoned, "Call Aunt Anna, Susie, and ask her to send a doctor."

Once contacted, the doctor replied that he could treat Mother better in town, so I helped Dad slip the clean, freshly pressed blouse over her underclothing, and then with shaking fingers, I tried to quickly fasten the long string of buttons down the back. Next came the full, heavy, cotton, black skirt over the petticoat, with more buttons at the waist. As much as we wanted to hurry, convention dictated modesty, even in these tense circumstances.

Dad, who was eager to get Mama into the car and be on their way, changed in record time from his striped bib overalls into the dark trousers and a clean white shirt which Mama had laid out on the bed for him. I wanted to ask if I could go with them, or at least ask if he would call home and report what the doctor said, but that just wasn't done, and I knew it. Dad would handle the situation, and he would call if he felt it was necessary, or if he thought of it. I settled for giving Mama a quick kiss on her forehead and ran ahead to open the car door on the old black 1915 Maxwell, getting out of the way so Dad could carefully lift her onto the front passenger seat. We tucked a blanket firmly on each side of her to help absorb the jarring ride. It would be a bumpy drive to Aunt Anna's little white house in Idaho Falls where Dr. Roy would be waiting.

For nine endless, dreadful, frightening days, I washed the dirty clothes, cooked the endless meals, did the countless dishes, scrubbed the brown linoleum kitchen floor, and baked the needed bread. For nine interminable days, through the heat and the monotony, I did everything that was required of me. Actually, it was exactly as we had all planned. Mama would be gone for a time and I would take over her motherly responsibilities. But the joy and even the frustration of serving my large family were gone. I didn't talk to Sam, fight with Ruth, or get angry with Rachel or Irene. I didn't remind them of chores or insist on an early bedtime. I didn't frown. I didn't smile. I existed. Foremost in my mind was the fact that Mama was lying at Aunt Anna's tiny, storybook house like an exquisite wax doll, frozen in time.

All the children eagerly went to see her five days after her collapse, threading our way into the parlor with great anticipation. We returned home silent—frightened by her appearance. So white, so smooth, so beautiful, and so—*still.* She laid on the gold plush day bed, dressed in her pert, white blouse and black skirt, just as she was when Dad carried her from the house—nothing altered and nothing out of place. She didn't seem touched by any of it: the interminable heat, the family movement, the whispers, the sighs. Life moved on but without her knowledge or concern.

Mama never came home again. For nine long, dreadful,

weary days, Mother was unconscious, having suffered a massive cerebral hemorrhage. And then silently, early in the morning of the ninth day, she slipped from this life and from our lives. This time she truly was gone—her spirit flown from her cold, lifeless body, her once animated voice stilled forever.

Mary and Sarah, my older married sisters, and Aunt Anna washed Mama's ivory skin and arranged her beautiful mahogany tresses softly about her face and up into the ever-present bun. They dressed her in her lovely white temple dress and sparkling white temple clothes with the emerald green apron and laid her in a casket lined with white satin. She was ready to be put into the dry, hard earth, and I couldn't believe any of it.

I just couldn't believe it. Surely it wasn't possible to have a mother—alive, vibrant, and in charge of all our lives—even if she was just a little ill—and then have her gone. Gone forever, it seemed. She wouldn't do that to us. She loved us so much and knew we needed her. We depended upon her. She was our stabilizer, our sustenance, and our lifeline. Why would she leave? Or, why would she be taken? What kind of God would do that to a family with small children to be cared for and a loving husband?

The sweltering day kept the black-clad women's fans moving steadily throughout the funeral service at the small Coltman church. Mama had been well loved and the mourners were packed into the chapel. Of course, the adults talked about us seeing her again someday in the next life—of her being in a place where she was well and happy, at last being able to put down her worldly cares. They spoke of her greeting parents and loved ones who had gone before her and even of seeing the Savior and basking in his love.

But my frozen teenage mind just couldn't come to grips with any of it: the bishop's inspiring funeral sermon, or the neighbors' murmurings of condolence. Mama couldn't possibly be as happy there as she had been with us! We were her life, and she definitely was ours. Constant tears ran down our cheeks as Mama's favorite hymn, "Oh, My Redeemer," was sung with reverence and feeling by the ward choir—unstoppable tears that mingled with the heat, the dust, the numbness, and the shock.

I hated the funeral. They were talking about my mother, but it didn't seem possible. My mind was closed into a box of hurt and despair. The void about my soul seemed as black as the ugly mourning clothes we all wore. I wasn't at all sure how I would go on without my dear, sweet mother.

I'm sure others were hurting around me as well, although I really wasn't aware of their pain. I honestly didn't see them at all. Who cared about anyone else? I was the one who was hurting inside like someone had ripped out my heart.

And then I looked up and saw Dad. His lined, weathered face looked like cracking, ill-tended leather. It appeared closed and stiff and years older than the week before. He seemed to have receded inside himself. He looked through us all, brothers and sisters, children, neighbors, and bishop, as he stared straight ahead. If we were raw and hurting, he was in mortal agony.

Sitting close beside me on the hard wooden bench, my youngest sister, Irene, insisted on holding my hand during the entire funeral service. As she gripped my ice-cold hand tightly with her warm, moist one, I felt almost impatient with the small, clinging body so insistently close to mine. I tried to at least get control of these feelings. Irene was barely seven years old and must be terribly confused. If I could hardly cope with Mother being gone, Irene surely couldn't understand what was happening.

Spreading oaks, graceful weeping willows, and stately pine trees lined the Idaho Falls Cemetery where Mama was laid to rest in a newly purchased plot. Faded yellow-green grass from the extreme summer heat scratched at our shoes as neighbors and ward members milled around for a time offering their condolences.

Stiff as a stone monolith, Dad, dressed in his best black

suit, white shirt, and plain tie, stood at the head of the casket to dedicate the grave. Rudolf, Mama's oldest son, had offered, but Dad felt he should shoulder this important priesthood responsibility. Because we had no living grandparents, the family members in attendance were Dad, eleven grieving children, two sons-in-law, one daughter-in-law, seven small grandchildren, and Mama's youngest sister, Aunt Anna.

Probably a week after Mama had been buried, I finally remembered the binding promise I had made to her. Up to that time, my mind had been such a blur I hadn't thought coherently about much of anything. Once I remembered, I could hardly think of anything else.

"Don't worry, Mama," I had blithely said. "I'll take care of the family while you're gone. As long as they need me, I'll take care of them. You just go and get well."

For the only time I could ever remember, Mama hadn't kept her end of the agreement—the get well part—and I felt abandoned and disillusioned by the thought that Mama would recant on her word. But then, in all fairness to her, she had never said she would get well. I had just assumed that a wonderful trip to California would rejuvenate her and make her as good as new.

When my mind finally got around the broken agreement part, I realized my promise was binding, and I was determined to keep my end of the deal. I would take care of my family for my mother. I had promised her. I had even volunteered without urging or coercion. I could do it and I would. Still, I missed her terribly. Slowly, subconsciously, I realized that this long-term commitment would not be an easy one to accomplish.

Each new day, as I awoke to the warbler's song in the tall cottonwood tree, and the rays of early morning sunlight in the girls' large bedroom, my conscious mind reverted immediately to all that had happened. I struggled to achieve some kind of comprehension, to assign some purpose in the Lord taking her. Even into the fall, the heat continued to be oppressive and stifling, just as the summer days had been, as though there would never be an end to this awful condition. Maybe Mama had moved on to heaven, and we were all roasting in hell.

One morning in late September, as storm clouds finally began to gather and rumble around the dense, gray sky, my feelings of frustration and anger were simmering near the boiling point. Aunts, uncles, cousins, and married siblings were finally all gone—gone home to their own responsibilities. The harvest in progress, the boys had left hours before, right after breakfast, for fields heavy with ripened grain. The little girls, after seeing to the daily morning chores, had left for the long walk to school. I no longer attended school. By wordless agreement, I was staying home to take care of things there.

I was standing in the too-quiet house by the white enamel kitchen sink getting ready to do the mountains of dirty breakfast dishes—again. I raised my clenched fists into the air, and shaking them at the heavens I wailed aloud, "If there's a God in heaven, he wouldn't take away a mother from children who need her as much as we do!"

I whirled around almost immediately, with my back leaning against the countertop, my hands pressing into my cheeks. I was aghast at what I had said. Such an outburst was against all my religious training. While feeling the terror and magnitude of the moment, I had, nevertheless, finally verbalized the thoughts that had been building inside me ever since the funeral. But for one brief moment, I wondered if God would strike me dead on the spot.

Then, mere seconds after I had spoken, my beautiful mother quietly appeared before me, standing there in the silent kitchen and smiling sweetly in her loving, gentle manner, an aura of light about her.

For one moment, I blinked through my instant tears, staring hard, not believing my eyes. Then, "Oh, Mama," I whispered as I tentatively reached out for her.

And she was gone, but not before flooding my being with the comfort and peace I had been missing. I knew then that

Mama would always be with me to help me through the difficult times. She knew what I was going through. She was aware of my longing, my hurt, and my frustration. My heart filled with overwhelming gratitude and love.

Chapter 3

It's one thing to make a sweeping promise like that, but it's quite an enormous, depressing weight on a sixteen-year-old girl's shoulders to actually try to carry it out. Granted, I could make nourishing bread, wash stacks of dishes, mop endless floors, do mounds of laundry, and braid three girls' hair, but to do it day after boring day without complaint or reprieve was another story. Sixteen is supposed to be a time for discovery of self and friends. Each day was a struggle to get everything done so I could do it all over again the next day.

My older sisters, Mary and Sarah, were married and had husbands and several youngsters of their own. Their lives were already full of responsibilities. Rudolf, my oldest brother, was married and had children too, but we saw him much more frequently because he supported his family by working with Dad on our farm. That was good for both Rudolf my brother and Rudolf my Dad.

Our Dad, born in far-off, majestic Switzerland, had never really enjoyed much of a father figure in his life. His mother, Anna Maria Magdalena Butikofer, made the tragic mistake of falling in love with a boy of means when she was only twenty years old. This rich heir met her on the sly for three years before he informed her that his parents expected him to marry a girl from another wealthy family. There was nothing Anna Maria could do. Her family was penurious—extremely poor. Heartbroken, she watched her beloved marry someone else in the social event of the season. Grieving was useless but necessary for Anna Maria because she had truly loved her young man and the grieving process dragged on year after long, tedious year. Finally, in an act of desperation and resignation, Anna Maria began a tryst with Johanas, a young man who had recently moved into the area. The relationship lasted long enough to father three illegitimate children: two girls, Rosina and Anna, and my father, Rudolf. Even though Dad's biological father was not married to Anna Maria, Johanas lived on and off with the family for several years, finally drifting away for good.

Heinrich, the third man in Anna Maria's life, moved into her household, and they began an intimate relationship that she hoped would keep him around so he would help her care for her family. Heinrich fathered six more children, all of whom died as babies, each one living as little as one day to as long as nineteen days. Finally after eight years of living together and just before Bertha was born, Heinrich married Anna Maria. Ironically, Bertha was born healthy, squalling, and vigorous, and lived to adulthood.

True to past experiences, Heinrich, also a drifter, was only in evidence occasionally, each time coming home just long enough to leave behind another pregnancy. The main legacy he left my Dad, Rudolf, was to teach him to shoot a gun with quick and amazing accuracy. Shooting was almost a national pastime in Switzerland, and Dad's second "father" was a well-known marksman. Target shooting was his favorite sport.

Bern, Switzerland, was picture-postcard perfect, with a fine view of the Alps and surrounded by the Aare River on three sides. With its picturesque bridges, beautiful walks, bubbling fountains, and quaint shops, it would seem an ideal place to live. But the heartland of Bern was textile manufacturing. Anna Maria had worked for many years in a factory, weaving raw cotton into cloth. The working hours were extremely long and the pay pitifully low.

One evening, after returning from a long, tiring shift on her feet, Anna Maria reported to her children that the tedium of her job that day had been interrupted in a horrible way. The body of a Negro boy, no more than nine or ten years old, had been discovered inside a new bale of cotton that had just arrived from the States. Most of the workers in the factory had never seen anyone with black skin. At first they thought he was rotting but finally realized he was preserved perfectly, his skin black because of nationality instead of decay.

The Butikofer children were always looking for some way to bring in another franc to supplement their meager income, and to that end, Rudolf delivered newspapers.

"Mother, while I was picking up my papers down by Yarne Street today, I heard two young men, wearing suits and bowler hats, standing on the street corner, preaching religion. Joseph, my friend from school, says they are missionaries from America. He says they have been in the Yagenstorf area of Bern for about three weeks now. I listened to them and what they were saying was really interesting. Could we have them come here and talk to all of us? Could we, Mother?" The questions came tumbling out as Rudolf finally took a breath.

"Oh, Rudolf. I don't know. What were they saying that you found so fascinating?" Anna Maria was a little distracted with stretching meager ingredients to make a supper for five, but her interest was piqued.

"They were talking about America. It sounds like a wonderful, rich, exciting place. Their families live in the United States, but they are here telling people about a book that is supposed to be an ancient record of people who lived in America centuries ago. You know you love to read, Mother. I think you would be interested in what they have to say." Rudolf had saved that argument for last, for he knew his mother could never get enough of reading and learning new things.

"Oh, I don't know, Rudolf. Young men! What would they know about an ancient record from America?"

But then, with mounting curiosity, for she did love to read—it was her escape from the harshness of life—"Oh well—maybe—I guess. Ask them to come to supper. We haven't much to offer," she mused. "But if you'll eat a little less on the night they come, it might stretch. Maybe they will enjoy warm, simple food and tell us more of their homeland, their message, and their book."

In a very short time, Dad, his sisters, and his mother had accepted the gospel and all were baptized, except for Bertha who was only three years old. The next time Heinrich, Bertha's father came home, the truth about the baptism slipped out, and he was furious. He hated the Mormon Church. Something had to be dreadfully wrong with a church that wouldn't allow a man a pint of ale occasionally. Truth be known, Heinrich's drinking was more constant than occasional.

The missionaries continued to visit fourteen-year-old Rudolf and the Butikofer household. The family didn't have much, but they shared freely what little they had.

"America is a wonderful place, Rudolf; you and your family could go there if you wanted."

"How could we possibly go, Elder Hansen? We are poor, barely finding enough work to feed ourselves from day to day. There is no way to put away money for ship passage. I'm afraid America is only a lovely dream for us," Rudolf lamented. Oh, America did sound *so* wonderful!

"But you see, others have thought of that already, Rudolf. The Saints in the West have set up a fund called the Perpetual Immigration Fund to help newly baptized Saints in England and Europe immigrate to America. The money is only on loan to them and has to be paid back from what they earn after arriving in the Salt Lake Valley, but it is available." Elder Hansen looked into Rudolf's big, round, staring eyes.

"You are a hard worker. You and your sisters could use the fund to travel, and then after you have paid it back, you could earn money to send for your mother and your little sister, Bertha. This is your chance to move to a new land and make a better life for your family. It really is possible!"

Eagerly, with hope springing brightly in their hearts, Rudolf and his two sisters, Rosina and Anna, took advantage of the fund. They found sponsors back in Utah with the help of the missionaries and booked passage on a sturdy old steamship bound for the States.

Oh, but to leave their precious mother behind was very hard! They loved her dearly. And Bertha! How do you leave one so young without a perpetual ache in your heart? Anna had tended Bertha from her birth while their mother worked. She felt almost as much Bertha's mother as Anna Maria actually was. Bertha would lose this constant association with her beloved older sister, and Anna Maria would lose not only her teenage children but also her necessary babysitter. Even with such a significant hardship and feeling truly frightened for what it meant for those who were going and those who were staying behind, she insisted they should go. In her mother's heart, it was the only way she could see any kind of a promising future for her young children.

Rosina, Anna, and Rudolf wanted to go. Oh, how they wanted to go! And they loved their dear mother for giving them the opportunity. They only hoped Heinrich would not abuse Anna Maria or Bertha when he found out the older ones had deliberately left home to cross the ocean and be with the Mormons. The constant prayer of Rudolf's heart was that he could pay back their loans quickly so he could honor the promise he made to his mother to unite their family again as soon as possible.

On boarding the ship, Rudolf could quickly see the need for someone to work with the cattle that were being transported. He made himself available and then indispensable. After only four days at sea, one of the more wealthy men on board lost his wife when she gave birth to their first child. Grieving, but unable to turn back, the man looked around for someone to tend the tiny red-haired newborn. He timidly asked Rosina if she would be willing to help; he would pay her well. On arriving in Utah, Rosina married the man and adopted the child she had so faithfully served. Jobs such as these helped defer some of the cost of the passage.

Even though Dad was a hard worker, he was unskilled in a trade, having only delivered papers to the textile mills. He didn't have the background to get a lucrative job upon his arrival in America. After several days of looking, he finally found a job laying railroad ties in Utah and Idaho. It took several years to earn enough money to bring Anna Maria, his mother, and Bertha, his rapidly growing younger sister, to the promised land. But, being true to himself, his dream, and his promise to his mother, he was finally able to pay their passage all the way to Salt Lake City, Utah.

My mother, Marie, came from a different city in Switzerland. Jacob Metzener, Marie's father, was a skilled brick mason, as well as an exceptional gardener. Marie had grown up learning how to grow just about anything edible. Almost as soon as the missionaries found them, father, mother, and children were united in their acceptance of the gospel. Their neighbors were just as united against the Mormons, and Jacob quickly discovered his mason skills were no longer profitable. Marie's family anxiously immigrated to be with the Saints, leaving behind a beautiful brick home and well-tended gardens and orchards.

In a red brick churchhouse in Salt Lake City, two young people from Switzerland, Rudolf Butikofer and Marie Metzener, met, fell in love, and married.

They tried for a time to live on love, but real life and children intruded. After living with Marie's family for a time and working with Jacob, Marie's father, to learn the brick mason trade, they realized it was time to be on their own. Through Mother's persistent persuasion, Dad decided to homestead a small farm in Idaho: a fertile place to grow food and raise their rapidly growing family. The farm flourished, the children came regularly every couple of years, and our home and several of our outbuildings were made of brick.

The Butikofer acreage was well established when Mama died. Our family boasted five boys, and they were all hard workers, so the farm thrived. But, boy, did they ever eat a lot at mealtime! I would have breakfast on the table in the morning at six o'clock sharp. About the time I had finished up the breakfast dishes, braided three girls' hair and got them off to school, tidied up the house, mixed a batch of bread, did some ironing, and started lunch, they would all be in to eat again, along with Dad. They were regular as clockwork, arriving again by suppertime, hungry as brawny Clydesdales. The little girls were some help, of course, but it was easier to do things myself than to argue with Ruth, and Rachel and Irene still needed considerable supervision in their activities.

Because Mother died in early September, before she had a chance to sew new school dresses for the girls, I decided to try to fill this need. Girls in farm families only received one new dress each year, so it was an important event in their lives. I, of course, wasn't returning to school.

I had told the boys often since Mother had died that I needed to be able to drive the car to go into town for the supplies we needed. They laughed at me and said I couldn't drive.

"Walt, I can *so* drive! I mean, I can if you'll just teach me!" This conversation was taking place out by Dad's old black Maxwell, with autumn's delightful pumpkin and mustard colors all around us.

"Susie, Sam will be driving the car before you do."

Now, that really rubbed me the wrong way because Sam was two years younger than I was. "Not a chance," I glared as I bounced my hand hard off the car's rear fender and kicked the dried leaves in the driveway. And then, wearing a look that would kill a less formidable opponent, with gritted teeth and scrunched up eyes, I challenged, "I am older, so I should learn to drive the car first."

Walt just laughed. "But Sam's a boy, and we're going to teach him real soon."

"Walt, that just isn't fair and you know it!" My blood was really boiling now. "I'm older and I'm going to be driving first even if you help him," I vowed.

"Right, little sister." Walt could see I was madder than

hops, and his mind was working quickly. Acting like he was really thinking this whole situation through carefully, he countered, "If you're so sure you will be driving before Sam, how about making a small wager?"

Taken by surprise, I defensively shot back, "Like what?"

"Like betting your potato money against Sam's that you will drive the car before he does."

Well! That was something to think about! Picking up potatoes in the fields, after they had been dug and lay on top of the rich, brown dirt, and filling large burlap bags with them at potato harvest time was the only time during the year we younger kids really had of making any spending money. We prized our potato money, and we worked hard for it.

"W-e-l-l-l, ma-a-y-be-e-e," I considered the possibilities. "But only if you'll let me sit in the front seat of the car every time we go anywhere," I blurted with a rush. "Every time we go to church, or into town, or to Aunt Anna's, you have to let me sit in the *middle* of the front seat."

Walt laughed uproariously to think he had actually gotten me to agree. "Yup, sure Susie, you can sit in the front. Shake on the bet?"

As I think back on this incident, I was *so* dumb! Here Walt was wagering *my* potato money against *Sam's* potato money. Walt didn't have a dang-blamed thing to lose. It wasn't his money that was in jeopardy. It was all a game to him—just something to get me going.

But, on the other hand, Walt wasn't so smart either. Every time Dad's Maxwell pulled out of our long, curving, gravel driveway, I was sitting smack-dab in the middle of the front seat. To go in the car was always an outing, with everyone laughing and joking, while I sat silently watching every move of Walt, or John, or Fred at the wheel. I could see that we would jerk forward if they didn't handle the clutch just right. It was also obvious that you didn't have to turn the wheel much to drive down the middle of the road, but you had to crank the wheel like crazy to make the car turn at the end of the lane.

Eventually it was Sam, two years my junior, who was the loser all the way around, without having anything to do with it.

One bright, crisp fall afternoon, about three-quarters of the way through potato harvest (we weren't picking potatoes that afternoon because the ground needed to dry a little from the soft rain received the day before), I told the girls to get prepared to go into town to shop. Of course, everyone in the family knew about the bet, so the girls were as excited and flighty as hummingbirds to think I was going to try and take the car on my own. Ruth even offered to jump out of the car to open and close the heavy, awkward gate at the end of the graveled lane—something that was completely foreign to her nature.

The day, slightly chilly but calm, was the perfect day for my attempt. I thought all the boys and Dad were checking the soil in one of the far fields, which would definitely give us a head start, even when they realized what was happening. Rachel and Irene were talking a mile a minute, but Ruth was as silent and tense as a hunting dog watching for geese. The four of us, wearing warm quilted jackets, piled into the car, and I started the engine.

Luckily it caught the first time. With a minimum of gear grinding, we were off—first hidden by the white brick two-story farmhouse and large red barn and then moving slowly down the pebbled lane, jerking only slightly. This was my first time ever behind the wheel. Up to this point, I had only watched like a hungry fox checking out the chicken coop as someone else did the driving.

"Hurry, Susie, hurry!" squealed Irene.

"Oh, they see us. Drive faster," yelled Rachel.

And sure enough, Sam and Rudolf, just returning home and in the nearest field, were churning up the dirt with their feet, making the slightly damp clods fly into the air. Rounding the corner of the barn at a run, they shouted angrily at the top of their lungs, "Stop! You can't drive that car! Stop! Stop right now!"

As the old black Maxwell reached the end of the bumpy lane, we slid to a stop, barely missing the cross-barred farm gate and almost killing the engine. Ruth was out in an instant—without being told—and working at pulling the wire latch over the pole as fast as I had ever seen her work at anything. She skidded to the side of the road, pulling the gate behind her so we could pass through, and then dropped the awkward gate right where she stood.

"Aren't you going to close it?" questioned Rachel nervously.

"Heck no, let's get going, and fast before Rudolf catches up to us." Ruth's straight, white teeth were chattering in her excitement. And she was right. We could hear Rudolf's mild cussing at that point because he was getting so close.

I gunned the motor and popped the clutch a little faster than I meant to, but we were on our way, smoking, jerking, and coughing, but moving quickly down the road toward town.

As we neared Coltman, I pulled over to the side of the road and parked well on the outskirts of the village under trees still covered with brittle fall leaves. "Hey, Susie, don't stop here. You're doing great. We're still four blocks from Harvey's Dry Goods Store," voiced Rachel.

"Yeh, I didn't think you could do it," laughed Ruth in a lightly teasing manner. "But you did and you did okay too," she stated with increased awe and respect in her voice and eyes.

"I appreciate your confidence in me, but I still have to turn the car around to go out of town when we go home, and it will be easier here than right on Main Street."

"I bet you could do it, though, Susie," Irene gushed.

"Well, let's not push our luck, okay?" I gulped. They finally agreed and piled out of the car to begin walking the rest of the distance to town.

At Harvey's, the only store in Coltman that sold material, Rachel, Irene, and Ruth had a hard time agreeing on the fabric we should buy for the school dresses. Each girl walked down the fabric isle, fingering the soft cotton fabric, trying to decide. "This is the best because it's dark and won't show the dirt as quickly. Besides it looks so chic." Rachel was always the practical one, much as Mother had been.

"Chic? It's *so-o-o* boring, Rachel. I know you love navy, but we need something a little more colorful. We'll be wearing these dresses all year, you know," chided Ruth.

Flashy clothing was much more Ruth's style. She was developing a cute figure and was a consummate flirt, with her dark hair and dark, flashing eyes. Navy was too subdued for her.

"Why can't we each just choose our own material, anyway?" Rachel turned to me with a pleading look on her face. "That way we will all be satisfied."

"Because, Rachel," I snapped, "as you know, I haven't had a lot of experience in sewing. If something goes wrong on one dress I may have to take some of the material from someone else's dress to use, and so it all has to be the same color. You wouldn't want one yellow sleeve in your navy blue dress, would you?" I finished triumphantly.

I had already given this a lot of thought and had previously decided all the dresses had to be the same material. This was a new experience for me, this sewing business, and I figured if I needed more material than I had planned on for Ruth's dress, I could make Irene's a little shorter or something to make up for it.

"Look at this material," Irene shyly pointed out. "It's kinda nice. It looks like tiny spring flowers have been tossed up into the midnight blue sky and stayed there, like stars twinkling— only in color. I love pink, Ruth loves yellow, and Rachel loves navy."

"I guess we would each get a little of what we like that way," admitted Ruth grudgingly. "You just make sure you buy enough, Susanna. I want my skirt nice and full, not skimpy like you ran out of material before you were finished."

Surprised that they had agreed so quickly, I then spent considerable time choosing thread and buttons. I didn't hurry them along as I normally did because I was not anxious to return home to the wrath I was sure was awaiting me there. Eventually, though, I knew we had better start for home so we could do our chores, or we would be in even more trouble.

As we approached the farm on our return, the sun was lowering in a pleasant water-colored sky that matched the land. I had anticipated the boys' fury and knew I had every reason to be concerned. They met us outside on the hard-packed dirt and gravel lane, taunting me all the while as we continued to pull slowly up to the house in the car.

"Susie, you had no right to take the car without asking us first," yelled John the moment he saw us.

"What if you had hit something with the car and wracked it up?" shouted Rudolf, who still hadn't gone home. He was waiting until he was sure I had returned safely.

Fred joined in. "This isn't funny, Susie, and you're going to be in a lot of trouble."

"Dad will skin you alive. You know that, don't you?" gloated Sam.

With the boys continuing to harass us, the girls and I moved nervously through the screen door at the side of the house and into the big farm kitchen. For once, however, the boys were all wrong. Dad, who always seemed to think the boys did fine and the girls weren't worth much, was lying on the burgundy divan with his eyes closed but obviously listening to the noisy ruckus. Suddenly he sat up, his face stern and foreboding. Everyone held a collective breath. He kept a straight face for a few moments and then broke into a huge grin.

"I guess my little Susie showed you this time, didn't she?" He laughed right out loud, slapping his knee. "You guys goaded her into this, you know. I think this is great! You never have time to take me over to Svensen's or up to Sarah's. Now Susie can drive me wherever I need to go. She can take a book to read while I visit. *She* won't be too busy for me."

Dad had been involved in a minor car accident soon after

Mother's death, and he was driving the car when the accident occurred. Since then he had been reluctant to take the car anywhere, always asking one of the boys to drive him; but the boys seldom wanted to drive him because they felt he stayed longer than necessary at each stop.

The boys could plainly see they had lost, so they tried to fade away before Dad remembered the money aspect of the situation. But Dad, for once, was on my side all the way. "And remember, Sam's potato money goes to Susie this year at the end of harvest."

Walt sat back, kind of grinning, and not saying a word. Sam was fuming, sputtering like a mad dog.

It's good the driving thing turned out okay because the sewing of the school dresses was another matter. Even though all three girls had to wear their dresses the entire year to school, Ruth vowed for years later that she would never wear another dress sewn by me. I had done the best I could, but after that, we hired Miss Leishman, Coltman's most eligible old maid, to sew for the girls.

Chapter 4

When I was younger, I was kind of a loner. I loved to read, and while I slowly churned the thick, rich cream into smooth, delicious butter in the dank, cool cellar I would always have a book open with my eyes glued to the page. Anyone coming to check on me would start talking to themselves loudly at the top of the stairs, "I wonder if Susie has that butter churned yet?" to give me time to hide the book and churn more vigorously. Other favorite reading places included being cocooned in warmth, lying on my back in the sunny, incredibly soft sand dunes, or walking to and from school in the mild, delightful spring air.

That is not to say that I didn't like to be active as well. I liked nothing better than to play with siblings in the frigid, clear water at the dappled, tree-shaded swimming hole on hot summer afternoons. Racing Maebell bareback across the gently swelling sand dunes, with the sand flying every direction and my long hair whipping in the wind, was another favorite release from work-a-day matters. Occasionally I would pull the boys on skis over the dunes, the lead rope tied firmly to the back of Maebell's saddle. It was a crazy ride with them whooping and hollering while I urged her forward at breakneck speed.

On my fourteenth birthday, Dad asked me what I wanted for a birthday present. Totally surprised that he would even ask, I answered that what I wanted most was to learn how to shoot the gun.

"Why do you want to shoot the gun, Susie? Do you think you can become as good a shot as your old dad?" he said with a slight smile.

I had heard many stories of his expertise in gun handling, and I knew my asking this of him would please him. It seemed I was always subconsciously looking for a way to have Dad acknowledge my worth. We struggled to like each other, or so it often seemed. Mama always told us that Dad loved us, but he was so strict that I just couldn't see it most of the time. So asking him to teach me to shoot was maybe a way of trying to get his attention, although I honestly did have an interest in shooting. I think it was the inherent tomboy in me.

"Well, Dad, maybe I could learn to shoot as well as Rudolf. You taught him, and he's a really good shot. I don't know if I could bag a turkey like he did, but maybe I'll . . . have to defend my family someday." I was only half teasing. Something inside me wanted to not only learn how to shoot well but to have the opportunity to prove what I good shot I was. From all my reading, I longed to be the heroine sometime in the story of life. Or maybe I just needed a self-esteem boost at that time.

"I'd consider that request, Susie, but you'd have to take it seriously. Part of shooting is learning how to take care of your firearm. It has to be loaded correctly, cleaned regularly, and put away properly every time you use it. The only time I could teach you would be in the early hours of the morning. Could you handle a lesson at four thirty?" He was quite serious now.

I gulped. At four thirty in the morning, it was still dark. The first wisps of daylight would just be touching the horizon. That would be before chores and getting ready for school. I had hoped for an after-school lesson time, but I wasn't about to back down now.

"Of course, four thirty would be great! You might have to call me the first few mornings 'til I get used to getting up then, okay?" I asked tentatively.

"Come down as soon as I call," was all he said.

Dad's gun was an old rifle with quite a kick. My right

shoulder soon resembled toad skin both in color and texture. The first time I actually shot the gun, it tumbled me over backwards into a patch of brittle weeds.

"You have to aim a little low to make up for the upward pull when you squeeze the trigger, Susie."

"Not that low. Concentrate on the mark you want to hit."

"If you take that long to fire, the rabbit will be over looking for breakfast at Sarah's before you get the shot off."

"Come on, Susie. You can do better than that."

And finally, "You are gettin' good. Your speed is increasing, and your aim is on. Keep practicing. You ready for a shoot-off tomorrow morning? See just what you can do up against your sharp-shootin' dad?"

What a morning that was. Dad beat me, of course, but not by much, and three mornings later I shot old tin cans off the weathered fence in the south field without a miss at forty yards. This was a wonderful one-on-one time for Dad and me. I seemed to learn quickly, and I loved the challenge. Dad actually acted quite proud of my accomplishments which helped our shaky father-daughter relationship considerably.

One frosty day, the winter after the driving episode, Rachel came tearing into the house, screaming, "Susie, there's a big cat outside. A really big one, and he looks scary." Rachel was shaking with excitement and terror as she husked her coat onto the hook by the door.

I was aware that a large tawny cougar had been spotted in the vicinity a few days before. One of our neighbor's dogs had been killed. We had discussed it over the dinner table two nights before. Without a thought, I hurried into the bedroom and pulled the gun off the wall behind Dad's bed. Just as I got to the screen door of the kitchen, I saw the cougar slink under the new addition of the house. The tracks he left behind in the sparkling snow were huge.

"There he goes, Susie. I saw him. He went under the corner of the house," whispered Ruth as though the cougar could hear us from inside the kitchen.

"I know. I saw him too. You guys stay in here. Don't come outside, no matter what. You hear me? Stay inside!" I ordered as I loaded the gun and slipped on my work coat with shaking fingers.

Carefully, I opened up the dilapidated screen door and tiptoed as quietly as I could onto the creaky porch. Skirting the icy spots, for I certainly didn't want to slip and fall, I peered intently toward the spot where the cougar had disappeared. The girls behind me weren't making a sound. I wondered briefly if they were still breathing, it was so quiet. Four sets of eyes were riveted to the corner of the house, where there was no basement, only a space tall enough for a cougar on his belly. We waited, and waited, and waited. The cougar wasn't making any noise, either. It was as though he and I were silently determining each other's mettle. I didn't know if I was the hunter or the hunted.

At first I felt really nervous, but the longer he waited, the more composed I became. I again became aware of the pale sun on the snow, the huge cougar tracks partially erased by the sweep of his tail as he had crouched to fit under the house. The winter air was calm. I could even hear Irene and Rachel moving around inside the house. They had become bored with the waiting.

After quite a long time, Ruth hissed, "There's his nose."

"Shhhh, I know, I can see him," I whispered back. "Stay inside." I moved out onto the porch further and knelt down, tucking my dress under my right knee and steadying the gun barrel on the solid porch railing.

After tentatively sniffing the air, the large golden-brown cat slowly emerged from his confined space. He was moving steadily but with great stealth, until he was totally visible, from his big pointed yellow teeth to the tip of his long, occasionally twitching tail. When he was free from the house completely, I could see he was assuming a crouched position so he could spring. His amber eyes were staring intently at me. I stared back at him, equally as intense. I took careful aim, waiting on him to make the next move.

It happened so quickly. I gasped as my finger automatically pulled the trigger of the gun. It was like his movement had activated my trigger finger. The huge cougar had leaped forward and seemed to be hanging in midair. My next nervous reaction was to drop the gun, sprint for the kitchen door, and dive inside. Ruth was quickly fastening the door shut as I stood up shakily, rubbing my slightly bruised shoulder where the gun had kicked me.

"I think you got him, Susie. He's still out there, but I think you might have wounded him. He doesn't seem to be moving." Ruth was shaking as well, with aftershock. At the sound of the gunshot, Rachel and Irene had raced back in our direction.

"Well, I'm not going out to find out. I've had enough of that cat. My heart is still pounding," I exclaimed breathlessly. "Except we'll have to watch when the boys come home so he won't attack them. A wounded cougar can be pretty dangerous."

"How will we let them know?" quizzed Irene. "Rachel and I will sit by the window and watch for them to come home so we can warn them. Okay, Susie?"

"Sure, you do that! Don't forget to yell *loud*."

The boys, arriving home shortly after to a screaming little-girl chorus of "Be careful, there's a cougar in the yard," were more impressed than they wanted to admit as they checked out the dead cougar lying in the crusted snow. It seems he had been killed with one well-placed shot.

So, as you can see, I was pretty busy without worrying about some fellow hanging around hoping to date me. Morris didn't really seem to count as a date anyway because he was around so much. I mean, a date is someone you drool over at school, dream about at home, fantasize about with friends, and who, when he finally calls you on the telephone, makes you have a happiness seizure on the spot. Morris simply didn't qualify in any of those areas. He was more like a comfortable pair of house slippers you didn't have to think about. No thought necessary, just dependable for contentment and pleasure.

Sometime in the evening of almost every day, Morris would show up at the house. On cold days, he would hurry along the gravel road, with his well-worn brown coat buttoned up high around his neck and his beaver hat pulled down low over his ears.

As winter gave way to spring, his stride shortened, and he sort of sauntered up to the house, usually playing a lively tune on his harmonica. Often he would arrive for supper, with everyone making him welcome. He especially liked to come at suppertime if he had a story to share about work. Because he was boarding with the Johnson family, he would have been welcome there too, but somehow our house worked like a magnet latching onto a pin, drawing him there regularly.

"Hi, Sam, what did you learn at school today?" was a typical opening remark.

"Aw, you know! Stuff! Did anyone fall into the canal today, Morris?" Sam did okay with his schoolwork, but he would much rather hear an amusing story from Morris than talk about boring school.

"Not today. Although that young Peterson kid got caught trying to catch a fish up by the headgates. He didn't have a line, of course, so he was up to the top of his wading boots in freezing water. Ol' Mr. Fish saw him coming and lit out of there fast, his tail moving him just out of reach of Peterson's hand at every grab. Gentry Peterson vowed he would bring his pole and a juicy worm tomorrow and fry Mr. Fish for supper."

"Which reminds me. I sure am hungry tonight. Is Susanna in the kitchen stirring up something good to eat?"

"I don't know. Probably. It is just about suppertime." Sam would trail Morris through the kitchen door just in time for Morris to say, "Hey, Sam, how about helping me set the table? Sure smells good in here, Susanna. Pork chops are my favorite . . ." or roast beef and gravy, or ham, or whatever was being served that night.

Lacy white jonquils and periwinkle grape hyacinths were lifted carefully out of Morris's pocket one evening to grace the middle of the table. "I just couldn't pass up their cheeriness," he laughed, placing them with a little water in one of Mama's bone china cups.

Always chipper, optimistic, and lighthearted, Morris brought a ray of sunshine into the day. He often helped wash the dinner dishes, joined the boys in their bedroom for a game of checkers, but never over-stayed his welcome. When he could see that he needed to be gone, he would stretch and yawn, saying, "Guess it's time I headed home to bed. Morning comes early in Idaho." He'd shrug into his coat, "See ya later alligator." And we'd chorus the rejoinder he had learned on his mission, "After a while, crock-er-dile," as the screen door banged shut.

I had faithfully stayed home from school after Mama's death for about two months, and then shortly after potato harvest was finished, Dad insisted I return. It made the full-time job of housekeeping a heavy weight to carry, but the association with other kids was important, as I'm sure Dad was aware. I was still struggling to understand his wisdom in many things.

There was one guy from school, though, more popular than I could ever have imagined would be interested in me, who started to ask me out. Jim was a looker—dark wavy hair, aquiline nose, broad shoulders, and slim hips. He was one of the popular athletes, and, of course, when he asked me out I said I would go.

The only problem was that when Jim would arrive to pick me up in his old jalopy, Dad would think of three or four more things that absolutely had to be done before I could go. His oldest worn-out work pants just had to have a patch on the knee before the following morning. The ironing that had been sitting for a week had to be sprinkled with water and rolled tight that night. Or maybe the eggs had to be washed so they were ready to send into town to sell the next day. I would hurry from job to job, trying to complete each one so I could go on my date, but inevitably by the time the chores were finished, it was too late to go anywhere, and Jim would leave disappointed. That didn't last long. I mean, a fellow can only take that for so long and still keep hoping and coming around. Besides, I wasn't that much of a catch.

My disappointment finally hit fever pitch the night Jim was picking me up to attend the school prom with him. In the first place, I was totally surprised that Jim had asked me out again. It must have been the challenge of the unattainable.

I was so excited and had planned carefully, hurrying through a multitude of jobs assigned earlier, as well as some extras given at the last minute, so I could be ready on time. The pleasant anticipation of this special date had been savored for weeks as I chose my best dress to wear, adding a bit of ecru lace at the neck to make it more special. My long hair had been put up in rags the entire day to make it float in a cloud of curls.

Just before Jim arrived, Dad came into the house. "Susie, have you got the eggs washed? John needs to take them into town tomorrow to Harvey's."

"Yes, Dad, the eggs are washed. They are all ready to go in the bucket in the back room where it's cool."

"Well, yes. Good! What about that ironing that needed to be done? If you leave it sprinkled too long, it will mildew."

"It's done, Dad. Your shirts are folded in the chiffonnier. Even the hankies are pressed and folded in the top drawer. I was able to finish every piece." I felt almost smug to think that I could answer yes to every question. My planning had been complete for this occasion.

"Well, Susie, I just need you to finish sewing buttons on these work shirts of mine before you go to the dance."

My jaw dropped, my shoulders tensed, and I looked at Dad like he was out of his mind. There were always buttons to sew on work shirts. The job would keep! I had planned so carefully, finishing every possible job ahead of time that I could think of.

I stomped over to pick up the sewing basket filled with pins, needles, thimbles, and thread—my tension building. And then in a fit of rage, I turned and flung the basket straight at my father.

With the contents of the basket flying everywhere, I screamed out, "Why? Why do you always do this to me? Do you think Jim will just keep coming back to sit in our kitchen and wait over and over again? Tonight is prom night! He's one of the most popular guys at school. He doesn't have to take that! You're doing this on purpose . . . and I hate it! I hate it!" I sobbed, sinking to the floor, red-faced, my dress billowing out around me, entirely without composure.

As soon as I let go of the basket, I was astonished by my own impulsiveness and half scared I would receive a good thrashing, but the anger inside of me had built up for such a long time, and I could not contain it any longer. My emotions were completely out of control.

Through my tears and misery, and to my total shock and astonishment, I saw Dad slump onto the sturdy wooden deacon's bench near the door and begin to weep. With big rough farmer's hands held over his light green eyes and tears cascading down his cheeks, he responded with the most astounding answer possible. In fact, a few minutes before I was sure he hated me, but now I had full proof positive of his care and love for me.

"Oh, Susie, I wouldn't do this if I didn't love you so much. You know what happened to the Wilkins girl—she got in the family way—and if that happened to you—! You're such an impulsive little girl—oh I wouldn't want you to go through that. I just wouldn't be able to forgive myself. And what would I ever tell Marie?"

And then after an emotion-filled pause, Dad whispered, "But if it ever were to happen, I would never drive you from this home. You would still have a home, and the little one would be cared for."

The accepted procedure at that time for unwed mothers

was to denounce them and banish them from their home. My dad was so aware of the lack of a mother in our home to guide me and so fearful of high emotions during the dating years that he was trying in the only way he knew to protect me—from others and from myself.

I had never been so sure before of my dad's love for me, and warm, tender feelings welled up in my formerly rock-hard heart as I threw my young, slender arms around his work-worn neck and mingled my tears with his.

A short time later, when Jim knocked at the door, I answered quickly.

"I won't be able to go out with you tonight after all, Jim," I said softly. "I was really looking forward to it, but now I can't go."

The red eyes and tousled hair must have presented quite a picture, and I later wondered what was going through his mind at that instant. But all Jim said was, "Okay, Susanna, but I won't ask you out again." Bitterly he turned and left—never to return.

My father and I sat up and talked for a long time that night. Dad finally promised he wouldn't chase the boys away any longer because he could see I could distinguish right from wrong and was committed to live as I had been taught.

Chapter 5

In this world, there are many things for which to be grateful. I was particularly glad to welcome my eighteenth birthday at the end of April and the conclusion of twelfth grade at the end of May. It had been uncomfortable around school for me after prom night and the "Jim disappointment." Thank goodness the school year was almost over when that occurred! No one could really understand why I hadn't gone to prom, probably because I was reluctant to open up and "tell all" about my relationship with my father and especially the understanding we had come to that evening. That was my business and I wasn't a tell-all kind of person. Let them think what they would. Schoolmates usually listen but then talk about it behind your back, anyway. Because of all my insecurities, it was so much easier to be home with the family than trying to cope with friends.

As the summer proceeded, my home chores settled into a routine that was rather boring, though necessary and acceptable. Housework would never be my favorite thing to do, but it was part of life. The weeks continued to move quickly forward in a constant ebb and flow.

In my butter churning and book reading days, a job that should have taken half an hour stretched out for the entire morning. Washing dishes for a family the size of mine would often take me from after breakfast until time to begin dinner preparation. There was no such thing as lunch at my house. Dinner was a much heartier meal, as was supper. The older I got, the faster I seemed to accomplish what needed to be done.

Somewhere along the way, the realization finally dawned on me that if I did the job more quickly, instead of daydreaming so much, I could have some time to myself. Some days I wouldn't have minded churning the butter again so I could have some reading time, but that was Rachel's job now.

It was well into June. The balmy, verdant summer days were lengthening, and the evenings were mild and delicious. For all the routine, life was good.

I had just finished up the dinner dishes when I heard a peculiar noise outside. I slipped into the little-used parlor to take a quick peek out of the lace-curtained window. Through the small glass panes, I caught sight of a motorcar I had never seen before, chugging *s-l-o-w-l-y* down our gravel lane toward the house! It had been washed and waxed so perfectly that the flaming crimson setting sun glinted off the fenders in several directions like flashes of lightning. The cautious driver obviously didn't want to stir up any dust.

And then I started to laugh. It was Morris, driving the car like he owned it, with pride in every bounce!

"Susanna!" he called out as he spied me in the window, the ring in his voice filled with excitement. "Susanna, come out here. See what I've got."

He didn't have to shout twice. I hit the side screen door on the run, equally as excited as he was.

"Morris, is this yours?" My eyes were huge and shining as I skidded to a stop a few feet from the car and then started looking it over carefully. Even though it was an old car, it was painted and fixed up just fine.

"Yup! All mine!" His exuberance was apparent.

"Where did you get it? And how? Are you rich?" I giggled. "Not rich any more, huh?" I could tease Morris. He was like my sixth brother—only better. He was my best friend.

"Do you like it, Susanna? How about the color? Navy blue!" and he raised and lowered his eyebrows in an ol' Groucho Marx gesture. "My personal favorite!"

I was much too entranced with the car to be entertained

by the man.

"I thought all Fords were black. Did you paint it? It's *beautiful!*" I tentatively touched the back fender, careful not to leave fingerprints.

"I didn't paint it, but Mr. Fenton did. He said he was tired of seeing only black cars on the road, except for the really expensive ones, and decided to try his luck with a paint job. Actually, I haven't quite bought it yet. I wanted you to see it first and—you know—see if you liked it. Do you?"

"Of course I like it. I love it! Can you afford it?" I knew Morris had been working an extra job at Mr. Fenton's service station in town three evenings a week.

"Actually," he said, showing off his straight white teeth with his cute crooked grin, "I can. Let's go pay Mr. Fenton right now."

And that was the beginning of going riding with Morris. I wasn't sure how Dad would take to that, but as reluctant as Dad was to have boys date me, he couldn't see a thing wrong with having Morris around our place almost constantly.

"I'm going riding with Morris," I would sing out after supper dishes were done, and Dad would call back from the settee in the parlor, "Don't be late."

Or, "Uncle Jake has a new pony. I'm going riding in the car with Morris to see it."

Dad's only comment would be to remind me gently, "Supper needs to be on the table at six sharp, Susie."

Or, "I'm just running into town with Morris to pick up a few kitchen supplies."

"Anything for an excuse, Susie," Walt would tease. "Check on my boot polish at Harvey's, okay?"

And so, Morris began inviting me to "go riding" with him fairly often.

"You guys headed into Coltman to the church dance?" Morris would ask the boys.

"Of course," assured Fred. "Birds fly, don't they?"

"You can head out now, if you want. I'll take Susie with me

after she's through with her chores," he would answer easily. Oh, it was lovely to always have a ride without depending on an older brother.

It seemed Morris and I could talk about almost anything comfortably. We laughed or were serious, depending on what the situation demanded. Sometimes as we chatted, we pointed out an antelope bounding through the fields and into the trees, or a black skunk, with a telltale white stripe, trying his darned-est to hide behind a fence post. At other times, we just sat in companionable silence. Often Morris would sing his favorite hymns in his rich baritone voice. If summer was in a hurry before, it was now hitting its stride at full gallop speed as we spent time together.

One especially fun outing took us clear into Idaho Falls to his parents' house. I had never met them before and was nervous about the prospect, but Morris laughed at my fears.

"They are only parents. Just like yours. Just like everyone's. My dad is a tease, and my mother is a sweetheart."

"Morris, my dad is not a tease. We are getting along better than we used to, but he is much too serious to tease us children."

"Susanna, your dad just has a lot on his mind. He's an okay guy. I get along with him fine."

"I guess I do too," I replied thoughtfully, "most of the time." I hadn't thought about that for quite a while. But, come to think of it—it was true.

Ransford, Morris's father, was a rather slight-built man, only about five feet eight inches tall. His thick, full, walnut-colored hair was worn in a slight pompadour in the front and then trimmed up neat and short on the sides. Round-lensed, wire-framed glasses made him look quite serious, until he started to speak, and then his smile broke through, and after that, his smile was all you saw. His wife, Lodisa, was easily as tall as Ransford. She was built like a grandma should be—round and full in face and body. Her hair was blonde, with a splattering of gray. With regular, even quite handsome features, she was easy to look at and, as I quickly found out, easy to be with.

When we arrived in Idaho Falls, Lodisa had arranged for us to go on a picnic with the two of them. A picnic! I had never in my life gone on an adult picnic. In a lovely, shady spot under a widely spread oak down by the Snake River, we spread a heavy quilt on the ground and sat down on it to eat our lunch—delicious thick-sliced ham, cheddar cheese, and leaf-lettuce sandwiches, washed down with cold, tart lemonade. What an adventure!

I quickly found out that although Ransford might often look quite serious, he was exactly what Morris had said—a tease.

"Susanna, what do you think of this poor boy of mine? Spending all his hard-earned money on a navy blue car! Ol' Fenton probably charged him double the price just for the paint job. And he tells us you think it was okay for him to buy it."

I wasn't used to being kidded by a father. My brothers teased me mercilessly, but I never joked around with my dad. And because I wasn't used to a father figure doing the jesting, I wasn't sure how to take it.

"Dad, you like that navy blue color as well as I do." Morris was right there, easing the way.

"Have Ransford tell you about when he bought his first car, Susanna." Lodisa too quickly realized I needed help with verbal fencing and adroitly stepped in, redirecting the harassment back to her husband

I had missed my own mother achingly since her death. She had always been my source of reassurance. Lodisa was much like her—interesting, peaceful, and easy to be around—much like Morris. In fact, the teasing qualities of Ransford and the calm assurance of Lodisa translated into a marvelous combination in Morris.

"Oh, come on, Dicie! Susanna doesn't want to hear about that old thing."

"You started this, Ransford." Lodisa wasn't about to let him off the hook easily.

"So, I got took a little." Morris's dad looked chagrinned. "Actually, that car was quite a looker!"

"Yes, it looked great! So great! It just didn't run! You tell her, Ransford." Lodisa was smiling benignly.

"Well," he began slowly, "it didn't run because there—there wasn't a motor in it," he finished quickly.

"Ransford just didn't happen to find out that little fact until he had already given the guy two hundred dollars." Now Lodisa's smile was huge and sparkling.

"Well, you have to remember that the quick-talking salesman could have sold a fridge to an Eskimo." Ransford was intent in his justification.

"Nope, just to a Teeples." We were all chuckling now. Ransford looked a little sheepish, but he didn't mind the joke being on him. It was obviously an old family favorite, and it was plain to see he actually enjoyed laughing about it again himself.

What a delightful day! I hated to see it come to an end.

Each day brought Morris out to the house on some excuse. If anything helped speed up the chores, it was the anticipation of seeing the navy blue bomb or hearing that familiar gurgling laughter. Bottom line—I enjoyed Morris's company immensely, but one perfect summer day in late August, he ruined it all.

Fields, a lush green turning slowly to gold, with the wheat beginning to head out perfectly, rippled softly like a wave moving to shore. It looked like the weather was cooperating for a bounteous and most welcome harvest. A smattering of soft, white, fluffy clouds—easily identifiable as a man with a wart on his huge nose, or a tortoise with tiny legs—moved lazily through the azure sky, prodded by the whisper of a breeze. Hot, lazy, replete—what a marvelous day! And then—

"Susanna, I was wondering—I mean—I know we really haven't talked about this before, but—I—um—have been wanting to bring up the subject all summer."

He continued to hesitate—actually stutter—like he was

scared to go on. "I—I've wanted to ask you, uh, I mean, what I really want to say is, I—uh—love you—Susanna, and I want you to marry me." Morris stammered haltingly, as he made his outrageous proposal.

We had just arrived at my house in Morris's car, having run a quick errand to the neighbors for Dad. The mood on the ride had been one of joking and laughter, and suddenly I felt we had picked up a too-somber hitchhiker along the way without even knowing it. I would have thought he was still joking if it hadn't been for his suddenly serious face and his even more serious tone of voice. The switch in mood was so sudden and total; I was completely taken by surprise by the shift in the conversation.

I had been anxious to get out of the car and into the cooler house to fix a tall, cold glass of orange juice for each of us, but that unexpected proclamation of love made me turn and look at Morris as if he were from another planet. Whatever possessed him to say such a thing?

With perspiration beading my brow, and my heart beating a hundred miles a minute, I answered him almost without conscious thought. "I can't marry you, Morris, I'm committed to my family. I thought you knew that. I promised my mother—"

"She didn't mean forever, Susanna. I think your mother would have liked me; the rest of your family seems to. I have loved you ever since I first met you, and I think—" He was warming up to his subject, but I wouldn't allow him to even finish his thought.

"No, Morris, I can't marry you. It's out of the question." With that, I quickly got out of the car and, on the run, headed toward the house.

Morris sat still for a few more minutes in the steaming car, trying to digest what I had just said. He backed out of the driveway, and not looking back, he headed slowly down the graveled lane.

Of course, I expected to see him on my doorstep the

following day. I wasn't sure if he would repeat his astonishing declaration or apologize for it. He might even tease me by asking if I didn't know how to take a joke. I mulled over in my mind every little detail of how our next conversation could proceed. He might ask again, giving me more justification for his cause; or he might drop the matter entirely, foreseeing my rebuttal and biding his time for a more plausible opportunity. In either instance, I was ready for him, with all my realistic arguments firmly in place. To me it wasn't a joking matter. And it certainly wasn't a possibility. Morris was just a very good friend, one I enjoyed having around. He was just a pleasant person—not someone to marry.

I must say, I was more than a little miffed when Morris didn't show up on schedule the following day. I fumed and fretted as he continued to stay away. On the outside, I was trying to act like nothing was amiss, but for all my good intentions, the rest of the family began to speak to me only when necessary because all they received were short, biting answers. No one else in the family knew of the proposal—or the refusal—at all. It was soon evident that they all wondered what was ailing me.

After receiving so much loving attention from Morris, I was hurt and disappointed by his neglect. It didn't help, either, to subconsciously know that I had brought it upon myself. But then, I was fully justified in my response to him. A promise is a promise, and I had definitely promised my mother that I would take care of the family in her absence. Nevertheless, my hangdog expression must have been more apparent than I had thought.

"Susie, for heaven's sake, stop moping around. Did you and Morris have a tiff?" Walt inquired.

"I don't know what you're talking about, Walt. And besides, it's none of your business."

"Fine, have it your way," Walt drawled. "I just wondered why you hurried to the parlor window every time you heard someone coming up the drive."

And then, for he had saved his punch line for maximum effect at the last, "Morris isn't working for ol' man James anymore. He took a job up in St. Anthony, spraying trees and cutting firewood. He's been gone since Tuesday."

If Walt had punched me in the stomach—hard—he could not have stunned me more. Turning quickly away so he wouldn't see the raging emotion in my eyes, I stumbled over to a kitchen chair and sat down. What a rotten way to find out that Morris was gone—maybe for good.

As the days and weeks passed without Morris being around, I began to reassess my impetuous answer. I missed his bright smile and his talkative nature, his happy countenance and his caring ways. Oh, what had I done?

So, toward the end of November, three interminably long months later when Morris wrote asking if he could come and see me, I was ecstatic and immediately answered back in the affirmative. Those three months had dragged on in bleak loneliness for me. Sweltering summer had turned into blazing fall, which slowly turned into wind-chilling winter. The swift-moving days slowed their forward rush. Suddenly, there was no end to my forlorn monotony.

Before coming to my house, even though he had to pass Coltman to get to Idaho Falls, Morris drove home to visit his parents. It had been the same three long months since he had seen them. He had been living in a lean-to in the forest area of St. Anthony: poor heat, a cornhusk bed, and a leaking roof. Now he was looking forward to a fire in his parents' fireplace, for he was chilled through when he arrived from his long drive. His navy blue car might look great, but the heater was pretty finicky and didn't work so well sometimes. Oh, to have a good home-cooked meal and a stimulating conversation!

He barely got inside the door before Ransford, his father, made a startling request. "Son, the Church authorities have put out the call for short-term missionaries to serve for the next six months. You are between jobs right now, and I think you should offer your services."

"Oh, gosh, Dad. Let me warm up and catch my breath." Morris removed his heavy coat, hung it on a peg in the back entry, and moved into the living room where the fire was burning brightly, just as he had imagined it would be. He sat down heavily on the hearth, and then with confusion on his face, Morris looked at Ransford.

"Dad, I've served my mission—two and a half years' worth in the Southern States under the direction of President Callis. You know that! It was a great opportunity, and I loved every minute of it, but I've given my service as a missionary."

And then, before his dad could respond, he added, "And besides, I'm headed up to Susanna's in just a couple of hours. I want to ask her again to marry me."

"Again?"

"Well, I kind of suggested it in August before taking that job in St. Anthony, but she—well—she—"

"You have asked her already, and she turned you down? Has she given you any indication she would say 'yes' this time to such a proposal?" inquired Ransford with raised eyebrows.

"No—but—well—I haven't asked her for a while. I haven't even been around for a while, as you know. And Dad, I want her for my wife."

Ransford ignored the plea in Morris's voice as he moved ahead with his own agenda.

"Morris, this mission is only for six months. Maybe in six months' time she'll be more agreeable to your plan. You know we think the world of Susanna. In the meantime, you can give a tremendous service to the Church. Six months isn't forever, and when the Church calls for missionaries, we need to respond." Ransford was full of the fervor of appealing to his son's righteous nature. He hadn't been able to serve a mission himself when he was young. What an opportunity for his son to be of service again so soon! He knew he had raised a boy who was anxious to serve the Lord and to do what was right.

"Oh, Dad, I don't know," sighed Morris.

His thoughts were churning. He had truly been taken by

surprise by this unusual request. His only thought had been to ask Susanna again to marry him, hoping she had missed him as much as he had missed her during his time away. He was well aware of her curt answer before, but she had seemed so effusive in her reply to his letter asking if he could come and see her again. On the other hand, she hadn't even considered the possibility of them being married when he first verbalized his feelings. She had acted like he had offended her when he proposed.

After a considerable pause, and considering the likelihood of Susanna saying "yes"—or more likely—"no" to his proposal, Morris softly muttered despondently, "I guess so."

Ransford arose immediately, went directly to the phone, and called the stake president. "President Crawford," he said, his voice ringing with pride, "Morris is willing to accept a call to be one of your missionaries."

"That's great, Brother Teeples, I'll make it official at once. He will probably be leaving in just a few days," was the president's ready response.

Chapter 6

I know I am stubborn. Whenever I have truly wanted something I have gone after it, like learning how to drive the car. But I had never seen a stubborn streak in Morris. He always seemed so laid-back and easy-going. The stubbornness was there, though—strong and healthy! His determination was relentless and therefore could not be taken lightly!

Morris had declared he wanted to marry me. Me! I could not imagine why! I didn't consider myself pretty or talented. I knew I wasn't social like he was. I didn't catch on to jokes as fast as the other girls. I got mad at people for some of the dumbest reasons. I liked to dance, and he didn't. He loved to sing, and I could barely carry a tune. I was only eighteen—well, eighteen and a half. I had the weight of many responsibilities on my shoulders and felt duty-bound to carry through with what I had been asked to do. What did he see in me? Why would he want to marry me? How did he ever get such a weird thought in his mind in the first place?

Nevertheless, I had said he could come. He must have figured *that* was worth *something*—that maybe I had more feelings for him than were readily apparent, considering my reaction the last time he had mentioned marriage. In his mind, I suppose, an invitation to come back had to mean something positive.

It was late in November. The day was so frosty that the air was almost difficult to breathe. Naked branches reached toward the sky, shrugging their up-lifted arms into their icy winter coats. Below, a light snowfall covered the ground, shimmering like tiny diamonds glittering in the weak winter sun.

The day was pleasing to Morris. He loved the seasons. Cold weather always made him appreciate a crackling fire, a cup of hot chocolate, and good company. Before leaving Idaho Falls, he had taken the opportunity to fix the car heater, and it was trying hard to cooperate. Mostly though, his warmth and pleasure were emanating from within.

As Morris drove to our farm, a delicious, plausible plan began to formulate in his mind. This would work—maybe! Yes, it just had to work! It was a good plan. He was anxious to try it out, so when he arrived and found I was in town with my sisters, he was quite perturbed.

"I'm sorry, Morris, but Susie isn't here, and I'm not sure how soon they are planning to return. I think Rachel had a dentist appointment, or something."

"John, I need a big favor from you. I need to talk to Susanna, and I don't especially want the little girls around." Morris then told John about accepting the short-term mission call for the Church. "I don't know how soon I will be going, but I think it's just a matter of days."

"A matter of days! Wow! Your dad really got you into something this time, didn't he?" whistled John.

"Would you come into town and drive the girls home so I could take Susanna with me for a while? It's important!"

John, reading between the lines, smiled knowingly. He had always liked Morris and readily agreed.

In no time, they found us doing a bit of shopping.

"Ruth, get Rachel and Irene so we can go home now," John called out, taking charge of his younger sisters.

"Hi, Morris! Oh, good, Morris is back! Good to see you again! Why can't we ride with Morris and Susie? Come on, John! Let us!" they begged.

But John knew Morris was depending on him. "Hey! Hey! They'll be home in a while and then you can see Morris! He's coming for supper, you know," John finished with an assuring wink and a quick smile.

The girls finally got in Dad's car with John as I slid into the semi-warmth of Morris's car with him. Morris tucked a blanket securely around my legs. He knew I was usually cold, and he didn't want me dwelling on the temperature because there were more important things to consider.

With such an exquisite winter scene, it was impossible not to appreciate the sparkling, clean look of the countryside. Burrowing deep with their noses through the crusty surface, hunting for clumps of grass, the sheep looked overstuffed in their thick, fleece coats. Their black noses and ears stood out in stark relief against the glittering snow. The barbed wire fences, dripping with shimmering crystals, divided the fields into tidy geometric jewels. As we neared the junction of the road, I was surprised to see Morris turn northeast toward Ammon.

"Morris, why are we going this way? It's the long way around, and I need to get home and start supper for the family."

"Oh," he kidded, "the long way around is the sweet way home."

"But where are we going? You must have some particular place in mind," I said. I just couldn't figure out what had gotten into him and why he was being so evasive.

"Susanna, I just want to be with you for a few extra minutes. We haven't seen each other for several months. I didn't think you'd mind the extra time!" He was beginning to sound exasperated.

"Well," my voice softened, "I don't, actually. It's great to see you again. Tell me about your job, or is it finished? What are you planning to do now?"

"Actually—" he paused, debating whether to talk about the St. Anthony job or the topic that weighed heaviest on his mind. *Why delay the inevitable?* he thought and then rushed ahead, "I have just accepted a short-term mission call for the Church."

Morris turned slightly to see my reaction.

"I stopped to see Mom and Dad on my way here, and Dad had it practically arranged. It seems they have been looking for young men who can serve a mission for six months. I wasn't sure I wanted to go on another mission so soon, but Dad was pressuring me, and I *am* between jobs—" Morris's voice faded slowly as he paused to let it all sink in. And then he added, "I finally said yes, I would go."

"Where will you be going on this mission?" I asked in a small voice, my eyes wide with wonder at the suddenness of his plans. I really hadn't expected such an announcement and in my heart was disappointed to think he would be gone again so soon. I knew Morris had already served a two and a half year mission in the Southern States, and I hadn't considered such a time commitment in his future any more than he had a few short hours before.

"I don't know yet. Dad just called President Crawford about two hours ago to tell him I would go, so I haven't got the official call as far as where I will be going. This wasn't really in my plans at all, but I've told you before how persistent my dad can be. For some reason—" Again he paused as if reassessing what he had done. "I just couldn't say no." Morris was looking steadily at the frozen gravel road now as he drove.

I pulled my gaze from Morris's stiff profile and stared out the side window at the frosty fence posts strung with jeweled wire. My eyes were blind to their pristine beauty as I tried to feel happy for Morris. Church missions were calls from the Lord. They were fondly anticipated and could be rewarding experiences. Why were foreign longings tugging at my thoughts and invading my heart? I didn't understand why he felt he needed to go again so soon, and I certainly didn't understand why I was feeling so moody and bereft.

By this time, we were about halfway home and were passing my bishop's well-kept farm. Before I could comprehend what was happening, Morris turned into Bishop Wooten's lane, pulled up to the neat, white farmhouse, and stopped. I looked at him like "now what?"

"I just have a hankering to stop and see the bishop," was his explanation. "Come in with me for a minute; this won't take long."

He must be more excited about the call than he sounds, I thought as I rather reluctantly followed him through the chilled air to the kitchen door from which delicious smells were emanating, *if he wants to share the news with the bishop.*

We knocked on the door, and Sister Wooten, a short, stout, gray-haired lady wearing a large white apron dusted liberally with flour, answered. She told us the bishop was out in the barn milking the cows, but he wouldn't mind having us come out there, so Morris and I trudged down the frozen path to the stately red barn.

Bishop Wooten was a short, stocky, cheerful man, and after a friendly greeting and some small talk, Morris told him of his forthcoming mission call. After looking intently at Morris for a moment or two, the good bishop turned to me, asking, "Susanna, would you mind going up to the kitchen and visiting with Sarah so I could talk to Morris alone for a few minutes?"

"O-o-o-k-a-a-y," I agreed. What else could I do? I was a little confused but assumed a private talk had something to do with the mission call. Maybe a worthiness interview—I didn't know. The only thing was, Bishop Wooten was not Morris's bishop, so that really confused me. Or maybe Morris was having second thoughts about going and just needed to talk it through with a bishop? That was almost the way it had seemed in the car. I turned around slowly and climbed the path back to the kitchen door alone as the cold seeped through the fabric of my winter coat.

"How is the family, Susanna?" Sister Wooten inquired as I reentered the warm, cozy kitchen.

It felt good to be inside. A brisk rub of my hands together quickly sent tingles of restored feeling to them. The action was automatic, as my mind was centered on the red barn at the bottom of the path.

"Oh, they are fine." As much as I loved to talk to Morris, I was rather shy around others and didn't have a whole lot to say to Sister Wooten.

"There are some fresh-baked cookies there on the counter, if you would like one. They're called snickerdoodles. It's my mother's recipe, and our grandchildren love them." She was trying hard to involve me in a conversation, but my mind was on Morris and the bishop, and I didn't respond.

"That's a fine looking car Morris has." Again she tried to include me in a discussion but finally realized it would be a one-sided conversation at best, as I said distantly, "Yes, it is."

"Susanna, why don't you wait in the parlor while I finish up here in the kitchen. I'm sure the bishop and Morris will be coming up to the house soon."

I was grateful for the escape. With my hands folded tightly in my lap, I sat silently on the stiff, horsehair sofa. Sister Wooten kept a pleasant house. Family pictures graced the Victorian wallpapered walls, homemade candy sat temptingly in a candy dish on the end table, and Church books were scattered around, convenient for ready enjoyment. My gaze took it all in quickly, and then my thoughts reverted back to Morris again and my eyes became glazed and unseeing.

All of this had to do with Morris and his life. I couldn't imagine why I was so nervous, my heart beating rapidly inside my chest. I wished we had never stopped here. But then, that was insane. I really didn't mind if Morris needed to clear up something with the bishop. I guess I just wished he had come by himself and let me go home with my sisters. Why had he pulled me along with him? Did he know all the time he was going to stop at the bishop's? Talking to a bishop was a personal thing. Whether he wanted to inform the bishop of his mission call, clear up an indiscretion, or discuss how to get out of this crazy, quickly made commitment was his affair. Morris had no right to make me feel uncomfortable and out-of-place here in the bishop's home. I could have waited in the car—although I probably would have been frozen—or he could have come to see me at home after this stop at the bishop's was over and taken care of. My mind raced around and around, over and over again on the same muddy racetrack, trying to assign some sense to this stop and to my jumbled thoughts.

Some time later—I had no idea how much time had elapsed—Morris and the bishop entered the house through the kitchen door, laughing and enjoying each other's company. They moved together easily into the parlor.

"I fear I smell of the barnyard," stated Bishop Wooten. "It will only take me a few minutes to change my clothes and then I will be much more pleasant company." And then, looking directly at me, "I hope you won't mind waiting, Susanna, because I would like to visit with you a few minutes when I return." Without waiting for a reply, he left the room.

"Morris, why would the bishop want to talk to me?" Now that he was back again, I felt more comfortable. "Did Bishop Wooten find you worthy to serve a mission? That talk took quite a while. I'll bet you had some high talking to do to convince him you should go." Gently teasing Morris seemed the best way to handle the situation. I could do that because I was sure in my mind that he was mission-worthy.

He grinned and then said, "Oh, I've had a really good talk with Bishop Wooten, and now he wants to talk to you." The way he said it sent off warning bells in my brain. Seeing my startled expression, he added, almost as an afterthought, "Probably just to ask how the family is and stuff."

All of a sudden, the air around me constricted. "Morris, the bishop can ask me about my family any time. Is he coming back to visit with us or talk with me alone? What's going on here?" My nervousness had returned in full force.

"Come on, Susanna. He's the one who said he wanted to talk to you. I guess you'll just have to wait and see what he says."

Before I could protest much further, Bishop Wooten returned, and to my chagrin, Morris quickly excused himself and walked outside like he needed a big breath of fresh air.

"Sit down, Susanna," invited the bishop. As soon as we were seated, he got right to the point. "Do you know that this fine young man wants to marry you?"

I stared at Bishop Wooten like he had just accused me of not being morally clean. "Yes—yes, I guess I do," I finally stammered. "He asked me last August to marry him, but—" the bishop had really caught me off guard.

"Well, do you love him?" The bishop wasn't being gentle or even considerate with his questions, as far as I was concerned. In fact, he was beginning to raise my ire. I just couldn't figure out what business this was of his. Besides, Morris hadn't even mentioned marriage to me since the last time I had seen him.

Obviously, that was what he had been talking to the bishop about, though. That made me kind of mad too. The problem was that I had been raised to show great respect for my bishop. I couldn't ignore his inquiry or be abrupt with him, which was what I wanted to do just about then.

"I don't know for sure, Bishop." My voice was stronger now. This was a subject I had given considerable thought to, although that thought had been right after Morris had popped the question last August, and I hadn't contemplated it much lately.

"I like him a lot. I feel comfortable around him, and we have fun together." And then, with my voice trailing off somewhat, "I must admit I missed him a lot more while he was gone than I thought I would. But do I love him? I don't know. And," I continued, my voice again strengthening, "I made a promise to my mother to take care of my family."

"Oh, yes, I know you did, and you have done a fine job fulfilling that promise; but Susanna, that wasn't meant to be forever. Your father will wish to remarry someday, and then you will no longer be needed or wanted there."

Not needed or wanted! The bishop's statement hit me like a roaring freight train. I had *never* thought of that. I just assumed my service would be absolutely necessary for years to come. How many years, I had never contemplated. I was only eighteen, and the younger children were still too young to be on their own. And they were certainly not old enough to take over running my father's household! That was my job, anyway, not theirs. In a way, my responsibility was like a security blanket for me. I knew what was required of me each day, and I was now fully capable of the job at hand, and indispensable—to my way of thinking.

"The real question is," the bishop said, pulling me back to the conversation, or interview, or whatever it was, "do you love Morris?"

"Bishop, I—I don't know," I stuttered. That was still the question I was avoiding, both in my own mind and out loud to anyone else.

Quietly contemplating my answer for a full minute, the bishop finally sighed softly and said, "Well, I know you haven't asked for my advice, but I am going to give it to you anyway. I would advise you to marry this young man. I am aware he is leaving on a mission in a short time, but while he is gone your father will have a chance to adjust to the notion of you being married, and he can make arrangements for when you will no longer be at home to help there. It's time he did that, anyway."

And then, to my utter amazement, the bishop continued, "Susanna, if you follow my advice and marry Morris, I promise you that through the years you will receive blessings beyond measure—so many that you won't be able to count them all."

I sat ramrod stiff like I was in a trance, my mouth slightly ajar, not looking to the right or the left, but staring straight into my bishop's eyes. I mean, what was I supposed to say to that?

The bishop returned my penetrating look for several seconds, and then he spoke again, normally, not at all like he had just delivered me a deathblow.

"Just in case you do decide to follow my advice, I am going to write you a temple recommend to be married. You still have your free agency, so you don't have to use the recommend, but if you want it, you'll have it."

Again I was totally speechless, and the interview ended with Bishop Wooten handing me a signed temple recommend.

Like a girl in a trance, I said my good-byes to the good bishop, left the house, and climbed into the open door of the waiting car.

"Morris," I whispered, once we were back onto the road and headed home, "I am so confused. I've been taught all my life to never go against anything a bishop says. Even a suggestion." I found myself nervously pleating my coat between my fingers as I struggled with my thoughts and the enormity of my words.

"I truly don't know if I love you, and also, I made that promise to Mama. It was not just a whim; it was a commitment, an oath, a pledge." I looked at Morris at last with pleading in my eyes. "I just assumed I was supposed to honor that for a much longer time. The girls are still young."

"Oh, Susanna! I love you! What did the bishop say that has you in such a quandary?" I could see the compassion in his eyes. "I never meant to put you through this."

"Oh," I said with a little half-laugh. "Only that if I marry you I will receive so many blessings through my life," I choked slightly on a half-sob, "that I won't be able to count them all. Morris—"

But Morris had pulled to the side of the road and set the car brake so he could take me tenderly in his arms.

"He said that before long I wouldn't be needed at home to take care of the family, or even wanted there." I was sobbing softly now, my wet face pressed firmly to his chest. "He said that Dad could possibly marry again, and then, I guess, the girls would have a new mother. I've never considered these things before."

"You have been doing such a wonderful job with your family. But, Susanna, he's right. You're not the mother, and you should be able to have your own life. You know I will support you in any help you still feel you need to give to your family, but I want you for my wife," Morris stated unequivocally. "That will never change."

"Well, I won't talk to Dad about it!" I stated defensively, stiffening, not knowing what else to say.

"That's all right. I never expected you to," smiled Morris. "That's my job." He kissed me gently and tucked me under his arm as he slowly pulled back onto the road to continue home.

When Morris and I arrived at the house, I quickly went into the kitchen to begin fixing supper. My mind was in a whirl. The promise I had made to my mother a scant year and a half before felt like a heavy weight I could not lay down, and yet the promise the bishop had given me was equally heavy in its import. What was I to do? And the time was so short! I felt the pressure of needing to make a quick decision because Morris was to leave for the mission field in a few short days.

Morris had told me one other important thing while we sat by the side of the road; he claimed he wouldn't go on the mission if I said no to marriage with him. He had already accepted the call, but he said he would get out of it somehow if he needed to. He didn't want to leave me again without knowing I would be his forever on his return. Oh, how I needed my mother as I had never needed her before!

No one seemed the least bit disturbed to have Morris there for supper. It had been such a usual occurrence for so long, and they were happy to see him again. He kept them well entertained throughout the entire meal, sharing stories of his job up in the forest area near St. Anthony. After supper, the girls scurried off to another room, knowing they could get out of helping with the dishes when this particular guest was around.

After finishing the dishes in almost complete silence—quite a change from the levity of the dinner hour—I pointed out my father, who was resting on the divan in the parlor, to Morris. He just smiled his soft smile and walked steadfastly toward Dad.

"John," I said, bursting into his room at the top of the stairs. "Could I talk to—oh, hi, Walt and Fred."

I had wanted desperately to talk to John privately for a few minutes. John was my closest family confident. I knew whatever I told him wouldn't go any further, and although he teased me at times like the other boys did, when I needed advice or counsel, he gave it freely or listened attentively, whichever was needed.

We all talked together for a time, but I just couldn't think of a way to get the other boys to leave. I finally blurted out to all of them what was happening. They were delighted. They laughed and slapped each other on the back, like they were the ones getting married.

"Come on you guys, what should I do? This is serious!"

"*Do?* Do, little sister? Marry the guy! He's so much in love with you he doesn't know if he's coming or going," Walt chuckled.

"Besides, he'll make a terrific brother-in-law," added Fred.

"But what about my promise to Mama?"

All three began to chuckle again, with even John joining in. "You don't have to worry about that. She never expected you to stay single forever."

I left the room in disgust. They hadn't helped the situation out one little bit.

Chapter 7

In desperation, I hastily pulled on my gray flannel coat and slipped out the back door of the house. I hurried across the porch and down the stairs, hoping the bracing winter night air would clear my mind and help me think. I headed in the direction of the canal, where I often walked when I had a problem. The soft swish of the constantly moving water seemed to have a soothing effect on me. Even in winter, when it should have been frozen over with ice, the water moved gracefully between the high embankments.

Somehow, it had always seemed easier to pray outside where I knew I wouldn't be interrupted. Maybe it stemmed back to my first real experience with having a prayer answered. As I stood watching the water slowly drifting by, my thoughts went back to that day long ago.

Spring, in the form of tender green grass and tiny purple crocuses, was beginning to peek through the small patches of snow, which were still lingering after a long, bleak winter. The red brick one-room schoolhouse had withstood the enthusiastic clamor of sixteen students of all ages for another day. Usually there were considerably more bodies, easily twice that number, but spring farm work had relentlessly whittled away at the attendance figures, with many of the older kids staying home to help. Some days Mr. Stucki wondered why the school board demanded he continue to hold school in the spring. And then again, it was rather pleasant to have just the younger children there on occasion. Their eager young minds made teaching a delight, for their active spirits were constantly wishing to rush ahead to the next exhilarating concept. Different types of learning activities could be offered on days when all the students were nine years old and under. However, when day's end came, these same children were just as anxious to be free of school as they were to learn during the pleasantly informative day.

"C'mon, Susie, hurry up. The other kids are leaving us. We'll have to run to catch 'em."

"I'm comin', Mary. Hang on a second." My short, almost eight-year-old legs were pumping to catch up with Mary and the gang. "You know, this is the first time I've ever carried the cream check home to my father. Usually John or Fred takes it home when they're given out."

"I know. Esther has our check. The teachers always give it to the oldest kid in the family at school. I've never carried ours home."

Each week, Dad took our extra cream into town to sell, as did several of the other fathers from surrounding farms; and every second Tuesday the cream checks were distributed at the school, with the oldest child in the family taking it home. Because my older school-aged brothers and sister were home preparing for spring planting, I was the oldest Butikofer child at school, and the check was given to me. My—was I proud! I felt so grown-up and responsible. Dad had specifically asked me that morning as I left the house if I could bring the check home for him because he knew it was the day the cream checks arrived. He had emphasized the importance of this responsibility—as if *that* had been necessary! I was already well aware of its importance. It was an honor to be asked to do this service.

"What are ya' doin'?" questioned Mary as I began lagging behind again.

"I can't decide if I should put the check inside my books or lay it on top so I can see it at all times," I muttered as I kept messing around with the precious piece of paper. "I think if I lay it on top of my books, I'll be able to see it every second.

That way I for sure won't lose it."

"Okay, fine. Just get hurryin'."

Actually I was in seventh heaven to think Mary, a new girl in school, was choosing to be my friend. She was outgoing and friendly and just the boost my quiet spirit needed, and I moved quickly down the country lane to catch up with her.

"Look at Jana. Billy's gonna get her with the snow yet," laughed Mary. "She's a fast runner, but Billy's legs are longer. She doesn't have a chance."

The boys ahead of us were taking clumps of the soft, wet snow and trying to put them inside Jana's mid-calf boot tops. Jana was a popular, highly excitable girl, and everyone seemed to like her. Mary continued laughing and talking to me like I was an old friend, and the new association felt good. "Run, Jana, you can do it!"

"Nice dodge," we shouted, as together we encouraged our classmate.

Home for me was a four-mile walk, with some students living closer to town, and some having to walk still further than we did. We were about halfway home when I casually glanced down again at the—my eyes widened, and my heart fell to my toes!

"No!" I shrieked. "Oh no! Where is the check? The cream check! It can't possibly be gone. It was just here!" I whirled around as my fearful eyes scanned the ruts in the road where we stood.

"Are you sure you didn't slip it back inside your book, Susie?" queried Mary as she hurried to my side.

"No, I'm sure I didn't," I sobbed. "It was just here. Remember, I was keeping it on top of my books so I could see it all the time."

I began quickly walking back over the road we had just traveled, my bright blue eyes darting left and right, trying to spot the valuable slip of paper. The road was anything but smooth. "Oh, Mary," I moaned. "Mary, help me look, p-l-e-a-s-e! I'll get the lickin' of my life if I have lost that check!"

Mary quickly called to the other kids to come and help us look. Everyone spread out across the road, and slowly we all walked back toward town, looking intently inside each furrow and crevice for the check. We were all farm kids. Every person there knew the importance of the cream checks, and all felt the dreadful weight of a lost check. But though we searched every rut and grass clump carefully, it was not to be found.

"Sorry," Jack finally apologized. "I've got to head for home, Susie. It's getting late, and my father'll be out lookin' for me with the razor strap if I don't get there soon."

"Me too, Susie. Sorry!" and, "We gotta go, Susie. You know that." My friends were reluctant to leave, but it was true. The sun was already beginning to get low in the sky, and we would all be in trouble if we didn't get moving toward home. So, with sincere apologies and sympathetic looks, they hurried on their way.

I knew I couldn't go home. The cream check was a sizeable amount of money, and I had been entrusted with the responsibility of bringing it safely to my father. I had broken that trust and been careless in my duty. I was truly frightened.

As I stood in the middle of the country road, horrified with what had happened, the thought came forcefully into my mind that I should ask my Heavenly Father to help me find the check. Because I had never prayed before without kneeling, I moved over into the barrow pit at the side of the road, looked for a fairly dry spot, and knelt down to pray. It was a simple, pleading, childlike prayer.

"Heavenly Father, my dad expects me to bring home his cream check, and I've lost it. I need to find it, Heavenly Father. My family needs the money, and I'm responsible. Please help me find the check. Oh, please help me! In the name of Jesus Christ, amen."

After I said "amen," I stood up, but I didn't feel any differently. With slow, dragging steps, I finally began to move down the road toward home.

I hadn't gone more than a couple dozen steps when—"The

check!" There, gleaming white in the semidarkness, buried in a rut in front of me, was a piece of paper that was just the right size. Quickly I reached down. It was indeed the lost check!

With tears streaming down my cheeks, I carefully, reverently, put the check inside a book and hurried down into the barrow pit again. I fell to my knees, this time not watching where I knelt. "Oh, thank you, Heavenly Father. Thank you! Thank you for answering my prayer." My throat was tight, my eyes were misty, and my heart was full.

I quickly moved up onto the road again and began running hard for home. After only a few breathless minutes, I saw a lighted lantern moving in my direction through the deepening twilight. It was Rudolf, out looking for me. We both knew I was in deep trouble.

Surprisingly, I didn't end up getting the anticipated lickin' for being late. Dad just said, "Well, you remembered your Heavenly Father, and you *did* bring home the check. I won't spank you this time. Sit down and eat your supper, and then you can go to bed."

Mother added softly, "We are so glad you remembered your Heavenly Father, Susanna. I think you will be ready to be baptized on your birthday."

So, maybe it was Mama reminding me to remember my Heavenly Father again. Heaven knows I needed help from someone! My thoughts were swirling and couldn't seem to settle on any one thing.

The night sky was peppered with stars, almost like the heavenly cooks had stubbed their toes while salting the stew. It was dark and rather crisp out, and I found myself unconsciously hugging my long, thin coat around my shoulders more tightly in an effort to keep warm. I hadn't walked far along the canal before Morris materialized at my side.

"Susanna," he said, putting his arm around my waist, "you're going to be frozen. What are you doing?"

"I'm okay," I said, shivering slightly. "Just thinking and praying, I guess."

We walked along for a minute or two in the stillness of the dark night, and then Morris broke the silence. "Well, don't you want to know what your father said?"

"Yes, what did he say?" I asked, turning to face him.

Morris was wearing a solemn face as he started slowly. "He said—" and then his expression changed to an elfish grin. "He said he was delighted!"

"No. Really. What did he really say?" I insisted.

"He said, 'That's fine, Mor-rees. You can marry Susie, and you can go on your mission, and she can come back here and do the work. When you get home from your mission, you can move right in here with us.'"

"But, I will tell you something, Susanna," said Morris emphatically, holding me tight to him. "When I get home from my mission, Mor-rees is not going to move in here. We're going to have a home of our own. Your father has asked too much of you, and we're not going to stay here where he can continue to do that."

We continued to walk for a brief moment, a feeling of contentment settling over both of us, and then Morris turned me toward the lights of the house that spilled out over the frosty yard.

"We need to get back so you can get packed. We'll need to leave quite early in the morning to get everything done. I will have to drive up to Bishop Walsh's house to get a recommend to be married, and then we'll have to stop by President Crawford's house to get both our recommends signed by him." Morris was bubbling as he outlined our agenda.

I was in kind of a daze. I still hadn't actually said I would marry him. I was still feeling a bit unsure of my feelings, but I had to admit the warmth of Morris's arm around me was very comforting. I was sure of one thing! Morris loved me *so* much! Maybe his tremendous love would be enough for both of us.

The next morning, December first, the day dawned somewhat more mild and cooperative, the temperature having risen slightly from the day before. Morris picked me up early, and we scurried to each place he had mentioned the evening before, finally ending up at his mom and dad's house.

Lodisa, Morris's sweet mother, took me in her arms as soon as we walked through the kitchen door and hugged me tightly. She was totally delighted we were getting married but equally as shocked to think we were going to drive to Salt Lake without anyone accompanying us. Idaho Falls would not have a temple for many years yet.

"Oh, Susanna, this is all happening so quickly. You need a woman with you for this most important event in your life. Oh, whatever will we do? I just can't go with you. Betsy Brown's baby is due any minute and she has so many problems having her children. I just wouldn't dare leave her at a time like this."

"Let them be," soothed Ransford. "They will be fine."

"Well, at least let me send my temple suitcase with you so you will have temple clothes," fretted Lodisa. "And you know, Logan has a temple, as well as Salt Lake. We were married in the Salt Lake Temple, but the Logan Temple would be considerably closer for you."

And so it was on that crisp, bright, winter afternoon that Morris and I drove to Logan, Utah, alone together to the temple to be married for time and all eternity.

For time and all eternity! Now that was a scary thought! I was still trying to come to grips with loving Morris enough to marry him at all, and the temple meant eternal marriage—forever and ever.

All the children knew our parents had been married in the temple. That seemed a good thing. We had always been taught that temple marriage was synonymous with a strong commitment to marriage, family, and the Church. About once a month, Mama and Dad would drive the one hundred fifty miles or so to the Logan Temple to do temple work. I had been taught you must be sealed together in the temple as husband and wife and as families to attain the greatest reward in heaven after this life. The sealing power also allowed you to live as families rather than individuals after the resurrection.

The whole temple work thing was a little vague in my mind. We had been taught that temple recommend holders did proxy work for their ancestors, allowing them the choice of accepting these most important ordinances at a later time. Mostly though, we were told the temple was a sacred place, and one didn't talk about the ordinances performed there outside its walls. The one principle I knew for sure was that because the sealings were performed by men who held the sealing authority obtained from Jesus Christ, the ordinances were effective eternally. My faith allowed me to believe all of that, even if the details were a little unclear.

My oldest sister, Mary, and my oldest brother, Rudolf, had both been married in the temple years before. Sarah had been married civilly four years earlier, much to the chagrin of my parents. But that was another story.

We left the Idaho Falls area later than Morris wanted to, but his mother, Lodisa, wouldn't let us go without first giving us something to eat. To send guests or family on their way without eating was a cardinal sin. "A full stomach rides easier," she'd always say in her most practical, caring tone of voice. "Besides, you will have to eat somewhere. It might as well be good, nourishing food from my kitchen."

The old navy blue Ford coughed and groaned as Morris tried to get some heat moving through the motor and into the interior of the car. As usual, the heater was trying, but also as usual, it was rather ineffectual. It was winter, with the snow crusted from the overnight chill, but even though the wind was brisk, it wasn't totally freezing outside. Morris had swathed my legs in blankets again to help me be more comfortable. The white frosting of snow over the ground was a gentle reminder that it was my wedding day.

Although the ride was a long one, there were many interesting things to see. The Blackfoot area was an Indian reserve, and there were still sod huts and some teepees there. We discussed the interesting Indian names of places, things, and people. Huge black lava rocks lined the road by Pocatello and Inkom. Morris told me that long ago there had been a volcano in this region of Idaho, but that it had been extinct for hundreds of years. The lava was now partly covered by wind-blown soil and sagebrush. Straw bales piled into stooks, or pyramids, were still standing in some of the fields. Stooking bails was a common practice, making it easy for the farmer to pick up fifteen bales in one place when they were needed. Lakes were pretty much frozen over as the winter season deepened. As we passed the turnoff for Lava Hot Springs, Morris asked me if I had ever been there.

"Lava's a great place. The mineral water bubbles out of the ground warm as a bathtub. Hotel owners have constructed their buildings right over the top of some of them, so that the water boils into cement lined pools in the basement to create a health resort. The state of Idaho has built outdoor pools where the water rises up through the rocks, keeping the temperature constantly warm and inviting. It looks like fish are breathing under the water as rising lines of bubbles break the surface." Morris's family was much more affluent than mine was, and he had traveled to many more interesting places.

"Are there really fish in the pools?" I wasn't sure that sounded so inviting, swimming with the fish.

"Oh no, there are no fish in the water," he laughed. "The rising bubbles just remind me of fish below the surface. The water is clear and warm and wonderful. Fish could never get through the layers of rocks, and besides, they probably couldn't live in the mineral water too well."

"Warm water that never gets cold. Now that is my idea of a heavenly bath." I shook my head in wonder.

"We will definitely have to stop in Lava sometime. You would absolutely love the hot water. There is a huge mountain of rock that looms close beside the hot pools. In milder weather, you can often see wildlife on the rock shelves above."

As I was trying to get my mind around such a lovely place, Morris saw the turnoff for Soda Springs.

"Now Soda has a spring too, but the water that bubbles

out of the ground there is cold and highly charged with carbonic acid gas. We could swim at Lava and then picnic in Soda Springs. If you can add the soda water to your drink, it tastes like it is carbonated."

"What next?" was all I could say.

Passing out of Idaho into Utah, we spoke of Utah also being an Indian name, derived from the Ute Indians. Beautiful, clear blue Bear Lake was to the east as we wove our way through many small villages and entered Cache Valley.

We spoke of inconsequential things the entire trip. Nothing would have been sweeter than to speak frankly of the vows we were about to take, but somehow we both shied away from talking about what we really should have been discussing. Morris had me in the car moving toward our marriage. That was a major accomplishment! I don't think he wanted to press his luck with talk of love or intimacy. If I had asked questions about the temple, he would have been only too glad to respond, but I was too naive to ask, and he seemed afraid to broach such a sensitive subject. He knew I was unsure in my feelings toward him. Maybe he felt it best to marry me first and then work out the details of our love later, when there was no backing out.

Actually, I had tried to talk to my older sister, Mary, about marriage and basically "the facts of life" after Morris had asked me to marry him the first time, in August. I hadn't planned on marrying him at that time, maybe not even in the future, but the subject of marriage had engendered several questions in my mind.

Even though Mary had been married a dozen years by that time and had borne six children, the conventions of the day made her too self-conscious and inhibited to talk to her little sister about any of it. "Oh, Susanna, shush! You know better than to talk about such things. You will learn all you need to know from your husband, when you have one. I—I certainly can't be telling you about married life before you are married. It just isn't to be spoken of, and you know the temple is sacred." So, without a mother's loving guidance or a sister's confidence, I realized I would have to rely solely upon a new husband for direction.

As we entered Logan from the north, the temple wasn't immediately visible, though our eyes strained to see it. Morris wasn't too familiar with the town, so he stayed on the main street, knowing we would see the temple from there, eventually. And then in the dusk of the evening, off to our left, there it was—huge, stately, and impressive, as the last threads of a beautiful magenta and gold sunset trailed off behind its two eloquent, white spires. Sturdy limestone turrets, giving the temple the look of a fortress, although a very dark gray, shone a lovely soft pink and then darkened to purple as they mirrored the ever-changing sunset. The individual window panes glowed momentarily as the last rays of sun caught them before the sky darkened completely. We followed the road up the hill, curving around the steeply sloping lawn to the entrance of the temple before realizing the temple workers were just leaving for the evening. The temple was closed!

"It's okay. We'll come back first thing in the morning when we are rested. Tomorrow will be a lovely wedding day," Morris assured me.

I could tell he was disappointed that we had arrived too late to enter the temple. He was so looking forward to sharing that experience with me. I think he also wanted the marriage ceremony performed as soon as possible, before I changed my mind. I still hadn't given him much encouragement in voicing my love for him. And so, his concern for my feelings and his own despondency mingled perceptively in his response as he tried to be positive.

My heart was in my throat as we drove to a hotel to get some rooms for the night. I couldn't imagine what people would think, although I wasn't sure exactly who I was worried about because everyone in our two families assumed we had been married that day. We certainly didn't know anyone in Logan, but staying in a hotel—an unmarried girl and an unmarried man! This entire situation was beyond my comprehension! Morris and I weren't married, and we knew it, even if no one else did, and yet we were going to stay in a hotel together.

As we stood in the brightly lit lobby at the dark walnut front desk, securing beds for the night, even through my extreme mortification I quickly realized Morris had everything under control.

"We need two rooms for tonight but only one room for tomorrow night," Morris informed the young, smirking desk clerk. "One needs to be a nice room, and one can be your least expensive room."

"W-e-l–l-l, my *least* expensive room is a bed in the hall, if ya' don't mind that. The bathroom's down the hall either way, so that don't particularly matter."

"In the hall?" I must have looked startled and upset, but Morris assured the clerk that would be fine; it was all he needed. "We'll keep the nice room for two nights, but the bed in the hall is only for tonight," he repeated, so the insolent clerk would have it right.

When we had our suitcases stowed away in my very adequate room, Morris took me to a cafe for dinner. "Oh, Morris, I've never been to a cafe to eat."

"Well, I guess this is a special occasion for a very special lady." Morris was playing the gallant to the hilt. And then his expression turned apologetic.

"I'm so sorry we didn't arrive in Logan soon enough to go to the temple tonight. This isn't exactly how I planned things. But tomorrow will be wonderful. Oh, Susanna, by tomorrow at this time, we'll be husband and wife—forever!"

If I hadn't been both excited and nervous before, this statement finished the job. I could hardly believe my father had let me go with Morris all by myself—unmarried and all—on this several-hour motor trip—and then to stay overnight too. It was the first time I had been alone with him this long, the first time I had ever eaten out, the first time I had ever stayed in a hotel, and yes, the first time I had ever thought of getting married. I wasn't nervous—I was scared to death!

"Let's walk around for a while and window-shop," suggested Morris after we finished our meal. "The stores are full of pretty Christmas things, and the evening's a little milder tonight."

Up one side of Main Street and down the other we walked, stopping at every store window to peer inside at the softly lighted displays. I had never seen so many beautiful things before. All the while, Morris kept his arm protectively around my shoulders.

Finally he said, "Should we head back to the hotel?"

"Could we get an ice cream cone?" I suggested shyly as we were passing an ice cream parlor.

"Of course we could!" Morris was anxious to please, and I was anxious to remain away from the hotel, although I supposed nothing of a wifely manner would be required of me on this particular evening.

When we finally returned to the hotel, with full tummies and cold noses, Morris asked if he could come into my room for a few minutes. At my unsure expression, he quickly elaborated, "I would like to have prayer with you before turning into bed." We knelt together for our first couple prayer, after which Morris kissed me tenderly but briefly on the mouth before he retired to the hallway to his bed.

Looking around the utilitarian hotel room, I was sure I would never be able to go to sleep that night, but after a quick trip to the bathroom down the hall, I also turned into bed and was asleep almost instantly. Peaceful slumber was a welcome companion after a long, full, stressful day.

Early the next morning, December 2, 1925, Morris and I, dressed in our Sunday best, again drove up the hill to the imposing Logan Temple. The air was crisp because the weather had taken a colder turn during the night, causing the frosty trees surrounding the temple to appear ethereal in the brilliant morning light. Perpetually green pines; long, bare, sweeping, weeping willows; hard, stubby grass; siliceous limestone temple, all sparkled like jeweled heavenly possessions of a loving Heavenly Father.

Because this was my first temple experience, I needed to go through a session to receive my own endowments. The whole occasion was so new, the implications so vast, the covenants so binding, my preparation so non-existent, I could hardly remember a thing afterward.

I knew the building was exquisite in its loveliness, with its beautiful paintings and woven rag carpeting. The curving stairways and elegant chandeliers kept me gaping in wonder and awe. Our pioneer ancestors had certainly put their best efforts into this magnificent structure.

I truly appreciated the warm, understanding help of the temple workers as they guided me to the appropriate rooms and through the needed procedures. Morris had gone a different direction almost immediately after we entered the temple. At first I felt so bewildered, but the sweet women quickly laid my fears to rest, making me feel like I was the most important patron in the temple that day.

The celestial room! I felt I was just this side of heaven as Morris and I stood reunited, hands entwined, gazing at the high vaulted ceiling displaying the most gorgeous chandelier I had ever seen. The elegant furniture; the soft, lush carpeting; the tall, stately windows were almost more than my senses could comprehend.

After a time, we were led to another, much smaller, room. This was the sealing room. There were plush chairs around the outside edge and an altar directly in the center of the room. Immediately when I saw the altar, I thought of my mother. On cold winter evenings, she had worked on tatting: a beautiful, lacy needlework art. Occasionally, she would edge the collar of a Sunday dress with her work. The temple altar was encased in an exquisite tatted cover. Not just the edges, but the entire altar top was covered with intricate tatting.

When we finally knelt across the altar of God and were sealed together as husband and wife for time and all eternity, my emotions were numbed by all that had happened. We were not accompanied by parents or siblings. Two smiling, white-robed temple workers, looking more like angels than mortals, were pulled into the sealing room to stand as witnesses of this grand event.

The sealer gave us some kind of advice, mostly scriptural references and quotes from General Authorities, which my mind just couldn't focus on for the moment. At first I didn't know where to look—at the sealer—at Morris—at the tatted altar cover? Through my confusion, Morris finally caught my gaze and locked his eyes to mine. My heart was full! I was now pretty sure I loved Morris, and I knew beyond a shadow of a doubt that he loved me. Suddenly, I subconsciously realized that my mother's spirit was there, adding her seal of approval. The peace she always brought into my heart returned.

We kissed shyly over the altar after the soft-spoken "amen." My angels hugged me and shook Morris's hand, patting him on the back and sincerely congratulating us both. The sealer, a white-haired man with a flowing white beard, and his petite, white-haired wife (I already couldn't remember their names) did the same.

I kind of floated down to my dressing room to change clothes. It had truly been a beautiful experience and a wonderful day.

Suddenly I felt a great weight of despair as I realized the heavy, high-necked, ankle-length, wrist-length temple garments Lodisa had thoughtfully left in her suitcase, and which had worked fine under her temple dress, now showed both above and beneath the dress I had brought to wear. My only nice dress had short sleeves, a slightly scooped neck, and reached only mid-calf, showing my ankles. I was so embarrassed. I hadn't thought of needing to purchase new garments to go to the temple. Of course, I had been aware I needed to wear the sacred temple garments after my marriage. I had washed garments for my parents for years, but in the rush of preparation, with so many other considerations taking precedence, I had not thought of buying garments. Now here I was, unsuitably dressed to meet my new husband.

Luckily my winter coat did up tight around my neck and was long—clear to the bottom of my ankles. So, not knowing what else to do, I dressed and then covered the visible garments with my long, gray flannel coat. I had never liked the coat much until now, always thinking it was too long to be stylish. Now I was ever so grateful for the full length and the tiny black fur piece high around the stand-up collar.

My flushed embarrassment, as I told Morris what had happened, paled next to his apologies for having let it happen. "Oh, Susanna, how could I have let this happen? I am so sorry. I was just so anxious to get to the temple this morning, to make you my wife, I didn't even think about purchasing garments for you to wear. I've been wearing garments for so long now, I didn't think of your needs. Come on, we'll go immediately and buy you some suitable ones."

Luckily the shop where they sold garments wasn't far from the hotel. We purchased some everyday ones for me and then hurried back to the hotel so I could change.

But that constituted the next problem. We had moved Morris's things out of the hallway and into the hotel room before leaving for the temple that morning, and I was much too embarrassed to change into the new garments with Morris in the room, even if he was now my husband. I scurried away down the narrow hall to the bathroom for privacy.

It was such a relief to remove the bulky garments I had been wearing and put on the lovely new ones we had purchased. Nevertheless, I worked slowly at changing because I was aware of my new status as a married woman and wasn't sure what would be expected of me next. I wasn't afraid of Morris, exactly, I was just kind of afraid of the commitment I had made and all that it signified.

After I had changed clothes, I washed my hands, neatly folded up the heavy temple garments, smoothing and pressing them with nervous fingers, and then finally sat on the toilet seat, nervously chewing at my fingernails. I knew I needed to be going back to the room, but I continued to stay in the old, dimly lit bathroom.

Finally Morris came to the door. "Is everything all right, Susanna? Do the garments fit okay?" The concern was evident in his voice. At last, I sheepishly came out to greet him.

We spent the rest of the chilly winter day strolling through the warm, brightly decorated shops in Logan, while talking of our future plans together. It was a lovely day and a cherished time, but as evening drew near and we again ate at the small cafe, I was quite terrified to return to the hotel.

"Susanna," Morris said quietly, "why don't we take turns changing into our nightclothes in the bathroom down the hall." He was aware of my distress upon our return to our room. "And then we can just sit in bed together and talk." He looked tenderly into my terrified eyes, and I hesitantly agreed. "I'll go first," he said.

When I returned, wearing my heavy, cotton, long-sleeved nightdress buttoned up to the top of the Peter Pan collar, I quickly slipped into my side of the bed. Morris, dressed in modest men's pajamas, was waiting patiently. Gently, but firmly, he gathered me into his strong, loving arms. "Oh, Susanna. All I want to do is hold you close to me. I love you so. I won't ever do anything unless you want me to. I will wait however long it takes for you to honor me with your love. I want this to be good and right."

The following morning, I knew it was both good and right, and I loved Morris with a love I thought would burst forth from every pore of my body, it was so wonderful. My face and spirit radiated from his exquisite, gentle loving.

The one other thought which seemed to run through my consciousness again and again was: *I would have died if we had loved each other so completely and not been sealed together in the way the Lord had ordained.*

Morris belongs to me forever—and ever kept reverberating reassuringly through my heart and soul.

Chapter 8

December 11/25

Dear Journal:

Oh, how I miss my husband. It almost seems strange to call him that, and yet I know he is mine forever. We have spent the last eight glorious, active, hectic days together, staying mostly at his folks' house. I am already calling Lodisa "Mother" because she is so good to me. I love her with all my heart.

The mission call came through on schedule, and Morris boarded the train in Salt Lake City yesterday afternoon for Tennessee and the Southern States Mission. It's interesting they should send him there, as that is where he served for two and a half years about three years ago. In fact, he will have the same mission president, President Charles A. Callis. That part will be wonderful for him, for he learned to love President Callis dearly when he served under him before.

I have now returned home and am doing the same tedious housekeeping jobs I did before our hasty marriage. Dad is delighted to have me back, of course, caring for the family as if nothing has changed. I hope with all my heart that Morris will remember what he said about living in our own home when he returns. And yet, even with saying that, I have this nagging feeling in my heart that I must honor the promise I made to Mama before she died. I know she is expecting me to take care of Ruth, Rachel, and Irene. I've come to realize the boys can take care of themselves, but the girls are still young, and they need some kind of a mother. Sam is 16 now and works with the older boys. I think he's okay.

February 3/26

Dear Journal:

I had wanted to write much more regularly, but every day seems so busy. Christmas came and went with little fanfare. Rudolf and Walt made sure the little girls each had a new doll. The rest of us settled for a new pair of shoes. I tried to do some Christmas baking. Most of it turned out pretty good. I guess I've helped Mama for enough years to know how to make the strudel and stollen Dad loves so much at holiday time.

*Morris surprised me with a book—*Little Women *by Louisa May Alcott. He knows how much I love to read and to actually have this book for my own is so special. He wrote in the front: "To my darling Susanna. I'm so glad you are mine. All my love, Morris"*

I sent Morris a long letter and tucked some white hankies inside, but after receiving the book, it seemed like a poor offering. At least he knows I love him, and he is always saying that is the most important thing.

I just found out that Dad recently answered an ad in a German newspaper and is now corresponding with a lady named Lydia Struhs. He seems to think she may be suitable for marriage, and I'm sure that is the end he desires. It seems strange to think he might marry again. I don't know how anyone could replace Mama, but I guess he needs someone to finish raising the girls. He knows Morris will be home from his mission in May.

March 23/26

Dear Journal:

I'm not so sure this correspondence of Dad and Lydia's is going smoothly. Dad wants to be sealed in the temple, and Lydia is not in favor of that—at least, not at the present time. Lydia has one daughter, Mamie, who is a little older than Ruth. If Mamie is as strong-willed as Lydia, she and Ruth ought to have a wonderful time trying to get along with each other. I hope this all works out for the best.

Morris is completely enjoying his mission, as I knew he would. He is such a people person. He loves to visit with people and especially about the gospel of Jesus Christ. It's too bad he couldn't have a permanent job as a full-time missionary. Of course, I would want him to be here with me, and he would have to get paid some money for it so we could live. I guess that isn't the way the job of a missionary works, but he would make a wonderful success of it, I know.

March 31/26

Dear Journal:

I just received the most astounding letter from Morris yesterday. He feels strongly he now knows why it was so important for him to serve this short-term mission and is now totally grateful to his father for encouraging—almost insisting—that he go.

He and his companion, Elder Wood, were trudging down the road after a discouraging day of tracting up by the Tennessee border. A man had given them faulty instructions as to where the road led, and consequently, they were lost. Although they were not familiar with the country, they suspected they were into the southeastern corner of Kentucky, just over the Tennessee border. Finally spotting a glimmer of light through the trees, they hurried in that direction.

Tom Burrows answered the knock on his door, well after dark, surprised to see two young men standing there, hungry and shivering. Because the Burrows lived in an out-of-the-way area, the likelihood of visitors was pretty remote. But Tom is a good Christian man who reads the Bible regularly, so he invited Morris and Elder Wood into his small cabin. Mrs. Burrows offered them some supper, which they gratefully accepted. They had traveled most of the day without eating, and the coon stew and dumplings were delicious.

Tom Burrows asked what business these two young men had in his part of the country. They explained to him they were telling people about the gospel of Jesus Christ and how it had been restored after a long absence from the earth. As they shared their message, the Spirit of the Lord testified to all in the room of the truth of what they were saying.

At first Tom was skeptical that men as young as these could know the truth and teach it so powerfully. He suddenly became quiet, and then he reached for his Bible, turned to the passage he had been reading to his family when the interruption came at the door, and read it to himself silently. He was reading from 1st Corinthians, chapter 2, where it talks about the gospel being preached not with man's wisdom but with the wisdom and power of the Lord. He shared the passage of scripture with the missionaries. After inviting Morris and his companion to kneel with them in family prayer, he invited them to stay the night in front of the fireplace.

In the morning, he wanted to hear more of their message. The Tom Burrows family is made up of nine people. Four of the children are under eight years of age, but Morris and his companion baptized Tom, his wife, Annie, and the three oldest children two days later. Tom just can't seem to get enough of the gospel. He is an eager student, having always loved the scriptures. In fact, he learned to read by first listening to his mama read the Bible daily and then reading it himself from age five on. The reason he waited two days to be baptized was because he wanted to finish reading the Book of Mormon before making that final commitment to the waters of baptism. Morris was thrilled with their golden find.

April 14/26

Dear Journal:

Morris now knows his release date. He will be returning to Idaho on May 29, 1926. He tells me he has been corresponding with his Aunt Belle, and she has a small cottage in Goshen we can move into for the next six months. Besides being in our own home, we will be close to Morris's parents because they now also live in Goshen, and I will truly enjoy that prospect. I think his dad even has a lead on a job for him upon his return. The Lord is certainly looking out for us.

Dad seems unhappy much of the time. I don't know if things are going well with Lydia or not—it would seem not. I guess it would be tough to think of marrying into a family of seven children still living at home. Even if the youngest child is ten and able to look after herself for the most part, it is still a huge responsibility. (As I can testify—and I love them all!) I'm not so sure how any one of them is going to accept a "new mother." Mama will be impossible to replace. Dad may get an acceptable new housekeeper, but I'm sure not even he can forget how wonderful Mama was. He may even break off this correspondence with Lydia.

I would not be sorry to turn the monotony of this job over to someone else, though.

June 6/26

Dear Journal:

Morris is home! Home to our own home in Goshen. The job with Anton Anderson came through, and he works each day on a threshing machine. We may be poor in worldly goods, but we are rich in love. Oh, it is so good to have him home again! How could I ever have possibly thought I didn't love him?

June 16/26

Dear Journal:

Morris just received his first paycheck from Mr. Anderson. We went shopping and purchased a mattress and two wooden chairs. Now this is living!

I have been going out to the farm the first four days of each week to cook and clean there, but I come home to Morris on the weekends. I can hardly believe the patience and understanding exhibited by my good husband. He is always sensitive to my desire to carry out my promise to my mother but is unwilling to have us move in with my father. Hopefully there will be an end to this unsuitable arrangement in the near future because Dad and Lydia are corresponding again.

Morris and I received two long-hoped-for gifts for our first wedding anniversary. The first gift was the confirmation that our first baby is on its way. I shared the news with Morris after we had climbed into bed for the night.

"Oh, Susanna, our own baby! Our own baby boy! I can hardly wait to teach him to ride a bike and throw a ball. What fun this will be!" Morris was ecstatic. As he held me close and secure and warm, he even talked about possible names—"We could name him Henry, after my grandfather, I suppose, or maybe we should name him a new and different name like Jeffrey, or Cade." What a thrill it was to know he was as excited about the new little life growing inside of me as I was!

The second gift was the marriage of Dad to Lydia Struhs. Their correspondence had dragged on and on, but they were finally married—though not in the temple as Dad truly desired. The ceremony took place on December 6, 1926, just four days after our first anniversary.

What a relief to think I could stop going out to the farm every weekday. With this marriage, we assumed that I would be released from my promise and responsibility to my family. That was a wonderful prospect indeed!

But we quickly found that wasn't to be the case.

"Lydia has such a strong personality, and Ruth fights with her constantly," I would cry to Morris as I returned from the farm to our home in Goshen. Even going out for the day to help with the large weekly wash was a strain.

"Rachel and Irene don't argue with her quite as much, or at least not as openly, but they are taking Ruth's lead more and more in expressing their negative feelings toward her. And Mamie, Lydia's daughter, just adds fuel to the fire. She's the oldest and feels that because she's Lydia's own daughter, she should get everything she wants. Or at least, that's the way the other girls see it."

And then one night, after a brief visit to the farm to deliver some baking, I arrived home laughing and shaking my head. "Ruth and Rachel were so rebellious and disobedient yesterday that in unhappy frustration Lydia told them they make her feel so sad and angry that she feels she maybe ought to just take poison. Rachel, having had quite enough of Lydia, marched right into the bathroom, got a bottle of carbonic acid out of the cupboard, came back into the kitchen and sat it in the middle of the kitchen table, saying, 'Help yourself!' Well, you can imagine how that went over with Lydia. She was furious!"

"I just hope she doesn't spread the rumor around the neighborhood that the girls are trying to poison her," Morris chuckled when he heard the story. But that is exactly what happened. Our good neighbors of many years were aghast, and the "poison story" was the topic of gossip for several weeks.

Finally, Dad, with his heart breaking, came to Morris and me and asked if Ruth and Rachel could come and stay with us for a couple of days. "I was so sure this marriage was the answer for all of us. But there is so much tension in my house you can cut it with a knife. Maybe if Ruth and Rachel could just visit you two for a few days, Lydia could get a grip on her emotions. Would you mind terribly?"

"Of course we don't mind," volunteered Morris. "If that will help the situation, we would be glad to have the girls stay here."

But in the end, this line of action made Lydia even more furious, and Ruth and Rachel moved in with us permanently. Irene stayed home with Lydia because she was younger and more apt to be obedient and useful there.

Although Morris and I greatly anticipated the coming of our baby, as did Ruth, Rachel, and Irene, I felt some cause for concern as well. The circumstances surrounding my own birth were unusual, as I had heard many times. I hoped I would have the presence of mind to handle any unforeseen situation that might arise.

At the time of my birth, my parents lived in a two-room log cabin, with the outhouse a sufficient distance from the house to endure the smell. As they were trying to pay off their farmland, their energies had gone into making the farm produce rather than in building a larger home. I was to be the seventh child, and so our little house was full to bursting.

On a clear, warm Monday in March, Mama was preparing to do the wash. It was a perfect washday. The sky, streaked with shades of blue and interlaced with giant billowing white clouds, held just enough of a mild breeze to dry and freshen the clothes in good order. Mama enjoyed washdays and was singing, as usual, as she went about her preparations.

Spring had been slow in coming, but this day the warming currents moved slowly around the legs and through the hair. The sun felt like soft velvet on the cheeks, sending pleasant rivulets down to the roots of tresses and seeping through clothes.

After the family had eaten breakfast, Dad left the farm with Rudolf, his twelve-year-old son, to clean sediment from the irrigation canals. It was a loathsome job shared by the farmers in the area, with each taking their respective turn.

Mama opened wide the kitchen door to let in the cooling breeze, filled a huge boiler with water, and placed it on the stove to heat. She was seven months into her latest pregnancy, but even with all the lifting and bending, doing the wash was a routine task. Mary and Sarah, at fourteen and nine, respectively, were a big help. They quickly moved through their responsibilities of doing the breakfast dishes, straightening the kitchen, and making the beds. Walt, although only seven, went to the barn to finish some chores there. Mama wouldn't think of starting the wash until everything was in order. Washday was just that—an entire day of doing the wash. Of necessity, it had to be carefully organized, with each person cheerfully and efficiently doing his or her designated job.

Mama sorted the laundry into several piles—whites separate from colors, sheets and linens, overalls and work clothes, dresses and shirts, dishtowels and towels. The first step was to jounce the clothes in hot, soapy water. The jouncer was a wooden stick, cone-shaped at the bottom, with a long handle on it like a broom. Mary, Sarah, and Walt took turns at jouncing the clothes up and down in the tub, their arms tiring quickly as they pushed the heavy, water-soaked mass around to release the dirt.

After the jouncing, Mary sat at the side of the boiler on a stool, picking up each article of clothing and checking for any stains still on the clothes. When she found soiled parts, she scrubbed them by hand on the ribbed scrub board.

On this washday, Mama had already taken the dishtowels, sheets, and linens and boiled them in lye water to make them sparkling white. Sarah's job was to take the whites from

Mama, rinse them several times in cold water, next putting them in a bluing rinse to whiten them even more. Sheets and linens were the first articles to be hung on the lines. After the laundry was finished, the lye water would be used to scrub the seats of the outhouse and then poured down the hole to help cut down on the fly population which resided there.

As the sheets and linens were finished, Mama moved the boiler of lye water from the stove to the floor to allow it to cool. And then she moved over to help dip the dresses and collars and cuffs of the shirts into starch water before hanging them on the line to dry. The warm spring sun and gentle breeze were already doing their work of drying, bleaching, and refreshing the laundry.

Next, Mama gathered the last load of overalls together in the kitchen. "Mary, Sarah, Walt, come outside and help me lay these out." With the lines full, the procedure was to spread the overalls around on the tall, thick grass to dry.

Fred and John, ages two and four, were wrestling and tickling each other, a game that often went on for hours. John was older than Fred, but Fred was blessed with a huskier build.

"I gonna get you," teased Fred, his fingers moving spider-like in the air. "You can't get away! I gonna get you!"

"No, don't tickle me, I can't stand it," giggled extremely ticklish John, as he quickly backpeddled across the kitchen floor. John was a good sport. As much as he truly hated to be tickled, he loved to tease and play with Fred in this manner.

"But, I gonna," squealed Fred as he lunged toward John.

Suddenly John was screaming at the top of his lungs. He had toppled backwards directly into the boiler of lye water that had just begun cooling on the floor. Automatically, John flung out his right arm to save himself, but the force of the back of his knees hitting the top of the boiler dumped him right into the tub. Only his left arm, which shot up into the air as if to grab some unknown railing, and his head and feet were not submerged.

Mama heard the air-piercing, heart-stopping scream from

outside the cabin and rushed in to see what was wrong. Her eyes scanned John's predicament and could see that although he thrashed and struggled, he was unable to get out of the tub. Immediately she pulled John from the boiler and started to undress him, but she could see that already in many places his skin was peeling away with his clothes. While John continued to scream because of the burning, Mama dumped the lye water outside and filled the boiler with a five-gallon container of linseed oil, all the while trying to soothe him with her voice. "Don't cry, Johnny, I'm trying to help you. Oh, don't cry, sweetheart."

She lowered John carefully into the oil bath to help dispel the effect of the lye and to allow the oil to begin to absorb some of the excruciating pain. Mama's mind was whirling. She knew Dad was working on the canals with their oldest son, Rudolf, and it was up to her to provide first-aid for John's terrible burns. Without stopping what she was doing, her prayers were sent heavenward in giant pleas to know the right thing to do *and* for Rudolf, her husband, to somehow know to come home.

"I need your help, Heavenly Father. Please help me to know what is best to do for Johnny. Please—oh, please. And Heavenly Father, help Rudolf to know that I need him at home. We need his wisdom and his priesthood power. Please bring him home to us."

Quickly she instructed Mary, Sarah, and Walt to bring in some of the newly washed and dried sheets from off the lines.

"Sarah, bring the quilt from our bed and put it on the kitchen table. Mary, cover the quilt with a clean, dry sheet, and push the table into the corner." While the girls were carrying out these instructions, Mama began to show Walt how to tear other sheets into strips.

As gently as she could, Mama lifted her shaking, shock-ridden little boy from the boiler tub and laid him on the padded table. Carefully she cut away the cloth, which was still sticking to John's skin. And then she proceeded to bind her son's body, wrapping each arm and leg, finger and toe separately with the clean strips of cotton cloth soaked in linseed oil and padded with oil-moistened cornmeal. She didn't want any parts of his body to stick to the table or to other body parts.

All this time, Fred was huddled in a corner, crying noisily, hiccupping and sucking on two of his fingers, frightened almost out of his mind. When Mama finally became aware of him, she instructed Mary to pick him up and rock him. "Talk to him softly and sing to him, sis. He needs you. Be gentle with him," she said with a catch in her voice. "Let him know he is loved and that Johnny will be all right."

The wrapping procedure took considerable time, but Mama was careful to have every part of John's burns covered with wrapping because she could already see body fluids oozing out of the pores of the raw, blistering skin. Within minutes after John's tortured body was completely wrapped and he was dozing off into an exhausted, painful slumber, Mama went into labor.

The pains started with a vengeance, as the exertion of the past hour began to tell on her dwindling endurance. As the pains tore through Mama's stomach and back, she clamped her mouth shut tight so she wouldn't cry out loud and further alarm the girls. Fred had finally cried himself to sleep, and Mary had tenderly laid him on his bed.

Finally, when the pain abated a little, Mama said, "Mary, put some more water in the big kettle to heat on the stove. I need you to be brave and help me. There might not be time to get the midwife here. This baby is coming."

"Walt, I need you to go over to Mrs. Jeppson's farm. Tell her your mother is in labor and needs her to come immediately." Walt's short, skinny legs were pumping as he left the house on the run.

Mary, thinking and reacting quickly, covered the exposed straw mattress with another clean sheet. She and Sarah, their eyes huge in their white faces, helped their mother lie down and put the water on to heat as she had bid them to do.

"Take one of the sheet strips that's already torn, Sarah honey, and tie it to the iron headboard. The knot needs to be nice and tight, and then let me hold onto the other end. I need something to hold on to as the pains get stronger."

Even as Mama said that, she wondered how the pains could get any stronger. They seemed to be tearing her apart with their intensity. There was almost no letup between the hurting!

I just can't give up now. Johnny needs me too much, and this new baby needs a mother. Please help me to hold on, Heavenly Father! she whispered in her mind. *And, oh please,* she petitioned, *bring Rudolf home!*

Mary and Sarah felt helpless as they witnessed the birthing process take place. I was tiny, which helped, but Mama's body was exhausted. The rigors of washday, mentally and physically dealing with Johnny's burns, and then premature labor had all taken their toll.

At the instant my head gave its final push from my mother's warm, cozy womb, Dad burst through the door. He took one astonished look at the situation and knelt by the bed to catch his slippery, newborn daughter.

Later, he was to explain to the family how he had an overpowering feeling while working on the canal that something was wrong at home. He couldn't understand what was causing it, but the feeling was too pressing to be ignored. Finally he went to his boss, explained how he was feeling, and was told to take a horse and go home to check on things there.

Instinctively Dad took out his pocketknife and cut and tied the cord. Only then did he realize that I wasn't breathing! In one smooth motion, he picked me up, holding me easily in one of his large, work-worn hands, and spanked me sharply a couple of times on the back. As the mucus in my throat dislodged, I began to scream.

"Wrap her in a blanket and lay her on a pillow feetfirst in the warming oven, Rudolf. Oh, I am so grateful to see you," sobbed Mother.

Again, with extraordinary presence of mind, Mary had anticipated the request and was holding out a small, well-used baby blanket.

Dad did as he was told, returning to the bed with a small container of consecrated oil. First, he gave Mama a blessing, and then me, and then John. In each he called upon the powers of heaven to give us the strength and the will to live.

A short time later, Walt arrived back at the house with Mrs. Jeppson in her old, much-used, black buggy. The midwife quickly checked me over, weighing me in at about four pounds. She was astounded at the method of keeping me warm but agreed it was probably the best possible answer. Next, she delivered the afterbirth from Mama and generally cleaned up the bed area. As she worked, she was told what had happened to John. She checked him briefly as well but stated there was no way he would live.

"Too much of his skin has been eaten off his body with the lye. You should call the doctor so John can be taken to the hospital. He can't possibly live through what has happened to him and should not be left here to drain your strength, Marie, or to die in view of the other children."

"I appreciate your help, Wanda Jeppson," said Mother firmly, drawing from deep, unknown reserves, "but I know Johnny will live! And our baby girl will live too! You see, Rudolf has called upon the powers of heaven through the authority of the Melchizedek Priesthood, and God will not fail us."

Mrs. Jeppson quickly finished her tasks, received her pay, and then left for her home, shaking her head at these strange Mormons. She could plainly see the Butikofer family would be lucky to save the life of one distressed child—much less two of them. With Marie's strength drained, Mrs. Jeppson had her doubts about the mother as well.

Although both John and I required special care, Mama was determined we would both live. She was equally adamant that neither of us should be taken to the hospital in town because *she* wanted to give the tender, loving care needed. She believed in the power of the priesthood and knew she was the emissary to bring about the blessing's fulfillment.

For several weeks after this fateful day, Mama never even undressed to go to bed. She would lie down fully clothed, ready to go to John whenever he needed her. At his slightest whimper she was at his side, trying to ease his pain and comfort him. I was so premature and frail that Mama had to feed me breast milk dribbled from a spoon, which she did day after day, with love and compassion.

Faith and tender care were finally rewarded as John slowly improved, and I gradually began to grow and learned how to nurse. John's skin always held the marks of his lye bath, looking shiny and smooth, and then terribly wrinkled, as any burned body area looks after it heals, but he did recover his health. I remained small for some time but finally gained weight as my tiny body matured enough to function properly.

I can't ever remember Mama taking credit for any of it, and we heard the story many times. She would quickly say, "No, it wasn't me. Through the Lord's mercy and kindness, he granted the priesthood blessings given in his name."

Chapter 9

"This baby business makes you feel like a clumsy ox," I complained as my twentieth birthday approached. "Truly, I want this baby, but I feel so huge. Why can't she just be born now so I can carry her in my arms, not inside my body?"

"*He* will be born soon enough. Stop fretting. You look so beautiful to me," laughed Morris. "It will be quite an occasion to increase our family with a new baby boy, rather than a teenaged girl."

I had to agree with the baby part, as Irene, my youngest sister, and Mamie, Lydia's daughter, had both moved in with us in February. The situation at Dad's house wasn't good. They were so unhappy there.

Dad had delivered Irene to our house one bitter cold, winter morning early in February, soon after breakfast. Outside, the bare-naked trees and brown, stubby grass looked achingly cold from the deep freeze of the night before, but because the cottage was so small, the kitchen almost glowed with the warmth given off by the black wood-burning stove. Morris, Ruth, Rachel, and I had eaten all the breakfast oatmeal and the last of the whole wheat bread. Because both Ruth and Rachel were old enough to be learning how to bake, a bread-making lesson was slated for later in the morning. And then there was a solid knock at the door.

"I hate to do this to you, Susie," Dad said as soon as he and Irene entered the house. Dad wasn't much of a talker, and when something was on his mind, he got right to it. This morning

his face was full of concern, mingled with hopelessness.

"Irene needs a mama, not a task master, and I know you will do right by her. My house is no place for her right now." He pushed Irene, carrying her small overnight bag, gently forward. "I'll send in milk, eggs, and later on produce on a regular basis to help out with the girls' keep."

"It's all right, Dad. The house is kind of small for everyone, but we'll make do." This was said while gathering Irene up in my arms and giving her a giant welcoming hug. "I hope you brought her bed along," I said as a practical afterthought.

Ruth and Rachel had already gone into the tiny living room to rearrange their double bed and a small chesterfield so that another single-sized mattress would fit in the room. Everyone was trying to make this as easy as possible for both Dad and Irene. We could see from her red-rimmed eyes that Irene had been crying.

"You know, Susie, you have a darned good husband." Dad continued to talk after he and Morris had unloaded Irene's mattress and a small trunk out of the back of the truck and returned to the warmth of the house. "I hope you know what a good man he is to accept half our family into his home like they were his own. Not everyone would be so willing to help out. I just hope you know!" Dad shook his head in resignation and in gratitude for Morris, while Morris blushed and waved off his comments with his hands.

"Now, Rudolf, you know the girls are welcome here anytime. We're just glad you realized that and brought Irene to us. She was probably missing her other sisters, anyway."

"Best thing I ever did, to say that young man could marry you," Dad muttered to himself as he left the house a few minutes later.

Morris was being wonderful about the entire situation, and no one knew it better than me. He wouldn't let me dwell on it but would shrug it off, softly making some remark like, "Someday I'll have to make my peace with your mother," or, "I knew what I was getting into, and I've never been sorry." I knew we were all being blessed by his generous attitude.

"Can I come in?" sobbed Mamie, one frosty, blue-black night later in the month when she arrived close to midnight, pounding on our kitchen door as if the devil himself was after her.

It took us a minute or two to come fully awake and respond. But when Morris saw who it was, he quickly pulled her into the house and slammed the door. She was wearing a long, red plaid wool coat and a black woolen tam pulled low over her ears. Her nose, running and looking almost swollen, was at least as red as her coat, and her cheeks were flushed a hot pink color, tinged with spots of white. The kitchen had cooled down for the night but was still infinitely warmer than the frigid, biting air outside.

Mamie was anything but quiet as she wailed out her story. Ruth and Rachel, who had been sleeping in the living room, awakened quickly, making two more sets of ears hearing the deluge. Only Irene, snugly cocooned in her favorite quilt and curled like a caterpillar on her own mattress, slept through the bitter onslaught.

"Mama is determined I will marry Mr. Farren!" Mamie had a captive audience, and she was making the most of it, her voice rising to a crescendo.

"Oh, Mamie, Mr. Farren is old enough to be your grandfather! Your mother wouldn't want you to marry him," I reasoned. "This is impossible," I was thinking to myself.

"Oh, yes she does!" Mamie was wound up, and her eyes were blazing. "He's wealthy! That's all I've heard about him for a month. 'He's so rich he can buy you anything you want,' that's all Mama ever says. 'You will have a lovely house, and beautiful clothes. You will have money to spend on anything you want. He has money, Mamie, and his money will give you a glorious life.'" Mamie was adamant in her telling. "And I tell her, 'Oh, Mama, who cares. I don't love him,' but she won't listen." Both deep hurt and raging anger were plain in her voice.

"Mamie, it's almost midnight and freezing cold outside! How did you get here, anyway? Did Dad bring you?" I suddenly questioned. The temperature had been hovering around the twenty below zero mark for several days.

With tears filling her downcast eyes and speaking considerably quieter now, as she slowly rubbed her hands together to restore the circulation, she said, "No, I didn't want to get him into trouble. He's been so kind to me." And then with the look of a changeling, Mamie lost her forlorn demeanor and said with a defiant pout, "I walked!"

"But, it's eight miles from the farm to our house!" I was shaking my head, almost not believing her. She did look pretty frozen, though. "Well, I'm glad you arrived safe. Come in and stay the night. We will call Lydia in the morning."

Thank goodness for the chesterfield in the living room that Morris's parents had let us borrow! Mamie would have a soft place to sleep off her anger. I thought I had one more homemade quilt on the shelf in the closet.

The next morning, as we were eating breakfast, Lydia called to report that Mamie had disappeared. When she learned Mamie had stayed with us for the night, she was furious.

"I was so worried about her. How could you not have called last night when she arrived?"

"Did you realize she was gone? Where did you think she would go? Would you have let her stay the night?" In frustration, the questions rushed out of my mouth one on top of the other.

"Of course I would not have let her stay the night," Lydia spat, addressing only the last question asked. "That foolish girl is running away from her destiny. She will make a great little wife for James Farren. He will treat her like a queen."

"But she doesn't love him. He's old enough to be her grandfather, you know." Why couldn't Lydia see the obvious?

"She'll learn to love him when he showers her with beautiful things," insisted Lydia.

I felt totally disgusted with Dad's new wife. "Mamie really

doesn't want to come home right now, Lydia." It was all I could do to be civil when she was so unfeeling for her own daughter. And even though I knew I was treading on eggshells and needed to proceed cautiously, I couldn't help but do what was best for Mamie. "She's frightened and upset. Could she stay here a few days until she calms down?" My words were meant to cajole Lydia until she got some common sense. But the steam inside Lydia was building like an overheated pressure cooker ready to explode.

"Frightened! Frightened and upset! Oh, that ungrateful girl. She can stay with you from now on. You bet! If you're silly enough to want to support her along with your sisters, go ahead and keep her, but you tell her she has passed up a mar-r-vil-l-ous opportunity." Lydia emphasized the words dramatically, as she ground them out in anger.

So Mamie stayed.

It was a grim group gathered for supper that evening. And then Rachel, the ultimate peacemaker, said, "One thing is certain, when this baby is born, Susie, you will have plenty of willing babysitters." With that platitude, the tension was broken, and we all enjoyed a fine, if somewhat sparse, supper together.

Yes, babysitters were aplenty. The problem was that Morris expected a boy, and frankly, my heart was set on a baby girl. When Sam, my eighteen-year-old brother came to visit, talking excitedly about the baby boy I was going to have, I realized all my brothers, as well as Dad and my husband, were set on this baby being a big, strapping boy. I think they expected him to be born with a baseball mitt on one hand and a hammer or a fishing rod in the other. But, even with all the teenage girls around, my soul yearned for a cuddly, petite, soft baby girl.

Over time, my dad and I had finally come to terms in understanding each other. Still, I was aware that boys were thought of as more valuable than girls by many of the menfolk. That thought hurt me deep down inside. I simply didn't believe it! Through the years, I had struggled with low self-esteem, beating myself up with the thought that I wasn't as important as the boys. If I had a little girl, I would lavish my love on her, and she would know she was important and adored. I believed the men in my family would love her too, probably even more than they realized they were capable of loving someone so fragile and feminine.

Morris had the habit of sleeping with his arms wrapped around me, a position that sometimes caused me to sleep less than restfully, but it was worth it because it always assured me of how much he loved me. One night we hadn't been in bed long when Morris's soft, even breathing let me know he was fast asleep.

I was thinking of girls' names I liked for the baby, which was moving regularly and quite strongly by this time. All of a sudden, as the baby gave a solid kick, Morris grabbed me around my neck, dragging me out of bed, as he floundered around trying to stand up. "Morris! Morris, what's going on?" I gasped as I tried to breathe.

"Save you . . . Don't fall, Susanna, I'll save you!"

And then he was awake and horrified at what he had done. "Oh, Susanna, I am so sorry. Did I hurt you?" he carefully picked me up off the cold, hard floor and placed me back on the warm, soft bed.

"I must have been dreaming. I thought someone punched you—really hard, and you were falling. I had—to—to—save you—" he ended weakly, looking into my sparkling eyes as I tried to subdue the laughter inside me.

The incident became a favorite family joke, and my brothers never stopped razzing Morris about dragging me out of bed by the neck in the middle of the night.

The icy fingers of winter finally thawed to the warm stirrings of spring. Years before, Aunt Belle, who owned our comfortable cottage, had planted daffodils and tulips along the side of the house. Tiny grape hyacinths pushed their heads up through the moist soil along the brick walk. I had even spotted a robin, its red breast heaving as it pulled breakfast from the mulch bed at the edge of the garden. Oh, what a lovely time of year to bear a child!

One day my dad thoughtfully brought us a wooden rocker, and Rachel carried it out by the warm, sheltered south side of the house so I could rock, read, or sleep.

During this special, introspective time, I often thought of Mary, the mother of the Savior. I had never thought I would have anything in common with her. She seemed so—special, so—*holy!* But now my scriptural wanderings often ended in Luke where I read again about her. She was probably about my age when she was expecting her first child. I especially loved the part about her "keeping all these things, and pondering them in her heart."

A lovely part of having all the girls around so much of the time was that they pampered me unstintingly, as I grew larger and larger. I guess because I was so short, I was destined to carry the entire baby out in front of me. I had known some girls who hardly showed at all during their first pregnancy, but that certainly wasn't true in my case. Because it looked like I was carrying twins, everyone was very solicitous of me.

Deep down inside, I hoped to deliver a baby girl as my own birthday gift to myself on April 26. That murky day dawned with a sky that looked like badly stirred chocolate milk. The overcast day mirrored my feelings, as it came and went very slowly, and although I felt huge and uncomfortable, my long-awaited baby girl didn't arrive.

Two days later, while sitting on a kitchen chair, resting from the exertion of ironing a shirt, I exclaimed, "Morris, would you help me into the bathroom? It feels like I need to go." But when we got there, it didn't feel like I really needed to go to the bathroom. It was just that there was so much pressure down low. Finally, it dawned on me. "I don't know what labor pains feel like, Morris, but somehow I think they may have started. The last pain didn't last long, though, so maybe not."

"Well, let's wait a while before calling Dr. Kimball and see if you have more." The pains started slowly, and though they gradually became closer, harder, and longer, it seemed the process would last forever.

It was late afternoon when I sighed heavily, "Oh, Morris, will this never end?"

"Only when we get our boy. Just hang on, Susanna. I've called Dr. Kimball, and he said to get you in the car and bring you to the hospital. He will meet us there."

There was still plenty of time to get me checked into my room, into a hospital gown, and into bed, sipping ice water. As early evening slipped silently into place outside my hospital window, the process began to speed up. Now I felt like I was on a roller coaster. The initial climb to the top was over, and my particular car felt like it was careening toward the bottom—over bumps, around curves—speeding toward destruction.

Dr. Kimball was making his rounds and checking me once again. This time he ordered Nurse Sally to give me some kind of gas as an anesthetic. Some of the gas must have gotten to Morris, for when the baby came, short minutes later, he exclaimed in a slow, drawn-out sort of drawl, "Oh-h-h, my gos-s-h-h, it's a gir-r-l -l-l!"

"Get him out of the room for a breath of fresh air," ordered Dr. Kimball. And then, in exasperation, he exclaimed, "Or better yet, just move the new mama over and lay papa down beside her. He's worse off than she is!"

Embarrassed by all the attention he was receiving, Morris quickly left the room for a few minutes and then returned to see his new little daughter. The moment he saw DeNiece for the first time, he lost his heart to that tiny bundle. Forgotten were the thoughts of the son he had so hoped to have.

DeNiece was everybody's baby. The teenaged girls played with her as they washed, fed, kissed, changed, and tended her. Morris rocked her and talked to her, giving her his full attention as soon as he arrived home from work. He had eyes only for his darling girl, and she responded with happy gurgles of contentment.

Dad and the boys came into town just to see DeNiece whenever time allowed. If they had to pick up supplies in Coltman, they made sure they traveled the extra few miles to our house in Goshen before returning home to the farm. I had been right in my perception of the boys and Dad adoring this girl. It was a wonderful, happy time for everyone. As is often the case with a new baby, she was the string that tied us all together in tight bonds of love.

As much as we all loved each other, our little golden cottage was bursting at the seams. Through the warm summer months, the girls sometimes slept outside under the stars, listening to the cricket chorus, for added room for them and some welcome privacy for us. Although Lydia, Dad's wife, seemed oblivious to the situation at times, we were soon to find out that she was busy looking for a working position for Mamie, her daughter. Lydia didn't visit often, but when she did, even she could see how crowded we were in this one bedroom bungalow. Most nights, all four girls continued to sleep in the living room.

One day, toward fall, Lydia called to say she had found a position for Mamie. "You know, Mamie needs to be working. She's seventeen now and out of school, and she really needs more to do than just babysit." Sometimes my stepmother wasn't too tactful, although I was impressed that she was talking over the situation with me before she told Mamie. "Mrs. Albough—you know, the older lady who lives on the corner across from the church? Well, she needs her housework done on a regular basis since her operation. She has enough work for a girl to do during the day, as well as on weekends, what with the house and yard and all."

"That sounds like a great situation for Mamie, Lydia. Ruth will certainly be jealous of Mamie earning her own money, though," I added truthfully.

"Well, maybe Mamie could work during the day and

Ruth could work some afternoons and on weekends. That way Mamie won't feel like she is working every minute, and Ruth can't complain about not working during the day because she's still in school, isn't she?" Lydia had mellowed a lot since Mamie had first come to live with us. It was a pleasant surprise to have her be concerned about Ruth's feelings too.

"Let me talk to Morris and call you back later this evening, Lydia," I said gratefully. "That is really good of you to find something for the girls to do to earn some spending money."

That evening, Morris and I talked over the possibilities. We felt it would be best if the two girls continued to live with us for the time being because rent anywhere else would eat up all they made. Lydia was in full agreement, and for several months this arrangement worked amicably for both girls.

DeNiece's butterfly whisper of a smile turned into the real thing, with outright giggles rebounding around the room as Morris tickled her tummy with his nose and chin. "DeNiece is *so* strong! Look at her hold up her head." Later, "Feel the strength in those little legs. She is standing by herself. Well, not really, but almost." Everyone rejoiced as she rolled over for the first time by herself. Her eyes were bright and radiated her active spirit within. Soon she was rolling from one auntie to another as they enticed her with bright bits of dancing yarn and rattling sounds of empty spools in a drawstring bag. Dad brought in a small cinnamon-colored kitten from the farm. Cinnabon, as the girls soon named the cat, was amazingly patient with this little person who stared at her and then reached for a handful of hair. Every day DeNiece managed a new accomplishment for the household to brag about. The telephone lines were ringing to announce that after some slight crankiness, DeNiece had cut her first tooth on the bottom. Her cheery disposition quickly returned. Again, each person who entered the room was greeted with garbled messages and a toothy grin.

And then, as is often the case when things are going too perfect, DeNiece became very ill.

"I just don't understand it. She isn't nursing well, and then when she gets a little milk in her, it comes right back up again. Oh, Morris, what am I doing wrong? She's never sick. Do you think something horrible is happening?"

Morris had come home from work and found DeNiece and me rocking and crying together in chorus. "I have tried everything I know to ease her distress. You know this isn't like her. She has been such a good baby."

"It sounds like we need to pay the doctor a visit," he stated, with a perplexed shake of his head.

I hated to go to the doctor. Such a visit cost money we didn't have. We had scrimped through Christmas and were just barely surviving financially in the new year. The work Morris was doing for Anton Anderson was spotty, at best. My mother had treated all sorts of illnesses without a doctor's help, and I was sure I could do the same. Now, though, I was desperate. Our unhappy girl was vomiting constantly and starting to lose weight and vitality. Finally, I agreed.

After giving DeNiece a thorough check-up, Dr. Kimball insisted on checking me over as well. When I complained, the doctor laughingly said, "Now, Susanna, let me do my job. You never did come back in after DeNiece was born for me to check you both."

"I never needed to, Dr. Kimball. DeNiece has done marvelously until now. She has been a total joy in our household."

"Well, that's good Susanna." Dr. Kimball patted my arm. "Slip your clothes back on. And by the way, DeNiece is just fine." Dr. Kimball acted amused as he gave his assessment. "She will need to stop nursing because your milk is not sufficient for her needs, nor is it treating her very well right now, but she's a healthy little girl."

"She sure doesn't seem healthy. She hasn't been able to keep any milk down for several days now." I was relieved but disbelieving.

"Put her on a bottle; she'll do fine. And, by the way," Dr. Kimball chuckled as he put his things away in his black bag, "you'll be fine too, as soon as your new baby is born—the end of October or the first of November, I'd say."

Shock was written all over my face. "But, Doctor, I'm still nursing."

"That's an old wives' tale that you can't get pregnant when you are still nursing, Susanna," Dr. Kimball informed me with raised eyebrows and a nod of his head.

I don't think Morris even heard that little exchange.

"New baby," he gasped and then laughed aloud for the joy of it. "Another baby, whoopee! I wonder if you could give me my boy this time, sweetheart," he said as he hugged me.

"Not if he'll take the place of DeNiece!" I stated defiantly. But Morris just grinned and shook his head. "You know better than that. No one could take the place of DeNiece. She'll always be my precious princess."

I wondered later if Morris would continue to think so kindly of her as he sat up night after night rocking her and trying to feed her a bottle. She was not happy about this new feeding situation. She hadn't wanted to be finished nursing so soon and fought taking the bottle. When I would try to give her a bottle, she would stubbornly clamp her mouth shut, turning her head wildly, and then try to nuzzle into my breast. Hence, the job fell to Morris. Finally her daddy's loving patience and her increased hunger won out, and she succumbed to a bottle and cow's milk.

That was in February. By the end of March, with spring again making feeble attempts to peek through the snow and cold, Lydia had sent Mamie to Salt Lake to a hair dressing school. Mamie had been begging for months for that opportunity. Dad was usually pretty tight with his money, and I was surprised when it was all arranged but delighted for Mamie's opportunity.

With Mamie gone, Ruth took over the entire housekeeping job for Mrs. Albough. Ruth was graduating from high school in May. Because she was such a good worker, Mrs. Albough was willing to work around her school schedule for two months. In the summer, Ruth knew she would have full-time work there. With the added wage, and some help from Dad, she and Rachel rented a small room of their own. Irene told me that when Ruth went to Dad she said, "It's only right that Susanna and Morris have a little more room to raise their own family. With the new baby coming and all—" Dad had interrupted her carefully worded monologue with, "You're right, Ruth. Susie and Morris deserve some space. I'll help you with the room rent."

From the spoiled girl who always got out of work when Mother was alive, to a young adult woman who could see exactly what needed to be done and did it quickly and willingly, Ruth was quite a girl. She and I were past our quarrelsome stage. Now I valued not only her willingness to help but also her solid friendship. Through some personal introspection, I realized that Mama had known us both very well. By not allowing us to argue and fight when we were younger, she knew that someday we would become best friends. Maybe part of the molting process to shed my chrysalis came about because, as a married woman, I felt like a beautiful, much-loved butterfly instead of a caterpillar needing to be squashed. Because of the attention and encouragement of my husband, I had come into my own as a person and wasn't so jealous of my sister's several abilities and accomplishments.

Ruth had turned into a delightful gamine with a petite face, sparkling eyes, straight white teeth, and slightly curly brunette hair. With a personality to match, she was always quick to laugh and see the bright side of any situation. She had a flair for choosing stylish clothes, liked to dress well, and wore her attire with charm and distinction. Ruth was going to be a wonderful catch for some lucky man.

I had always thought, though, that Rachel was the beauty. Her fair, smooth skin that tanned easily set off her light biscuit-colored hair to perfection. She was unpretentious, soothing, and pleasant to be around, much like Mama had been. At fifteen, her personality matched her looks.

And then there was Irene—just beginning to develop pleasing body parts and becoming such a good help with DeNiece. At twelve, she was willing and eager to mimic all that her older sisters did. How blessed we were to have had them all living in our home!

During the ensuing months, Morris didn't predict the sex of our unborn baby or tease me about giving him his boy. I think he was just a little superstitious after the first experience, thinking maybe too much talking and hoping had jinxed the whole thing. Besides, Morris was truly happy with his little girl. I don't think he'd anticipated that a girl could be so much fun. At any rate, he was much more casual about the whole baby experience the second time around.

"Morris, this time I know it's time to go to the hospital. I'm sure these pains are worse than last time with DeNiece, and I'm not sure I'm going to survive. I'm not even sure I want to survive at this point. Oh, how did I ever get myself into this situation?" I cried out with a mother's instinct that this was going to hurt a lot. Funny thing how you forget so quickly the pain of childbirth when you are holding a newborn infant in your arms, and how quickly those fears and memories come washing back when you are in the throes of the experience once again.

Upon arriving at the hospital, my anguish didn't improve. Dr. Kimball checked me over and then solemnly declared, "The baby is lodged the wrong way in the birth canal, Susanna. I need to go up inside you with my hand and try to turn it around to speed up the process, but it will probably hurt a lot. Try to focus on what Morris is telling you while I work at this," he advised.

"This baby is worth it, Susanna. Truly! Whether it's a boy or a girl, it's worth all the pain and effort. In fact, another girl is just fine. DeNiece could probably use a little sister for a playmate." (I didn't know if Morris was trying to convince himself or me, as he continued to grip my hand and encourage me to hang in there.) "Try to hold on. Dr. Kimball is only trying to help out." And, "I love you, Susanna, you know I love you. DeNiece and I need you. Hold on, sweetheart."

Late the following evening—a day, a night, and a day after the pains had originally begun—Elred Morris Teeples was born, his head molded cone-shaped by the long, laborious birthing. The remark I had so glibly made on the first day of labor, "I'm sure these pains are worse than last time with DeNiece, and I'm not sure I'm going to survive," seemed trivial as the ordeal finally came to an end. I felt like minced ham, and Morris looked haggard with the dark stubble on his face scratchy and uncomfortable. But he had gotten his boy. Thank goodness DeNiece was home in her warm, snug bed with Grandma Lodisa at her beck and call!

After a week in the hospital, we were finally home and trying to function again as a family.

"Morris, what I need most of all is to sit in a tub of hot water to help heal these stitches. I hurt so badly, and I just know the warm water will soothe my battered bottom." Morris was stubbornly shaking his head, as my eyes filled with pleading tears.

"Oh, Susanna. I can't put you into a hot bath. You know what my mother says: it will kill you!" Morris whispered.

Lodisa had been wonderful about coming to check on me regularly during the last stages of my pregnancy. She had taken DeNiece and Irene home with her during my hospital stay. When I returned home, she promised to arrive daily to help with DeNiece and Elred. What a sweet, devoted mother-in-law! I appreciated her cleaning, her cooking, her changing babies' diapers, her bright disposition and cheerful humming. What I didn't appreciate was her insistence that I could not bathe.

"She told me baths are dangerous for new mothers, and that I should only allow you to have sponge baths for at least a month," declared Morris for the hundredth time.

"Morris, I love your mother dearly, but how could a hot bath kill me? I remember my mother taking what she called sitz baths after she had a baby, and they always helped her. Honey, I promise I won't tell your mother when she comes over during the day about taking the baths if you will just help me get into the tub at night after she has gone. They will help, I promise, and I need them badly."

I knew Morris was only trying to do the best for me and was torn between the advice given by a seasoned mother—his mother—and my insistence that the warm water was what I needed to get well.

Eventually he carefully helped me into a tub of hot water, saying all the while, "Don't you dare tell my mother." And then he hovered around asking, "Are you all right? Is the water too hot? Don't you think it's time to get out?"

I'm sure he was waiting for me to drop over dead. Instead, periodically, I'd purr, "Honey, just add some more hot water, this is cooling down a little."

Finally after an hour of soaking contentedly, I allowed him to help me out of the tub and into bed. I rested so well that night and was so improved the next morning; the hot bath became a nightly occurrence until I was completely recovered. We never told Lodisa about my magical formula for healing. Meanwhile, our new son's head straightened out to its proper shape, and he turned into quite a handsome little boy.

Chapter 10

After you have children, your life is never the same. Before you have a child, you might yearn for one, imagining the joy of holding a tiny new infant close to your heart, but you truly cannot fathom the changes that a small human being will make to your life. What begins in marriage as your choice of when to work, to read, to bathe, and to sleep, suddenly changes to what is required of you—on someone else's schedule. The newness of this neonate makes you a willing slave to their demands. Isn't this what you desired? Waited nine months for? Beforehand, you just have no idea.

As the birth moment nears, you think you are ready. Let me have this child outside my body. Let me carry her in my arms. Let me sing and read to him, play with him and teach him, as I have envisioned. When the labor begins, you reach back to the dark recesses of your memory, trying to discover why it was you wanted a child at all. You knew there was pain in childbirth, but not this kind of hurt and stress. Not this overwhelming urgency to expel this thing from your body. And then the child is born. Now all will be well.

Thus begins the all-consuming time commitment. But it is so much more than that. Now you care for another—this vulnerable, helpless, trusting, demanding soul. You would not have it any other way—really. But you realize you can never go back. The responsibility and the love will always be there. Arms will get weary, hearts may be heavy, emotions may surface that seem foreign and sometimes overwhelming. Suddenly prayer is essential, not to be taken lightly. Your life is altered forever. But oh, the joy of it! A deeper source of fulfillment is present than you knew was possible to feel. And so you would not wish to go back—well, maybe some days you would wish that—but you realize you are in it for the long haul. Selfishness recedes, parenting has arrived.

As much as we desired to get wrapped up in the raising of our family, there were outside pressures—as there always are—pounding at our door. This was a time of scarcity. Aunt Belle had decided to move back to the "Golden Cottage." We had always known it was a temporary living arrangement, and besides, we were so crowded there! That tiny cottage was soon to seem like a mansion, for when we looked for other housing options, we could only find two rooms to rent in a home in Shelley. Dad realized that we would never move back to the farm ourselves, but Irene could move home again to relieve the overcrowding we were experiencing. As Irene had matured, she had become her own person and was able to handle her stepmother in a much more diplomatic manner. Lydia had mellowed as well, through her disappointments and disagreements, and she welcomed Irene's return.

Morris was out of work. Anton Anderson had been good to us, providing work as long as he could on the threshing machine. His boys were now getting to an age that they could do the work and were pressed into service. Jobs, such as water master for the canal, were now shared by several farmers, with no one getting paid for doing them. The government had no money to spend on such "trivialities." Many essential jobs were done free of charge as the nation experienced economic paralysis.

People throughout the country were out of work and close to starving. Finally, the government provided some small help in the form of food rationing coupons, where basic foods in meager quantities were dispensed. Rice, potatoes, and beans, with an occasional piece of bacon or cheese but more often a chicken, could be obtained using the coupons. As much as fathers and husbands hated using the coupons, their families had to eat something.

Dad was good to send butter and eggs, wheat and flour in from the farm, and that made the difference for our family. Regularly, in the spring and summer, Morris would catch a ride out to the farms and work during the planting and harvesting seasons. Putting in long days in the fields, without pay, made him feel better about the food we gratefully accepted from my brothers and dad throughout the year. On the heels of food coupons came gas rationing, which limited the boys' trips into town. One day they arrived in Shelley with a cow and some hay in the back of the farm truck. What a godsend! This not only provided us with fresh milk daily for our small children, but we were also able to share the milk with our landlady to defer some of the cost of the rent.

As grateful as we were for food to eat and a roof over our heads, we didn't dwell on our deprivation. Children were still children, with delightful smiles and winning ways. DeNiece and Elred had never experienced any other way of life, so they didn't realize how hard up we were. Store-bought toys were non-existent, but birds still sang, trees blossomed in a profusion of pink and white fluff, meadows were dotted with colorful wild flowers, creeks gurgled and splashed. Tickling, laughing, and singing were still allowed. Long walks made sturdy legs and strong lungs, and we didn't pine for what we couldn't have but were happy with our blessings from God.

No thought was given to getting an education or even apprenticing a trade. Those things were just not a possibility. Morris could see, though, that living in Idaho Falls would provide some potential part-time work. Eventually he found a run-down house on East 19th Street that was empty. The rent was minimal because the clapboard house was very old and was not insulated from the elements. The winter after the move was made, Morris insisted he kept warm by chopping firewood out in the backyard, to keep me warm on the inside of the house. Thank goodness for each other, to not only chop wood but to snuggle close together on the cold winter nights. It wasn't uncommon for the snow to blow in through the cracks in the walls and drift across the bed, covering us with a lacy white quilt. We layered the children in several sets of furry pajamas. Sleeping together in the same bed helped them to keep warm. The last job of the evening before turning into our bed was always to check their little trundle bed to make sure the blankets were tucked under them carefully.

During the formidable winter of 1933, Morris was again out of work. Each day he would get up and leave early for the central board office in downtown Idaho Falls where potential employers would post jobs that needed to be done, hoping a day job would come in and he would be chosen to work it. The employment office boasted a black, pot-bellied stove and other men with the same woes for company. Many of the days were spent in hunting for the elusive job, which never materialized. If nothing turned up, Morris would return home and putter around the house, feeling useless and restless. Some days he stayed at the office for a while hoping to pick up a lead for even the smallest task.

One clear, bright, sub-zero morning, as soon as breakfast was over and Morris was out of the house, Elred stood before me, his dark hair standing up in a shock, his bright blue eyes shining, "Can I go play with my coal shovel Daddy brought home last night, Mommy? Pl-e-e-a-s-e?"

A heavy, black coal bucket, which sat by the cook stove in the corner of the room, had a flared spout in the front where I could pour out the coal. I often felt frustrated as I tried to control the amount of coal falling into the stove. I would ever so carefully tip the bucket but often wasted precious coal when extra pieces would quickly slide out of the bucket and into the fire. Morris was aware of my frustration in my efforts to economize and just the day before had brought home a small coal shovel, just the width of the bucket spout, so I could put just the right amount of coal into the stove.

Elred was so excited about the shovel. New toys didn't

arrive often, and he felt the shovel, being just his size, was his. It wasn't a toy, of course, but household items often became toys for a short duration to fill in the long hours. He knew he must let me use it as I needed it, but in his mind, the shovel was only loaned to me occasionally. Now my active five-year-old was anxious to go outside and use it in the recently fallen snow.

"Oh, sure. But you'll have to bundle up real good 'cause it's awful cold out there. Do you want me to call Keith's grandma and see if he can play with you?"

"Oh, boy, Keith is gonna love my shovel. Bet he'll wish he had one."

"Well, maybe you can share it with him. You can dig some with it, and then you can let him try it out. What do you think?"

"Mmmmm, yeh, I guess so," was Elred's muffled reply as he pulled his knitted brown toque low over his ears. "But I'll have to show him how to use it first."

As Elred left the house, toting his little black shovel, I gave Mrs. Browning a call.

"Oh, Keith can't go outside and play today," she explained. "He has a terrible toothache. I'd love to have Elred come over, though, and play inside. Maybe it will get Keith's mind off his hurting tooth."

"Well, Elred should be there any minute. He left the house on the run a few minutes ago."

As the day progressed, I was pleased with the chores I was able to accomplish without my busy boy around my feet constantly. About 3:30, I bundled up and went outside to feed our three chickens. As I did, I had the strange feeling come over me that something was wrong—very wrong. The feeling persisted as I hurriedly finished the job and then walked around to the front of the house just in time to see DeNiece coming home from school.

"Hi, sweetheart! I was wondering if you would run over to Mrs. Browning's and bring Elred home. Daddy isn't home from work yet. I hope everything is okay with him," I hesitated, wanting to vent my worry, but not wanting to alarm my six-year-old daughter. "There's a storm brewing. It looks like there's going to be a real blizzard tonight. I'll just be glad when everyone's home," I smiled at her thinly. "Thanks love."

DeNiece returned promptly from Brownings but without Elred.

"Mrs. Browning said Elred didn't really want to come into the house to play at all because he was so anxious to shovel snow. Keith talked him into coming in until lunchtime, but then Elred said he had better shovel his way home, and he left."

"Are you sure, DeNiece? You know how Elred loves to hide at the Brownings when it's home time, just like they do here when Keith's mother comes to get him. The boys think it's a great game—hiding effectively in strange places and pretending they aren't here so they don't have to go home."

"Oh, I know that, Mama. They have played that game with me lots of times. But I'm sure!" declared DeNiece. "Keith wasn't feeling all that good. You could tell they weren't playing this time. Elred wasn't there."

"Well, run over to Parley's house. Maybe Elred talked him into going outside for a while. I'm sure Elred was looking for someone to shovel snow with him. And hurry, I'm still worried about Daddy and would like to have everyone else home when he comes." Silently I was still fretting, "I wonder why I still have this strange, unsettled feeling inside."

In just a few minutes, DeNiece returned from Parley's house. "Not there either, Mama!" she reported as she burst through the kitchen door.

"I'll make some phone calls to other houses to help locate that active boy. You stand by the fire and get warm, DeNiece, while I make the calls, and then you can go and walk home with that little scamp when we find him."

All up and down the block, phone lines rang, but no Elred. I began to call houses further away to see if he was there.

As word spread through the neighborhood that I was looking for Elred, who seemed to be lost, someone from each household bundled up and came outside to help look for him. No one had seen him that day. The men were arriving home from work by this time, and without stopping to eat, they joined in the search. The search, which began as an inconvenience, was quickly turning into a distinct concern.

"Have you looked through Browning's barn?"

"We've looked everywhere. That barn has been searched several times now."

"What about Layton's, where the big, mean dogs live?"

"Mrs. Layton has assured us no one has been in her yard today. The dogs haven't barked at all. She put the dogs into the house so that men could look through her yard for signs of disaster, but nothing has been found."

As the search intensified, the men held hands, so the line stretched from one sidewalk to the other, and walked down the streets trudging through the snowdrifts so they wouldn't miss a spot where a little five-year-old boy might be. Another group of men moved the piles of snow made by the snowplough from one location to another, in an effort to check every possibility.

About five o'clock it began to snow again; big heavy flakes of white, clouding the deepening dusk.

"You know, this snowstorm looks like it is going to turn into a blizzard. We are going to have to get Susanna into the house before long. I just don't know where else we can look for Elred," announced our next-door neighbor.

"We've tried to get her to go inside, but she's determined she must find her boy first," a burly man, who lived three doors away, replied.

Finally the police arrived to join in the effort, bringing searchlights with them. But as the snow continued to fall harder and harder and as darkness descended, people decided there was nothing more they could do.

"Mrs. Teeples, there isn't any more we can do tonight. You really need to go into the house, it's so cold out here," the police announced. "We will come back bright and early tomorrow morning to continue the search for your boy."

"Tomorrow morning! What good does that do us? I can't go inside. My little five-year-old son is still out here somewhere." I looked at them incredulously. What were they thinking? What were they asking me to do, abandon the hope of finding Elred?

"But Mrs. Teeples, it's too dark to see anything now. It is snowing so hard—the barns and outbuildings have all been searched. Maybe he will turn up at someone else's house after all."

"Well, until I know that for sure, I can't possibly go in where it's warm. That is just impossible." My heart was despairing. I never wanted to be inside in the warmth again if Elred wasn't found.

The policeman shook his head, not knowing what else to do for me. "I'd advise you to go inside," he said once again in a small voice, while turning to get back into his truck and leave.

"What am I going to do now?" I wondered.

And then, through my anguish, a still small voice seemed to whisper, "Have you asked Heavenly Father to help you? He knows where Elred is." Immediately I fell to my knees in the middle of the street to plead with my Father for help. My mind had no more than formed the words, "Please help us, Father," when my good neighbor from across the street, Barth Lambert, was lifting me up with his strong arms.

"What is wrong, Susanna? I saw you fall as I walked down the street through the piles of snow. I had to leave my car in the next block because the snow is getting so deep. What has happened here?" he looked around at all the snow, which had been shifted from one place to another during the intensive search.

"Oh, Barth, we can't find Elred. He has been missing for hours now. The entire neighborhood has been out looking. Even the police have been here. In fact, they just left, but we haven't found him. They all say we will look again in the morning. In the morning, he will be dead!" My voice broke as I looked at Barth with pleading, brimming eyes and an ache deep in the pit of my stomach. "I will never go in, knowing he's out here somewhere."

Feeling helpless, Barth replied, "Well, have they looked in the Browning's barn? There are lots of places there where a little boy could be."

"They've looked there. They've looked everywhere," I murmured hopelessly.

"Well, let me just take one more look," Barth mouthed as he turned to go, his mind pounding out the thought, *I've got to get her out of the cold somehow. She's exhausted!*

Barth moved down the alley toward the barn, but even in the swirling snow, he could see footprints everywhere, though they were filling rapidly with new snow, and he knew the area had been well checked. The barn itself was pitch black, and he could see nothing inside, although the two big workhorses could be heard chomping their grain and moving around in their stalls.

"I need to get back to Susanna," he thought, "and the fastest way to do that is across Morley's chicken run. With all this snow, it should be easy to climb over and return to the street. It will be a lot faster than going around," he reasoned.

The chicken run was a high, wire enclosure, which gave the chickens a little more room to move around in a protected area. During the day, the snow had drifted to about a man's height up against the wire fence on the west. As Barth clambered up the slippery, steep drift, he suddenly felt his feet slipping out from under him, and he fell heavily from the drift into the chicken run. "Ouch," he muttered, "what did I land on that's so hard?"

Digging around with his hands by his right hip, he discovered a small pair of boots, the bottoms sticking up slightly out of the snow. "Oh, my gosh!" He sucked in his breath in disbelief.

And then, "Susanna, Susanna, I've found him! I've found Elred!" he shouted excitedly.

With the wind growling and the snow swirling, I wasn't sure what I was hearing. "Barth, Barth," I called frantically. "Are you calling me? What are you saying?" For some reason, I had thought I heard Barth call that he had found Elred. Surely I was hearing only what I wanted so desperately to hear.

"Susanna, over here," Barth shouted again. "He's here! Elred's here, but I need help to get him out." Barth was screaming to be heard over the storm.

On the road, on the other side of the chicken run, I hollered to Barth. "Barth, have you found him? Are you sure? Oh, my baby!"

"Yes, Susanna, I've found Elred. Go for help! I need help!"

Almost hysterical—half laughing, half crying—I ran to the nearest house and beat on the door with all my might.

"What the—" exclaimed George Smith as he swung the door wide. And then, seeing me on his doorstep, he pulled me quickly inside.

"Barth Lambert has found Elred. Inside the chicken run, I think. That's where his voice was coming from. Can you come and help?" But before I had even finished my sentence, George was pulling on his heavy coat and yelling at Mary, "Call the police and have them get back out here."

"You stay here, Susanna," were his last words as he ran out the door, his shovel in his hand.

"I can't stay here," I told Mary. "I think they've found my boy." With tears coursing down my reddened cheeks, I too returned outside into the chilling, roaring elements.

Mary was on the phone to neighbors immediately. In a matter of minutes, out on the street, the neighborhood men streamed from their homes once again, dressed warmly and with shovels, ready to give whatever assistance they could. The city truck returned with its searchlight and ladders, ploughing slowly down 19th Street to where the men were gathered. By the time the police and city truck arrived, George and his crew had dug down into the chicken run, retrieving Barth and releasing Elred from his almost inaccessible position.

Quick-thinking Mary, George's wife, and her daughter, Louisa, had been busy at the Smith house. Mary had called a doctor, admonishing him to hurry, and then with Louisa's help began to make a big pot of chicken noodle soup.

"Mrs. Teeples, you must go inside now." Mr. Morgan, a slightly built man from down at the corner house, took my elbow and guided me home. "Mary Smith called our house to say the doctor is coming. You need to be home when he arrives." What a good man, this neighbor, with a heart condition that prevented him from shoveling snow, but who cared for everyone around him and wanted to be of help. Mary had known I wouldn't fight going inside with those encouraging words and this kind man to help me home.

As we entered our house, I could see DeNiece, white-faced and staring out the window. "What is happening, Mama? Where is Elred?"

"We have found him, sweetheart. Oh, love, you were so good to stay inside. Thank you! You are such a good girl." I pulled her to me and hugged her tight. "Here, help me stoke up the fire."

The minutes ticked by, and finally we heard the men's heavy work boots outside the kitchen door. "Mrs. Teeples, here is your boy."

Mr. Morgan was immediately at the door, opening it wide so George Smith could enter with Elred cradled in his strong arms. His toque, scarf, snowsuit, and gloves were stiff with caked ice. His staring, half-open eyes seemed sunken into his tiny, frozen, white skull. Behind him, most of the neighborhood men pushed inside the door and crowded into the tiny kitchen.

As if by magic, the doctor appeared and immediately took charge of the situation and my frozen Elred.

While he reached for my child, George assessed him of the situation. "This boy has been outside in the cold most of the afternoon, Doc. I don't know how long he was in the snow-drift, but quite a while, I would guess. He's pretty lucky that ol' Barth Lambert, here, didn't stop looking for him."

"I was just the Lord's instrument," Barth stated quietly but surely. "I actually fell on top of his boots, Doctor, when I slipped at the top of the chicken run. Elred must have climbed up that high snow bank on the west side of the run, same as me, and then slipped off the other side too. Only trouble was, he was head first in the snow."

As the men talked, the doctor was gently undressing Elred to check his vital signs. "The blood in this little boy's arms and legs is actually slushy rather than liquid after so long in the cold. Proper circulation has to be restored if his life is to be saved." The neighborhood men who had been a rivulet of rescue action now stood as if rooted to the floor, watching with wide eyes as if the boy were their own.

"Mrs. Teeples, you prepare a tub of cool water and put him in it. It must be cool, not too warm. You will need to rub his arms and legs continuously to thaw him out carefully." Even as the doctor spoke to me, taking in my dazed countenance, neighbors filled the tub and began working with Elred. The house was crammed with people wanting to help.

I wanted to help Elred myself, but the shock of all that had happened was finally registering in my confused brain, causing me to feel like my useless limbs were unrelated to my own cold, shaking body. DeNiece was pressed close by my side, afraid of what was happening all around her to those she loved most.

And then the kitchen door opened again. Into this teeming, animated scene walked a bewildered and frightened Morris. "What is happening? Why is everyone here?" he inquired softly, his blue eyes big and scared, his hands shaking slightly. The story poured out as one neighbor after another told of our hunt and our fear.

Someone pulled up a chair, and Morris sat down heavily. "I finally found work today. Only a day job, but because it didn't start until almost noon, I had to stay at it until now to get finished." He shook his head ruefully. "If only I had known what was happening at home."

As the cool water began thawing out Elred's skin and blood, he began mumbling out loud, the words slurred together. "I's sure I could jump across that ol' chicken run." The men rubbing his body signaled for us all to stop talking and listen.

"I wuz just hungry and wanted to get home fast."

"Were you playing in Browning's barn, Elred?" one of the men prompted.

"It'z okay—Ms. Brownin' doezn't care. Shez let us play there before, lots a times." He drew out his defense slowly.

"Oh, I know, Elred. I just wondered if that was where you were playing."

"Just playin' there cause it wuzn't sa cold. Shovelin' hay and horse biscuits." Elred coughed slightly.

"But I wuz hungry and wanted ta go home. I wuz sure I could jump that ol' run. The snow pile wuz clear up to the top of the wire."

"Was it slippery?" Barth asked quietly.

"Yeah, slip-ry." The word came out a little indistinct. "My feet slipped and I stubbed my toe on the wire and it flipped me upside down."

"Oh," Barth shook his head up and down as the light began to dawn. "So you were going to dig yourself out with your shovel, right?"

"'Course. I wuz takin' the shovel home for Mom-m-y to use. I figgered she'd be needin' it."

"I'll bet you're a good digger with that shovel," said Barth.

"I'm a good digger," agreed Elred. "I knew I could do it. But that snow was *s-o-o* heavy, and I think I wuz diggin' in the wrong direction."

Silence prevailed in the room. And then, Elred spoke again sleepily, "I waited and waited for someone to come and get me, but no one came."

As the incredible story came to an end, Morris reached out, gathering me into his arms and onto his lap to comfort me and get control of his own galloping emotions. DeNiece, looking forlorn, tears sliding silently down her cheeks, sidled over to her daddy. He wrapped his free arm around her waist, kissing her softly on her flushed, wet cheek.

"Okay, Elred doesn't need to stay in the cool bath anymore," the doctor said soon after the story had been told, adding seriously, "but you can see he is very tired—and he must not be allowed to go to sleep until 8:00 in the morning. If he sleeps before then, he will never wake up."

And then, such a beautiful thing happened: neighbors who had worked or looked for work all day and were tired and hungry offered to stay and help. The police and men from the town who had brought the searchlights and ladders refused to leave. Even men who were supposed to go to work that night said they could get off to stay and help. Morris assured them that they needed to go to their jobs. Work was hard to keep and harder to find. He didn't want people losing their jobs because they didn't show up for work. But they insisted it was fine; a phone call would fix everything. They just wouldn't leave.

In shifts all night long, those men tickled and played with Elred. They tossed him; they bounced him; they walked him; they carried him; they laughed with him and at him; they pushed him on his trike. They didn't let him relax for a second. When one set of men wore out and needed a rest, there were many other willing arms there ready to play hard with him and keep him wide awake and going strong.

A little before eight the next morning, the doctor arrived again. He could see that Elred was happily, if a little groggily, playing with a police officer and George. "You have done your work well. He will be okay. You may let him sleep now," he told all who were assembled. After a quick but solid hug, George carefully laid Elred down on his bed, and our exhausted five-year-old was asleep instantly.

"Are you sure he won't die?" Morris and I asked anxiously.

"No, Elred will live. You have many to thank, but Elred will live." I knew in my heart that brotherly love and an answer to prayer had achieved a miracle.

Chapter 11

After the prompt arrival of our first two children, I thoroughly expected more children to arrive at regular intervals. My own mother had produced another child about every two years, with a slight three-year variation, occasionally. Having eleven children in twenty-three years was a lot, but it wasn't considered all that unusual among our relatives. Although I wasn't sure I wanted ten or eleven children, I was mentally prepared to have several.

Our little princess, DeNiece, was only one and a half years older than Elred. They were active children—busy with each other, with school, and with life in general. At first the respite from having a new infant in the house every couple of years was appreciated, but by the time Elred was three, I was yearning for a tiny baby again. And then he was four, and then five, and still no sign of any more babies at our house.

"I'm certainly glad Elred was a boy for you, Morris. We have my girl and your boy, and it looks like that is going to be as big as our family gets."

I had just returned through the dreary October slush from a doctor's appointment and now sat dejectedly at the heavy wooden kitchen table, talking with Morris.

"Oh, another baby may come along. We aren't that old yet," Morris said with a half grin, but he couldn't lighten my gloomy mood. "Besides, I claim DeNiece as well as Elred. You told me I couldn't have a boy if he would get in the way of my loving that little girl, remember?" Rolling my eyes, I looked at Morris with raised eyebrows, a deep sigh, and a shake of my head. "So, these children are mine. You'll have to have some more if you want some for you," he teased.

"It's been five years since we've had a baby," I complained. "I just don't think there are any more coming."

When I didn't elicit another comment from Morris, I went on, "I've been thinking. Why don't we sell our baby crib and the high chair? DeNiece and Elred certainly don't need them. It would give us more room to move around, and—" my countenance brightened considerably, "we could put the money toward Christmas presents for the kids." Subconsciously, I realized, I had been thinking of this scheme for quite some time.

"As soon as we sell them," Morris chuckled slightly, glad for the diversion, "you'll probably have another baby. But, whatever you want to do is fine with me," he agreed.

When I get an idea into my head, it doesn't take long to carry it out. In fact, I already knew a family who could use both the crib and the high chair. Within days the deal was finalized, and the baby furniture was sold and gone. Morris and I had a great time purchasing two shiny new bicycles, a baby doll with a cradle, and a train set complete with engine, caboose, and yards of train track for DeNiece and Elred. A month to the day after the furniture items were hauled out of the house, I found out I was pregnant.

"If I had known it would work so fast, I would have sold that old crib three years ago," I exulted.

It took us the nine months of my pregnancy to scrimp and save enough money to buy another used crib and high chair—neither of which was in as good a condition as our old ones had been. Our friends offered to sell ours back to us, but we jokingly told them we were loaded and would buy some more. We weren't about to go back on our deal with them. They were as poor as we were. If selling the furniture was what it took to get pregnant, then it was definitely worth it.

This time it didn't matter if the baby was a boy or a girl,

as long as it was healthy. DeNiece, of course, wanted a little sister. Elred thought a brother might be pretty good—as long as he grew fast so he could play ball with him. Barth was born the following August, six years after Elred. Yes, we named him after Barth Lambert—our good friend, neighbor, and rescuer—to whom we still felt indebted for Elred's life.

During the summer of 1934, most August mornings started out mild and lovely, but by ten o'clock the heat of the day would already be increasing. By late afternoon, the dry, hot day felt like it was choking on its own dust, making it almost unbearable. At three weeks old, it was apparent that Barth was a very sick baby. He could hardly breathe as the heat wave continued. All of us felt parched by the stifling heat. But that wasn't the worst of our problems—or his.

Barth wasn't eating well, and what he did take into his little body flew back out as fast as he had gobbled it down. We knew we were in trouble. Morris would arrive home from work to find me, hot and sticky, with tears running steadily down my cheeks, holding our dehydrated, near-naked baby on a feather-down pillow as I rocked him back and forth in my mother's old wooden rocker.

"I just can't get him to keep anything down," I sobbed. "I feed him so carefully, and he eats it like he is starving, but the milk comes shooting back up almost immediately."

"What formula do you have him on now?" Morris inquired gently.

"Oh, the newest one," I waved my hand in the general direction of the kitchen. "I forget what the name is. It's not working any better than the previous six have done. I am so frustrated—not with Barth but with my inability to help him." And then, looking directly at Morris, my eyes tearing again, "And I'm starting to feel kind of scared. What are we going to do?"

"Come here, little fellow," Morris cooed as he took Barth from my shaking arms. "I'm really worried too, honey. This boy is so thin his skin looks almost transparent."

"I've been sitting here thinking. I wonder if Joyce would nurse Barth along with Jerry?" Joyce was our neighbor, and Jerry was her infant son. "Maybe her milk would be okay for Barth. How I wish my own would agree with him!" It was a great sadness to me to think I could give birth to a baby but could not feed him effectively. Because of my constant concern for Barth, I couldn't seem to be effective in much of anything these days. Meals, housework, even playing with our other two children, had all been delegated to a back burner. DeNiece and Elred were helpful, but they tired quickly of a baby who was always crying and a mother who was always on edge.

"Would you dare ask her?" Morris asked with trepidation in his voice. "That would really be asking a lot."

"You know, I would. And I even think she'd do it. Joyce and I have talked about how frightening this is getting for Barth."

And then I voiced my greatest fear, the one that plagued me constantly, the one that made all other considerations minor: "I don't know if he can continue to lose weight and live."

Standing at Joyce's door—afraid of knocking—afraid not to—was how Joyce found me as she rounded the house from the backyard early the next morning.

"Joyce, I have this huge favor to ask of you," I started, my voice trembling slightly.

"Susanna, before you say anything, let me talk." Joyce interrupted my carefully thought-out request. "I have been thinking that I should try and nurse Barth. Maybe my milk would agree with him." She could see the moisture building in my eyes.

"The only reason I haven't offered long before this is because he is so fragile. I know you carry him around on a feather pillow, and I'm half afraid to pick him up in my arms and hold him close. I wouldn't want him to break," she laughed nervously.

"That is what I am here for this morning, Joyce, to beg you to try feeding him. We've just got to try something." Now the tears were streaming down my worried cheeks.

"Susanna, no begging! You do not have to beg! You don't even have to ask. I would be glad to help. I don't know if it will help, but I'm ready to give it a try. Maybe if I can just get him to nurse for a few minutes at a time, he will be able to keep some down." Joyce, standing before me in a clean, faded house-dress and sandals, looked like an angel.

"Thank you! I love you!" I said while giving her a solid hug.

Joyce arrived at our house about fifteen minutes later, putting Barth to her breast gently, exercising great care. At ten o'clock, she was back to try again. By noon, she had fed her active two-year-old daughter and was back at my house, trying to nurse Barth. At two and four and six o'clock, Joyce was there.

"You can't possibly keep up this kind of schedule," I objected. "When do you have time to nurse Jerry and play with Veronica, much less do a load of wash or mop your kitchen floor?"

"Oh, Susanna. Jerry is getting fed. Does he look hungry?" she chuckled as she laid him on a blanket on the floor, where he playfully tried to put his chubby big toe into his mouth.

"Veronica loves to spend time with DeNiece and Elred. They are so good with her." And then Joyce looked directly at me. "Susanna, this is the most important thing for me to be doing right now. I guess our houses will just have to be a mess for a while."

With that kind of attitude, it was much easier to accept this most charitable and valuable service. The commitment was a solid one, and Joyce arrived at regular two-hour intervals for the next two weeks. At night I would feed Barth a little formula so she could get some sleep.

"There's still a lot of regurgitated milk, but a small amount seems to stay down and nourish Barth. What do you think? He doesn't seem quite as fussy, does he?" I asked Joyce for the hundredth time to give her opinion.

"I actually think it is helping some. But frankly, Susanna, I don't think the little bit he is getting from me is really enough."

"I know." Again I was teary-eyed. The water pump seemed to be directly hooked up to my watery eyes.

"Sorry," I waved my hands as I tried to get control of my emotions. "I feel the same. I'm so grateful for your help, but somehow—oh, Joyce, I think he is fading away before our eyes."

"What did your doctor say yesterday at your appointment?" She knew Barth and I had seen the doctor the day before.

"He admitted he doesn't know what to do. We have tried every formula on the market. Cow's milk doesn't work. Goat's milk doesn't work. My milk was horrible for him. Now, of course, it's not coming in any more anyway. Morris and I have prayed, pleading for help. Grampa Teeples and Morris have given him priesthood blessings. Sometimes I get mad at Heavenly Father, asking him what he is doing, taking this precious child from us. Other times I plead with him to spare his life. I'm afraid to lie by him at night because I don't want to roll over and crush him. But, I'm also afraid to leave him alone, thinking he will surely be gone in the morning."

Crisp autumn had arrived and gone. This was usually a time for all of us, as a family, to put the garden to bed for the winter and rake the cut grass into giant piles to insulate the perennials. Crunchy stacks of leaves served as mattresses for jumping on and blankets for burrowing under. Even though Morris made an attempt to do all the normal activities with DeNiece and Elred, he couldn't put much heart into it.

The cinnamon reds, nutmeg browns, and burnt oranges quickly gave way to dust bowl browns and then swirling white. As Thanksgiving approached, we knew we had much to be thankful for, but our happiness and security were marred by the stress we were feeling from the ill health of our tiny son. Joyce had continued her feeding vigil, without notable success, but refused to give up on the possibility it might be keeping Barth alive. It almost seemed a sacrilege to cook and enjoy a Thanksgiving dinner when we could plainly see Barth was starving to death.

And that was the terrifying reality of the situation. Barth's skin had taken on a brownish, greasy-looking sheen. He had been losing weight steadily since he was born, and at three and a half months was two pounds lighter than his birth weight. With his skin stretched tight over his tiny skeleton and his body lying still as death, with only a slight up and down movement of his chest like softly fluttering butterfly wings, he no longer cried but only occasionally whimpered softly. This long-hoped-for, tiny person was quite a frightening sight.

In the early evening on Thanksgiving Eve, we were surprised by a distinctive knock at the front door. Our surprise turned to astonished pleasure as we opened the door to see Lodisa, Morris's mother, standing there. When she saw we were home, she waved at the man and woman who had given her a ride, picked up her medium-sized carpetbag, and quickly entered our home. At the questioning looks on our faces, she chuckled softly and said, "Hope you don't mind if I stay a while."

"Of course not," Morris finally found his voice. "Where's Dad?"

"In Salmon. You knew we planned on spending Thanksgiving with the twins this year, didn't you?" The "twins" were Morris's twin brothers, Harold and Arnold. They lived in Salmon, Idaho, some two hundred miles away, up by the Idaho-Montana border. The drive was a long one, and Ransford and Lodisa didn't make the trip very often, staying at least a week to make the visit worthwhile.

"Yes, we knew that. So why are you here?" questioned Morris and then rushed on, "I mean we're glad to have you and all, but this is rather unexpected." And then, with growing exasperation in his voice, he asked again, "Where is Dad? Why isn't he with you?"

"Well, we were both in Salmon," explained Lodisa as she moved toward the coat tree to hang up her black wool coat and rabbit-fur hat, "when I was talking to one of Harold's neighbors there, and the subject of Barth's condition arose. Mrs. Taylor listened attentively to a description of Barth and then told us of a doctor in Pocatello who had helped the little Bergman baby that everyone else had given up on."

Lodisa moved over to the old, well-worn sofa and sat down. Her movements were always precise, without wasted motion. "I couldn't be waiting around to come and tell you. Any possibility of help for that dear, struggling boy needs to be checked into as soon as possible. I just told Dad I was coming immediately! He insisted that was foolish because we couldn't get in to see a doctor on Thanksgiving Day." Lodisa's stubborn, charitable spirit was shining through her eyes fiercely.

"So he stayed and I came!"

Morris was almost chuckling, in spite of himself. This independent, forthright attitude was so typical of his mother!

"And," Lodisa went on quickly, "Friday morning I think we should be on our way to Pocatello to see this doctor. I just feel in my bones that this is our answer. We've prayed and given blessings until we are blue in the face. Now is the time for action. I truly think I was supposed to be talking to Lizzy Taylor in Salmon, Idaho, this morning. It's through others that our prayers are answered, you know."

The hope and determination in her voice penetrated our hearts. We readily agreed that early Friday morning we would make the trip to Pocatello, even without a previous appointment, and try to see this supposedly remarkable doctor. We had prayed long for a miracle for this child, and now the flicker of hope grew bright as we discussed what Lodisa and Mrs. Taylor had talked about earlier in the day.

"Tell us exactly what Mrs. Taylor said about the Bergman baby," pressed Morris.

"It seems that the Bergmans had a baby girl about three months before Barth was born. She had some stomach problems—I forget what Lizzy Taylor called it—but anyway, that little tike couldn't relax night or day. She would pull her legs up tight to her chest and cry and cry."

"Well, that's not really like Barth's symptoms, Mother. Barth can't hold down any food. He isn't getting any nourishment."

"I know. I know the circumstances are not the same, but the point is that no doctor in Salmon could help that baby. The Bergman family heard about this Dr. Christensen in Pocatello from their sister who lives there. They decided to take the chance. They traveled all that way in the heat of summer to see him." Mother Teeples stopped talking as if her point was made.

But then she went on when she could see the skepticism in our eyes. "Dr. Christensen called the condition by name and treated that little girl successfully." Again she stopped talking, as we looked at her and then at each other.

"Listen," Mother said, her voice impatient now, "I saw that little girl rolling around on her blanket and laughing at her brothers. There was nothing wrong with her. She was healed. I know Barth has different problems, but I still think this Dr. Christensen is the answer we have been looking for."

We talked on for some time, and around ten o'clock when the three of us were considering turning in for the night, we heard a car pull up outside and stop in front of the house. In a minute or two, there was a noise at the front door. Upon investigating, we discovered Ransford, Morris's father!

"I'm not surprised," teased Lodisa. "It doesn't matter where I go, that man always tags along." But she spoke with great love in her voice, and we were all so glad Father was there as well.

Thanksgiving was a mark-time day that stretched out endlessly. The wind blew furiously outside, stiffening the already hard snow, but we were cozy and warm inside. The possibility of help for Barth weighed heavily on our minds, our souls yearning for relief for this special child.

Bright and early Friday morning we all bundled up, loaded into Dad Teeples's car, and were on our way to Pocatello where the doctor's office was located.

The four of us—Ransford, Lodisa, Morris and I trudged into Dr. Christensen's small waiting room. Joyce had insisted that DeNiece and Elred should stay at her house for the day. There were two young mothers sitting there, waiting for their appointed time to see the good doctor, with their little ones on their laps: one sleeping, and one coughing with a rattling croup.

Morris was carrying Barth, bundled up against the cold, on his familiar feather pillow. We just didn't dare hold him in our arms because we were so conscious of how brittle his minute bones had become. As we sat down, Morris carefully removed the warm, fuzzy baby blanket covering Barth, while Lodisa went right to the pleasant, middle-aged receptionist to ask for an appointment.

But Mother's efforts were unnecessary. The shocked receptionist was staring wide-eyed at the little form on our pillow. She quickly stood, entered Dr. Christensen's office, and we could hear her saying, "Doctor, come quickly. You won't believe the child that was just brought into the waiting room. The family doesn't have an appointment, but I think you will want to see this child immediately."

Within seconds, the doctor was standing in front of us.

Dr. Christensen gently picked up the lightweight pillow and child and moved into his office, saying at the same time, "Mrs. Johnson, thank you for coming in. I'm sure Melissa will get some relief from her congestion with that medicine." His receptionist gently but efficiently urged Mrs. Johnson and her daughter to leave the room, although Mrs. Johnson was curious and then astounded to see why she was being ushered out so quickly. One look at Barth and the retort at being so summarily dismissed died on her lips.

"Mrs. Bowman, reschedule the rest of my morning appointments. I will see them this afternoon, or I will come in tomorrow morning if I need to." And then he continued, almost whispering, "Send in the parents of this child."

All four of us trooped into the examination room. The doctor had invited the parents into the room, but Lodisa wasn't about to be left outside, wondering what was going on.

After carefully setting the pillow on his large mahogany desk, Dr. Christensen himself began slowly undressing Barth. As he worked, he directed, "Tell me everything that has happened since this child was born. Do not leave out even the tiniest detail."

I began my recitation, and he began his examination. Within only a few short minutes, Dr. Christensen stated calmly, "I think I know what the problem is."

My heart stood still. Was this doctor a quack or a savior? Lodisa had said he could help, that he was the answer to our prayers, but—he had spoken so softly and quickly the words we had longed to hear for such a long time, I didn't know whether to trust him or not. It is strange to want something so intensely and then have a person you hardly even know make it sound so simple and reassuring. You wonder if it can possibly be true. We sat in trepidation, our hearts in our throats.

Dr. Christensen went on, "Don't misunderstand what I am saying. The situation here is very serious. I'm not trying to minimize the difficulty this child is experiencing. He is critically ill, and we will have to change his course immediately if he is to survive." After this statement, our elation rose steadily as we could plainly see the doctor was earnest, knowledgeable, and caring.

"Mrs. Bowman," Dr. Christensen called to his nurse, "Leave the office and go into town to the pharmaceutical and then to the five and dime." We could see that Mrs. Bowman was very efficient as she quickly wrote down the list of supplies Dr. Christensen was requesting.

While she was gone, Dr. Christensen explained what he was going to do.

"There's a fairly new drug on the market which will relax

this baby's stomach muscles. Right now, when milk or formula hits the bottom of the stomach, the muscles are so tight, like a spring, that the food is literally thrown back up the esophagus and out of his body. This medicine will relax the stomach muscles—removing the tension or spring—and help keep the food down so that it has an opportunity to digest." Dr. Christensen looked around the adults standing in a circle, and we all nodded slightly.

"Ten minutes before you are going to feed him, you must give this drug to Barth with a medicine dropper. A second drug, which curdles the milk and will aid in digestion, will need to be added to the skim milk and water you are going to feed him. This concoction must be beaten up very fine so it will pass through a bottle nipple and be easy for Barth to swallow."

A key turned in the office lock. Mrs. Bowman had returned in record time. She had locked the office on her way out so we wouldn't be disturbed. Quickly removing her purchases from the bag, she set them on the desk and arranged them in the order the doctor would need them.

After filling the eyedropper, Dr. Christensen ever so slowly fed Barth the first drug, one tiny drop at a time. Because Barth was so hungry, anything put into his mouth was swallowed immediately. It was pathetic to see how our baby worked his tiny mouth, begging for more when the drops subsided.

While waiting for the ten minutes to pass, Dr. Christensen took the newly purchased bowl, added an equal portion of skim milk and water, and the second drug. As soon as this medicine was added to the skim milk, tiny curds formed which the doctor beat furiously with an eggbeater until no curds could be seen. He poured this mixture into the baby bottle, checking to make sure the mixture could easily be drawn through the nipple on the bottle.

Again, when Barth was fed, he drank ravenously. Instinctively, I moved toward Barth, holding a small towel with which to wipe up the regurgitated milk but found that precaution was unnecessary. Miracle of miracles, the milk did not shoot up out of his stomach minutes after it was consumed!

Dr. Christensen asked us to stay in Pocatello for three days to make sure this new food source was working. Before we returned to Idaho Falls on Tuesday morning, he would check Barth again.

Our immediate concern was for DeNiece and Elred—or rather, for Joyce, who was tending our children and had only thought it was for the day. A phone call assured us that they were all getting along fine, and we didn't need to worry about our children staying there with Joyce and her family until we returned—whenever that might be.

"I might as well be babysitting because I'm not running next door every two hours to feed my 'other' son." The delight in her voice was obvious as she welcomed our good news. "Besides, that gives me a great excuse for not mending that basket of clothes. With this many small children in the house, we had better make a triple batch of cookies instead." What a sweetheart that girl was, and what a true friend!

Gertrude, Morris's older sister, lived in Pocatello and was delighted to have us stay at her house. The unexpected turn in events would give us a good excuse for a visit, something that didn't happen often with so many small children. There were moans and groans from her children as they learned DeNiece and Elred were not with us, but still they all made us feel so welcome.

As grateful as we were for Gertrude's hospitality, we were even more thankful for her refrigerator. The drugs prescribed for Barth had to be kept cold. That was a definite concern for when we did return home. We not only did not have a refrigerator, but we didn't even own an icebox.

To our sincere delight, the treatment continued to work. On Tuesday, Dr. Christensen was very positive in his comments.

"Mrs. Bowman, make Barth an appointment for one month from now. I expect to see a mighty change by then."

And then, turning toward me, he said, "Of course you

know where I am if you need me before then—even without an appointment," and he chuckled at his private joke.

"Are we finally ready to head north?" Ransford inquired.

"We are, Dad. Let's go home."

"Well, actually, Bryan wanted us to stop by the house for one more minute. I think Gertrude and Bryan have something for you." Ransford was acting pleased with himself and life in general, as he swung the car back in the direction of Gertrude's home.

"Why?" Morris questioned. "We have already said our good-byes. I mean, they have been wonderful, but let's get going." Morris was anxious to see DeNiece and Elred again and tell them the good news about their little brother.

"It will only take a minute," Ransford said. Dad was never in a hurry to leave. He loved visiting his kids.

As we pulled up in front of Gertrude and Bryan's house, there was an icebox sitting on the driveway. Refrigerators were new, extremely pricey appliances. Gertrude and Bryan were the only ones in the family who could afford such a luxury. Iceboxes were more affordable, although still too expensive for our pocketbook. An icebox was basically an insulated box, with a hinged door into which a new block of ice needed to be put every two or three days. An iceman, driving an insulated truck and delivering ice to those who were fortunate enough to own an icebox, was a regular feature in every town.

"An icebox! Morris, it's an icebox! For us?" My water works were beginning again.

"As much as we need this, Gertrude," said Morris as he got out of the car, "we just can't afford it. It's cold outside most days. Somehow we'll keep this medicine cold."

"Oh, Morris! Accept it gracefully for heaven's sake. It's our gift to Barth, not to you," she said as she smiled slyly. "Mom and Dad put in some of the money, and even some of our neighbors contributed a little. Let us all do this for you. It really isn't a luxury anymore; it's a necessity. Now give me another hug and get on your way."

Chapter 12

The 1930s were the time of the Great Depression, the Dirty 30s, and in the central United States, the Dust Bowl. In our area, winters were colder than we had ever experienced. Snow would have been welcome. It did not come, but the temperatures continued to plummet. The freezing winters were followed by summers so hot and dry that nothing grew. Idahoans were used to irrigating their farmland to get abundant crops. With little rain, empty canals, and heat searing the land, the crops that were planted turned a sickly yellow and then a deathly grayish brown. Animals were too skinny to sell. The new crop of calves and lambs were sickly and malnurished. Town and city workers were unemployed, the machines standing idle. Everyone was hurting from a collapsed productive power, as the once-healthy economic life of the United States ground to a frightening halt. Our family's motto soon became: "Use it up, wear it out, make it do, or do without."

The country listened hungrily to President Roosevelt's fireside chats on the radio on Sunday evenings, straining for a glimmer of hope in his Works Progress Administration reports. He spoke glowingly of dams, bridges, parks, and airports being built to help the economy and provide industry for out-of-work Americans. Subsidies were offered to writers, artists, ballet dancers, and actors. One of the programs started by the president to fight the depression was paid photographers traveling through the countryside taking pictures. Few families had the money to pay for the picture, but they fed the photographers from their meager food supply and always received a copy of the photo in the mail some weeks later, which became a treasure in later years. The programs all sounded so good until reality hit home, and you realized that the man of your household was still out of work.

It was a troublesome, difficult time, and we were struggling like everyone else to put food on the table. But try as we would, we could not feel depressed as a new life for our tiny son began. Progress wasn't instantaneous, but little by little, gains were made. Before too long, we recognized the outward signs of Barth beginning to recover his health, reinforcing our former assumption that he had literally been starving to death. When we were finally allowed to start him on solid food, it wasn't baby cereal or strained pears as you might imagine. The diet was strict: mashed bananas, Jell-O—either warm liquid or cold set, skimmed milk, and scraped beef. I would sear the thin strips of lean beef on both sides in a frying pan, and then scrape off the slightly burned portion with a knife, repeating the procedure until the all beef was scorched and scraped. All of these items, especially Jell-O, were extremely scarce. Our doctor's "prescription" for Jell-O allowed us to buy well beyond the normal rationing amount for most families.

One thing every family did own was a radio. We were no exception. On biting cold winter evenings or sweltering summer nights, families gathered around the radio for entertainment. Will Rogers, Jack Benny, George Burns, Gracie Allen—and DeNiece and Elred's personal favorite—Dick Tracy, all allowed us to put aside frayed nerves, knawing stomachs, and disappointed dreams and permitted us to grin and find some joy in living. We also listened weekly to the promise made by President Roosevelt that the country would get through this depression because he was literally lying awake nights, thinking of all kinds of programs to help people out.

We soon realized that doctor's visits would be much easier to make if we actually lived in Pocatello instead of Idaho Falls. Morris still did not have a steady job because they were extremely difficult to come by. Rulon, a younger brother, thought he might be able to get Morris on with the railroad if he lived in Pocatello where the main line was headquartered. To relocate definitely seemed like the right thing to do, but moving that short fifty miles was out of our financial range. As usual, family came through. Soon we were renting a small, two-bedroom house in Pocatello. We knew it was temporary, but we were grateful for it and soon made it home.

With the tension of Barth's poor health lessening and the move completed, you would have thought I would feel wonderful. I was only twenty-seven years old—really in the prime of my life. But for some strange reason, each day as I arose, I felt worse than the day before. One day, just as DeNiece danced through the back screen door from school, anxious to tell me of her wonderful day, I fainted dead away and fell to the floor right before her eyes.

"Mama," she screamed, as she rushed to my side.

Luckily I had just laid four-month-old Barth in the crib, and the bath towels I was carrying weren't harmed as they cascaded to the floor.

"Mama," she whispered again in a scared, tight voice. "Oh, Mama, what's wrong?"

Not knowing what to do, DeNiece knelt down beside me, trying to revive me. As she worried over me, wondering whether to run for the neighbor or call the doctor, I came to.

For the next few weeks, I passed out several times a day without warning and would remain unconscious for several minutes. I could feel the blackout coming, with just enough time to ease myself to the floor. DeNiece and Elred soon learned to lift my head, put a pillow underneath it, cover me with a blanket, and within a short time I would be up and moving again. Of course, DeNiece told her daddy about my fainting spell the moment he arrived home that first day, and he was instantly concerned.

"You must go to the doctor and see what is wrong," Morris insisted.

"If it happens again, I will," I promised. But the children and I worked out the blanket routine and that sufficed for a while. I knew we didn't have money for another doctor's bill.

One Thursday, an exuberant Morris arrived home about lunchtime. "I've got great news! You know that little service station on the corner of 5th Street and 2nd Avenue? Well, the owner is moving to Burley to be closer to family, and we have worked out a deal where I can run it for him for at least the next six months. The wage isn't huge, but it will be steady."

"That sounds wonder ..." and I slid to the floor.

As you can imagine, we were sitting in the doctor's office within the hour, and I could hardly comprehend the doctor's diagnosis.

I was pregnant!

Of course, I wasn't nursing Barth, but how could I possibly be pregnant again—already! Barth took constant care, and I just wasn't ready. No, we hadn't been doing anything to prevent it. After all, we had been married ten years and only had three children. Somehow we just didn't think such a thing would happen.

But it had! I struggled to come to grips with the "exciting" news, not telling any of the family. I made Morris promise he would not tell, either. Not for a while yet. I knew they would know soon enough, and I could imagine the talk—"Susie is already pregnant again!"

As the weeks went by, I grappled with the thoughts of another baby coming. Meanwhile, my doctor talked quietly with Morris about his concerns, for as the time progressed, I did not feel the baby move at all. The doctor was grim about the chance of this baby being born healthy—or even alive.

One blustery spring day, Lodisa arrived on my doorstep, full of huff and puff.

"Okay, what is going on? Someone told me they found you resting in bed in the middle of the day, and I knew immediately something was wrong. Susanna, you don't have a lazy bone in your body, and you wouldn't be lying down in the daytime unless you were ill. I'm here to take care of you."

As I looked at her sweet, compassionate face, so full of love and concern, I broke down and blubbered, "Oh, Mother Teeples, I'm pregnant. Can you believe it? I'm expecting another baby. Barth will only barely be one year old when this new baby arrives."

Lodisa calmly put her arms around my shaking shoulders and guided me toward the couch to sit down.

"Oh, Susanna, what a blessing. A new baby!" She hugged me to her ample bosom. "How fortunate you are."

And then, somehow, she had a flash of insight. "Is there something wrong? You and the baby are okay, aren't you?"

"We don't know!" I sobbed. "The baby doesn't move. I am well past four and a half months along now, and I have never felt the baby move. Not even a twinge. Oh, I am so frightened! One part of me is wondering how I can be pregnant at all with Barth still so little, and another part is achingly afraid that this baby will not live. We have talked and worried and prayed. Still everything is unsure. What am I to do?"

"Oh, Susanna, trust in the Lord. He loves you! All will be well, however it should be. You must trust in the Lord."

My confirmation that the Lord was still very much aware of me and my needs came sooner than I expected.

My darling younger sister, Rachel, whom Morris and I had practically raised, had been living in California taking her nurse's training. After Rachel's graduation from high school, she ardently wanted to become a nurse. Aunt Rosa, Mother's sister—remember, the sister Mother was going to go visit at the time of her passing—lived in California and arranged for Rachel to take her training there and work at a French hospital in her area. The entire family was delighted for Rachel. Each family contributed a dollar or two each month, according to their individual circumstances, to help with her tuition. Aunt Rosa, with her big heart, was good to buy uniforms and other necessities to help out.

In return, Rachel kept us well informed of her activities and successes, writing delightful excerpts from her daily routine. Many a supper was enlivened by Rachel's wit as she shared her experiences through letters. Some days she made us cry, but usually the anecdotes were full of charm and humor, often telling of some naval officer who had recuperated enough to make a pass at her from his sickbed.

At the time of Rachel's graduation as an RN, she had a picture taken of herself in her nurse's uniform, with the traditional white nurse's cap positioned precisely in place on her head. She was such a pretty girl, and the sparkling white uniform set off her brunette beauty and smooth olive skin to perfection.

Rachel received full-time employment immediately and moved from Aunt Rosa's house to an apartment with five other practicing nurses—all young single girls. She was enjoying her life, and we were thrilled for her. Sometimes I was a little envious of her carefree lifestyle when she wasn't on duty at the hospital. She described the early morning hours along the Pacific Ocean, with the fuchsia-tinted clouds riding low over the horizon, the rising sun touching the water with a Midas touch as it lapped lazily up onto the shore.

One letter stated: "It's like our Heavenly Father takes a paint brush and palate and delicately changes this beautiful work of art slightly each morning for our own personal enjoyment. My roommates and I run down to the beach from our apartment, dressed in swimming suits, our bodies tingling with the early morning air, our towels waving like brightly colored flags, while we race to the water together.

"There is a long, stout sewage pipe that runs far out into the ocean almost directly down from where we live. It snakes out for over two miles, providing us a walkway out to the deeper areas where we can dive and play until we have to return for our showers and work. What a marvelous way to begin our day!"

As our Idaho weather began to warm—certainly not like sunny southern California yet, but warm for Idaho—I thought often of Rachel. It was almost the end of May. Sitting in the rocking chair on the front porch in the heat of the day reminded me of Rachel carrying that same chair outside for me to sit in when I was expecting DeNiece. I loved the sun's warmth as it penetrated my body. I yearned to see Rachel again, but I was happy for her stunning sunrises, refreshing swims, and fulfilling life. This little sister had done well for herself. She had graduated with high honors from her nursing program. Recently she had been made a night supervisor over the maternity ward at the French hospital where she had completed her training. What an honor for one so young! We were all so proud of her.

As the rocker creaked in rhythm, I breathed in the lily of the valley scented air, fed Barth, and felt heavy with child. I knew my life was good, and I was tremendously blessed. But, oh, to be twenty-two again!

I wasn't sure if I really wanted to go back to those years, but it sounded pretty good, sometimes. I mean, I wasn't ancient, but ten years of marriage and three and a half children made quite a difference in the responsibility field. So, when things got depressing or the work felt burdensome, I dreamed of Rachel's life, rejoicing in her opportunities.

That night when Morris and I turned into bed, we were both very tired. His day at the station had been especially taxing, with new supplies coming in, but that was good news because it meant the business was progressing. I think it was mostly due to Morris's friendly nature, rather than his business acumen. Morris was an okay businessman, but it was his natural charisma and genuine interest in people that steadily built his customer pool.

I just couldn't seem to get comfortable. This baby seemed so heavy, and I seemed so huge. All my babies poked right out in front, making my short, five-foot-two-inch frame seem square. I tried hard to stop tossing and turning, realizing Morris needed his sleep.

Forcing myself to lie still on my back, my eyes remained

wide open as if my eyelashes were glued to my eyelids. I had been so tired when we finally went to bed, and now I couldn't seem to clear my mind, close my eyes, and sleep. Faintly, in the moonlight streaming through the narrow bedroom window, I could make out the small yellow roses on the peeling, faded wallpaper. I watched the sheer chintz curtains as they ruffled slightly in the welcome, cooling breeze that slid under the open window and over the sill into the room.

A slight movement drew my attention to the foot of the bed. There, standing together with their arms tucked lovingly around each other, I thought I saw my mother—my dear sweet mother, and Rachel.

In my wonder, I struggled to sit up, as if that would help me see and comprehend better what was happening. It was Mama! It truly was her! Oh, it was so good to see her face again! And Rachel? Why would she be visiting me in my bedroom with Mama? Why would she be with Mama at all? I saw them both clearly, distinctly! Within moments, they were gone.

While I was pondering the significance of their visit, trying to decide whether to awaken Morris, someone began pounding on the front door. Morris woke with a start, mumbling unintelligibly, "Who could that be?" as he headed in the direction of the front of the house.

It was a telegram! Aunt Rosa had wired:

"Rachel swimming alone. Stop. Knocked unconscious on pipe. Stop. Drowned. Stop. Body discovered later in day on shore. Stop. My heart is aching. Stop."

My Heavenly Father knew I needed the forewarning to be able to stand the shock, but to provide it in such a sweet, loving way was almost beyond my comprehension.

If I had felt huge at the six-month mark of my pregnancy at the time of Rachel's passing, I now felt like the proverbial hippo at nine months. Would this baby never arrive?

Early in August, three days before Barth's first birthday, I finally went into labor. The entire pregnancy had been so different from all the others, I was inwardly fearful of the outcome, but nevertheless more than ready to have the baby.

Finally, finally, the labor began, and Morris took me to the hospital immediately. Everything progressed at an even rate for the first three hours, then, like a freight train changing its mind, the labor came to a grinding halt and did not resume.

"Just let me go home again," I cried. "I don't want to stay here being a burden to everyone if nothing is happening."

"You aren't going anywhere tonight," my doctor stated emphatically. "The night's rest won't hurt you at all, and if the contractions don't start by themselves by morning, we will induce labor."

The next morning arrived. Nothing was happening.

"I'm going to induce you, Susanna, but it usually takes hours for this to work. However, you need to stay right here at the hospital. Call Nurse Rasmussen if you need anything."

I fretted and stewed, but Dr. Adamson was adamant and left the room for his rounds so he didn't have to listen to my murmuring. He did call Morris at the garage from the nurse's station to keep him informed, suggesting he come by sometime in the afternoon to see how things were progressing. Morris thanked him for calling but said he was on his way to the hospital right then and was going to spend the day with me.

Within the hour, as Nurse Rasmussen tried to press me to drink some broth to keep up my strength, I knew the baby was coming.

"This baby is coming now," I insisted. "Please page Dr. Adamson. Please! I tell you, it's coming!"

"Susanna, the baby couldn't possibly be coming yet. It's much too soon after being induced. If you think the contractions are hard now, you really need to take a little nourishment because you will be at this for a long time yet."

"Just call the doctor," I breathed through gritted teeth. "Just let him check me, and then I'll stop pestering you." I closed my eyes tightly to endure another contraction. "Ple-e-a-s-s-e call the doctor."

"Just call the doctor," Morris cajoled softly. "It won't hurt to have him check and see what is happening."

"You would never suppose that Mrs. Teeples had had three other children, and one of them only a year ago," muttered Nurse Rasmussen with a heavy sigh of disgust, as she left the room to page the doctor. "What a baby she is! She won't have that child for hours yet."

I don't know if Dr. Adamson had a premonition or was just guided to come and check on me, but he actually entered the corridor as Mrs. Rasmussen was dialing the phone to page him. Hurrying into my room, he briskly began his examination and then began yelling at the top of his voice. "Nurse Rasmussen, come immediately. Susanna needs to be in the delivery room! This baby is on its way out!"

Within minutes the baby delivered!

Nurse Rasmussen, Dr. Adamson, and Morris stared in horror. The baby was a boy, but he was black. Black as good coal. Black from lack of oxygen. In an instant, after the umbilical cord was cut, Nurse Rasmussen gasped and then grabbed up the baby and literally ran with him to an incubator, trying to prolong his life. Dr. Adamson quickly followed behind, making a cursory check of the tiny baby before returning to my room. I never had made it to the delivery room, the baby had come much too fast.

"Is there anything we can do for you, Susanna?" he began. "Anything at all?"

"Doctor, I don't understand. Just take care of my baby."

"Susanna, this baby is probably not going to live."

My worst nightmare was happening. The haunting worry of the past months descended again in full force. Morris could not soften the blow. He had seen the infant and knew he was in trouble.

"Morris, could you call Mother Teeples?"

Lodisa, Morris's mother was as close to me as my own dear mama, and I definitely needed a mother right now. Lodisa would know what to do.

Within a short time, Lodisa and Ransford were standing at my bedside. Ransford had not even been allowed to change his shoes from working in the barn as Lodisa insisted they come immediately, bringing with them consecrated oil, blessed for the healing of the sick.

Dr. Adamson had examined our new son more carefully by this time. "Our machines show that the baby's lung cavities appear to be almost entirely empty. There is a single, tiny black dot in each cavity, surrounded by nothingness."

As Dr. Adamson went to retrieve the baby and bring him to my room to be blessed, Nurse Rasmussen followed him down the hall, objecting loudly.

"Even if you are a doctor, you have no right to take that baby from the oxygen. It has a right to every moment of life it can hold on to."

"Mrs. Rasmussen, these parents have the right to give this baby every chance at life they can, and that is what they are all about right now. Do not—I repeat—*do not* follow me into Mrs. Teeples's room. When we are finished," he softened slightly, "I will bring the baby to you, and you can take him back to the incubator."

By the power of the Melchizedek Priesthood, Morris, Ransford, and Dr. Adamson took our tiny, black, barely breathing baby in their hands and gave him a name and a blessing. Lodisa was the one who insisted the baby should be given a name—and the only name Morris could think of was Daryl, the name of the young boy who was covering for him at the service station. And so he named his third son Daryl Teeples.

During the short blessing, Dr. Adamson was reverently silent, but as soon as it ended, he quickly took Daryl and whirled around to leave the room. In the back recesses of his mind, he registered what he thought he saw—a tiny pink flush showing on the baby's skin. Mrs. Rasmussen was not in the hallway, but she had everything in readiness in the nursery to return this tiny human to the oxygen he so badly needed.

We knew that Daryl was in the hands of the Lord. I hoped

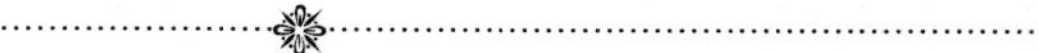

he would not be taken from us because I had not wanted him when I first found out I was pregnant. It wasn't that I hadn't wanted *him.* It was that it was so soon after the birth of Barth, and we had been through such a struggle to save his life.

Now my heart pleaded with my Heavenly Father, "Let him live—oh, please, Heavenly Father, let him live." Everyone in the room was silent, as if communicating personally with God.

In time, Dr. Adamson returned. He was as white as newly fallen snow, a look of awe and reverence on his face. His first words were: "I have seen a miracle, but I didn't cause it or perform it." Lodisa pushed a chair forward so the good doctor could sit down before he collapsed.

"We put that tiny boy back under the oxygen and then hooked up our machines again to observe his lungs—I should say, his lung cavities. He had no lungs that we could discern. As we watched, the little black dot inside each cavity began to spin around, so fast—you cannot imagine how fast. As they were spinning, they looked as if they were swelling and filling with air. What had appeared as dots were actually the lungs, and they expanded more and more within each cavity until each was full and normal. At the same time, you could see the black being pushed out of Daryl's body as a healthy, pink, newborn color moved down through his entire frame. Now, as he lies in the incubator, you can see his chest gently rise and fall. He is peacefully asleep. And he is perfect!"

By this time tears of joy and gratitude were coursing down our cheeks.

And so, Daryl lived!

Chapter 13

One cherished mother was taken when I was sixteen. My second beloved mother died suddenly a short twelve years later. There was even less notice than with my birth mother, if that were possible.

Lodisa, Morris's outspoken, determined, capable, caring, dear mother was taken as she sat in her rocking chair, knitting a sweater for one of the boys. One minute healthy, vibrant, singing softly to herself—the next, slumped to one side as her great heart gave out in an instant.

My heart achingly mourned her passing. During the last year and a half I had learned to anesthetize my feelings as one calamity after another had been forced upon us. Now I felt a final, solid pillar of outside support had been torn mercilessly from our lives. Lodisa had been there for us—for me—when my own dear mother could not be. She was supportive and optimistic no matter where our boat of destiny took us on rough and uncharted seas. Her constant reminder, merely by the way she lived her own life, that faith in God's mercy, omniscience, and constant care was imperative, set an example for me that lifted my spirits and often calmed my troubled heart. I not only missed her intensely, but I felt guilty for never having expressed in words or a letter how I loved her and appreciated her goodness to me. Did she know that? Was she aware of my love and devotion for her? How I longed to have her hold me close to her heart once more!

Barth, at a year and a half, was running at full speed like

there had never been a life-threatening moment in his life, while Daryl stretched and grew daily after his traumatic birth. Lodisa had truly been a rock of support with both children's problems. Now she was gone, and I remembered all over again how abrupt and unfair life could be.

Ransford couldn't stand to remain in the house where Lodisa had been his light and sustenance. He asked us to live there instead. It released him from the constant, daily reminders and at the same time enhanced our living conditions significantly.

While our family was attempting to regain our equilibrium, Fern, Morris's younger sister was struggling with the demands of single parenting. She had lost her devoted husband and then her beloved mother within four months of each other. Our move to a larger house motivated Morris to offer our services to take her two little boys for a time so she could regain the financial and emotional stability she needed. As reluctant as Fern was to have LaMarr and Verlin live away from her, she could see both the necessity and wisdom in such an arrangement. Her two boys fit age-wise into the family between Elred and Barth like they had been born there. At seven and a half and looking forward to baptism, Elred felt pretty grown up, being the oldest brother. Fern's two boys, LaMarr and Verlin, were six and three, respectively. Barth was a year and a half, and Daryl, the baby, was about eight months. Even with a bigger house, it was full to bursting.

As spring timidly peeked out through the lingering winter snow patches in May, the air tantalizingly mild but still cool, Fern arrived on our doorstep insisting I attend the Mother's Day program at sacrament meeting with Morris and nine-year-old DeNiece.

"It will be so good for you to get a reprieve from these five little boys for an hour or two," she persisted.

"Fern, you know I love the boys, and besides, I just couldn't go sit through an entire meeting devoted to mothers," I vented bitterly.

"Oh, Susanna, please let me do this for you. I feel so guilty never being here to help. It can't be easy keeping up with these scamps no matter how much you love them. If nothing else, the drive to the church and the change of scenery will be good for you."

I turned beseechingly to Morris for support of my reasoning, but he could plainly see Fern's need to perform this service. "It will be wonderful to ride—quietly—into church and enjoy the entire program without having to take someone to the bathroom or to get a drink of water. I'll bet you can't remember what it is like to sit without a squirming youngster—or two—on your lap," Morris reminded me, laughing softly to himself while envisioning what most Sunday meetings were like. "Let's do ourselves a favor and take her up on it." He grinned and then turned and whispered quietly in my ear, "She needs the time with her sons too. We need to do this for her."

That is how I ended up at the red brick church, sitting through a lovely Mother's Day program, numbly wishing I were anywhere but there. Lodisa had only been gone three short months, and my heart silently ached to be in her presence again. DeNiece was snuggled in by my side, enjoying my warmth and our oneness. I held her hand like she was a little girl again, and she was reveling in the nearness. Usually she was busy helping to entertain and keep quiet one or more of the boys all through sacrament meeting. Her closeness would have undoubtedly comforted me had I been aware she was there. Somehow I was wrapped up in my own emotions, my thoughts filled with my own selfish need. I longed for a mother's listening ear and heart. I was tired of being that mother to so many others, with no woman to turn to with my own cares.

"M is for the million things she gave me," the Primary children sang out. "O is only that she's growing old—"

But they weren't *old!* my mind objected. Neither mother had been old. They both should have still been here with us, enjoying the service.

Staring at my navy blue, worsted lap, subconsciously aware of my work-roughened fingers entwined with DeNiece's smooth, girlish ones, and again wishing I had not come, my gaze moved briefly upward. Startled, I quickly looked up again. There, walking toward me hand in hand, I saw Lodisa and Mama. They turned slightly, smiled lovingly at each other, and then, in unison, radiated that smile at me. Like streaks of saffron light extending in a bright circle from a lantern reflector, they stood in warm radiant beams as they both gazed peacefully at me, emanating a feeling of deep harmony and contentment. My bitterness and grief fled. Once again I had been granted a vision of eternity.

As was so often the case, Morris had been right in his gentle insistence that I come to church with him. When we arrived home, Fern had enjoyed a marvelous few hours with all the boys that had rejuvenated her spirit and "made her feel young again." DeNiece was basking in her feeling of maturity and was secure in my love. I shared with her and Morris what had happened during the service. That day was the true beginning of a closeness that continued through the years with this special daughter.

Within six months, Fern had remarried, taking her boys from our care to establish her own family again. Fern's new husband was a gem, and we were thrilled for her happiness. Nevertheless, a true bond had formed with LaMarr and Verlin, and we were sorry to see them go.

With Fern's boys gone, we began once again to look for another place to live. Ransford wanted to sell his home. That might have been difficult for us to bear, except that we could see it was situated too far from where Morris worked anyway. In addition, the ten acres required too much upkeep, because Morris now had a part-time job at the railroad yards in Pocatello.

Our inquiries into housing finally took us to an old, fairly large, extremely run-down house in Alameda, which was a suburb of Pocatello.

When we first walked through the house, it was apparent the rooms were large and roomy. There just weren't too many of them. A kitchen, living room, two bedrooms, one bathroom, and two large airy porches—one on each side of the house—completed the tour. When Morris first saw the house, he could see all sorts of possibilities. The first time I saw the house, I cried.

The holes from the rotten boards in the larger bedroom floor were so big I could easily look into the crawl space underneath the house. The floors that were solid in construction were rough and full of splinters. They were neither covered or painted. There were no cupboards or sink in the kitchen, only an old dilapidated coal stove and a bare pipe that brought water into the house. The bathroom was a small room plumbed for fixtures but presently without them. The outhouse, out back, was standing, but barely. Sunbaked quack grass and prickly brown weeds covered the hard-packed dirt, in both the front and back yards. Two giant apricot trees, begging for a drink and badly in need of pruning also graced the backyard. I didn't mean to act ungrateful; it just was not what I had imagined when thinking of a new home. It really was in terrible shape.

"I can gradually fix it up in the evenings after work," Morris pleaded. "I know it looks pretty terrible, but—" and this was the kicker, "the price is right—only nine hundred dollars."

"I know, honey," I sobbed, trying unsuccessfully to get my emotions under control. "After living at your dad's place—it just isn't what I expected. What will we use for a down payment?"

A down payment! The owner was as desperate to sell as we were to buy. He agreed to accept three small pigs and an old, broken-down automobile to seal the deal. We hoped our payments of fifteen dollars a month would be manageable.

Little by little, with scrimping and saving every available penny and Morris doing the work, the house did become livable. Morris and I took the smaller bedroom, putting the three boys in the larger one. DeNiece needed a room and some privacy and was delighted when her daddy suggested he close in one of the porches for her to use for a bedroom.

After painting most of the floors to prevent slivers, we wanted to repair the holes in the boy's bedroom floor, but we just didn't have the money for the lumber. As I visited with my new neighbors, I realized many of them took a daily newspaper. They readily agreed to save the papers for me for a couple of weeks. My idea worked, and when the papers were carefully overlapped on the floor, they formed a smooth, thick mat. We were careful where we placed the bed, and everyone was aware of the "safe" flow pattern for walking in that room. One day Morris surprised us all by bringing home a slightly worn piece of gray and blue linoleum, which we immediately rolled out over the newspaper mats. Wow! What luxury! The boys could run and play without falling through the floor.

Starting out housekeeping with two small tables in the kitchen, one to eat at and one to prepare food and wash dishes on, seemed adequate. One weekend, not long after we had moved into the Alameda house, Dad and Lydia came to visit. They only stayed a short time, but the next day, my brother John arrived driving the farm truck with the tall plywood sides nailed together to form a box. In the back of the truck was Bessie, the milk cow.

"It's a gift from Dad," he said when I objected to receiving the charity. "He sent in some hay too, but it won't last too long. He said to tell you the Indians come through the area selling first-crop hay, and when they come is the best time to buy it. She's just been freshened, so he thinks you can probably get plenty of milk and cream for the family and have some left over to sell for house improvements." I cried again at the goodness of both my father and brother.

Every house in the neighborhood was fixed up nicer than ours was, and we were the only ones on the block who still sported an outhouse instead of indoor plumbing. Neighbors were good not to complain—much—but we were just as interested as they were to have that eyesore removed from our backyard and be able to have indoor facilities.

"Morris," I began one evening after he returned from work, "I have been shopping around for a toilet and bathroom sink, and today I found a used set. It even has a bathtub."

I paused, hoping he would be impressed with my resourcefulness and also because I hated to say the price out loud.

"How much, Susanna?" He got right to the meat of the deal.

"All three pieces are only forty-five dollars."

"That's actually a great price. I have been looking for bathroom fixtures too, and that is definitely better than anything I have found."

And then in unison, we spoke, "But where will we ever get forty-five dollars?"

"Well," Morris was thoughtful when we had stopped laughing, "why don't we just go talk to the salesman and see what we can work out? Heavenly Father has been watching over us pretty good up until now, maybe we can pay some each month for a while."

"I'd need to run a credit check on you before I can sell these fixtures to you on time," the salesman drawled. "Come back tomorrow, and I'll have an answer for you."

The next day, he met us at the door. "Your credit's better than mine in this town. You can have the merchandise; I know you'll make the payments."

With Morris doing all the plumbing and installation himself, our indoor bathroom was finished in no time. As much as we wanted to have a ceremonial burning of the outhouse, we couldn't afford to waste the wood, and so we just knocked it down instead.

I've often marveled at the joy of having a man around the house. Not only do they provide a listening adult ear, a warm body to snuggle up against on a cold night, and a sensitivity to family needs, but they quickly learn the art of fixing almost anything. At least that was true of my man, and I was grateful for him. When he was working on a project at home, he would softly sing a favorite hymn. Morris really liked to whistle too. When the project was progressing smoothly, he whistled, and when it became a little more difficult, he would sing, but when complications arose, he was silent. I loved to hear him sing or whistle.

Work at the railroad yards was still far from steady. When Morris worked, he got paid. When the times were slow, the workers were forced into idleness and were not paid.

One evening, Morris returned from a partial day of work with the news that his boss was encouraging him to go to southern Utah and become a railroad machinist.

"You are thinking our family would move to Utah? How could we ever afford a house there? We're just now getting this one livable. And besides, the boys' doctor is here." My mind was racing through jumbled thoughts.

"No, the family would stay here in our home. I would live in Utah."

"You would live in Utah? And we would live here?" I asked in a soft, quavering voice.

"That is the way it would have to be," he answered while his eyes searched mine.

I was almost afraid to ask, "For how long?"

"I'm not totally sure. To become a full-fledged machinist takes four years."

"Four years? Oh—" It took my breath away. "Four years. Why—why, DeNiece will be all grown up by then."

"I think I will have to go for a year or two to southern Utah and then maybe I can finish some of it here." Morris was trying hard to soften the blow. "It sounds like an awful lot, doesn't it?" He could plainly see the concern in my eyes. "There are pros and cons to doing this. Maybe we could list them down on paper and see if that helps our decision making," he rushed on.

"Yes, let's do that together. Maybe I just need to understand it better." I could see Morris was being pulled to do this, wanting so hard to finally provide for the family with steady work, and I truly did want to be supportive.

The pro's listed included:

1. The railroad needed well-trained machinists, so the work would be steady.

2. Others already working for the railroad were not interested in applying because they would lose the seniority they currently held (Morris didn't have any seniority, so that didn't apply to him), so there was a good chance he would be accepted into the training program.

3. When he was finished with the apprenticeship, he would make twice his current salary, or possibly even more.

4. Occasionally, on a weekend, he could ride home to Idaho on the train to visit the family free of charge.

5. He would make a steady but low full-time wage while being trained.

Looming large on the con side was the unavoidable fact that he would be away from home for months, and possibly years. By being gone, he would be unable to help with the cow, unable to continue working on the house, unable to be there for the children and me. The decision was a difficult one.

In the end, after considering it from every angle, pouring out our despair to our Heavenly Father, and attending the temple, the decision was made: Go for the apprenticeship. Put our faith in the Lord.

The week after Morris left, I could see that this was going to be a long four years. On Thursday evening, after getting Barth and Daryl to bed, DeNiece, Elred, and I sat down together around the kitchen table for a family council.

"I miss Dad," Elred began, with a long face.

"I miss him too," echoed DeNiece.

"I miss him—three," I said glumly. "The thing we need to realize is that he misses us four—actually five," I continued with a hollow laugh at the sad little joke we had just made. "Daddy doesn't want to be away from home, but he needs to for a while so he can get some more training for his work. He is depending on all of us to work together and take care of things here while he is gone."

"Well, I've been thinking," DeNiece offered without prompting and with a slight rising lilt in her voice, "Elred and I could do some of the things Daddy used to do."

"Like what, sweetheart?"

"I don't think I could milk Bessie because she still kind of scares me, but I could pour the milk into the separator to remove the cream." And then she stopped and her eyes lit up. "Elred and I could even take the buckets of cream down to Mr. Mike's store in the wagon. If we went slow and easy together, we should be able to do it without spilling any."

Now Elred was starting to get the idea. "Sure we could do that, Mommy, and I could bring in coal from the shed for the coal bucket by the stove. You would still have to build the fire in the stove, but you wouldn't have to go outside to get the coal. I could have it all there for you, easy."

"All of those things would be a great help," I stated, outwardly nodding my head while smiling inside at their resourcefulness.

"We could play with Barth and Daryl more too, Mom, and keep them occupied," DeNiece went on.

"Yeah, I probably could help with that too." Elred was a little reluctant to commit to such a thing. Being several years older than his brothers, he really liked to play with his peers, and babies definitely cramped his style. "Maybe DeNiece and I could take turns so we still had some time to be with our own friends." He looked up hopefully.

"That all sounds so good. DeNiece, maybe I could show you how to help with a little more of the cooking too."

"Oh, that would be fun, Mom."

That night we made up a chart for helping around the house and with the year-apart-twins, as we called them. More than the actual help DeNiece and Elred gave was the assurance that they realized I needed moral support in trying to be both father and mother most of the time.

That support was especially important because I had not been feeling well for several weeks. It seemed I had a sore throat all the time and felt so run-down and tired. A trip to the doctor finally verified what I had known all along—I needed to have my tonsils removed.

"Can't this wait until next summer? You know Morris is gone right now, and I can't be gone as well," I told the doctor as I sat in his office.

"Will Morris be home during the week next summer, Susanna?"

"No, but at least DeNiece and Elred won't be in school, and the 'year-aparts' will be older and easier to handle."

"Susanna, this surgery is getting to the urgent stage. I really feel that it needs to be taken care of now. I'll just send word for Morris to come home for a couple of days so you can be in the hospital—"

"Oh, Dr. Clark," I interrupted, "please don't call Morris home from Utah. He just can't miss work; we cannot afford that."

"I don't know what else to tell you, Susanna. You could go into the hospital the day before the surgery and then the surgery would be performed the next morning. By that night we could probably have you home again. It's about the best we can do."

"Wait a minute. Why do I need to be in the hospital a whole day before the surgery?"

"That's just the way it's done. And then we can make sure you don't eat anything after six o'clock in the evening and—"

"I can do that at home. If I shouldn't eat anything after six o'clock, then I won't. You just give me the instructions, and I will follow them. Really! Please let me do it this way. You said yourself that I can have the surgery in the morning after Elred leaves for school and be home by that evening in time to milk the cow."

"No, what I said was the surgery would be in the morning and you could *probably* be home by that evening. I didn't know you were going to take everything I said so literally." The good doctor was beyond frustration.

In *my* mind, my course was plain, and I wasn't about to be deterred. "See, that would all work. DeNiece could miss one day of school to take care of Barth and Daryl. I'm not nursing Daryl, so she could probably handle him for one day. I could have the operation over with and—"

"It might work," the doctor conceded reluctantly. "I would have to have you at the hospital no later than eight-thirty in the morning, though, and you absolutely could not eat anything after six o'clock the night before."

The entire week was a busy one. The day before my surgery, I woke up an hour earlier than usual and had six loaves of bread ready to go in the oven by the time DeNiece and Elred left for school. Casseroles kept cold would last well, so if I didn't feel so well after the operation I would have supper easily ready for several days. Thank goodness we had the icebox that Gertrude and her neighbors had bought for us. Cooking, assembling meals, and cleaning up the kitchen took me all afternoon. If I just hadn't had to stop to fix lunch and change diapers, it would have really been much easier. Of course, I wanted the wash done up too, and that included diapers—soaked, washed, dried, and folded—ready for another week. Diapers were my least favorite job and the one that seemed the most full-time. Oh, to have Barth potty trained, but it just hadn't happened yet. I guess he was still plenty young.

After school, DeNiece and Elred played with Barth and Daryl so I could finish hanging clean, wet diapers on the line. I certainly didn't want to use up the casseroles I had made in the afternoon, so I put DeNiece to work making hamburger patties to fry for supper. I was certainly looking forward to a good rest the following day.

After listening to Elred read for fifteen minutes and helping DeNiece with a couple of math problems, it was bath time for everyone. The time was going so quickly, and I still wanted to mop floors and straighten up the rooms. I certainly didn't want anyone to come to the house and find it a mess while I was gone. I thought the four children would never stay in bed and get to sleep, but they finally did. About two-thirty in the morning, I turned in as well, with the alarm set for six-thirty. Not that I would need it—Barth seldom slept past six.

I had followed instructions explicitly. I didn't eat anything after six o'clock in the evening, even though I was only about halfway through supper by then. I had given my word to the doctor, and I wasn't about to go back on it.

As they were preparing to give me the anesthetic, I was just so grateful I could finally relax and rest. I wasn't sure they even needed anesthetic I was so tired. I could probably just sleep through the operation without it.

Finally, I awoke! My, how good I felt! Maybe anesthesia was a good thing. I hadn't realized that an hour or two under its influence could make you feel so refreshed. I was barely opening my eyes when a nurse sitting by my bed jumped up and left the room.

"That's strange," I thought, a little groggily.

She quickly returned with Dr. Clark in tow.

"Susanna, it's so good to see you are finally waking up."

"What time is it, Doctor?" I questioned, dully realizing I could see stars twinkling outside my hospital window.

"It's nine o'clock, Susanna. You have slept all day and into the evening."

"It can't be nine o'clock!" I started to get out of bed. "I've got to get home and milk the cow!"

"You are not going anywhere, Miss," Dr. Clark said, as he caught me by the shoulders and gently pushed me back into bed. "You had us scared to death. What did you do yesterday, anyway?"

"Yesterday, before the operation? Well, I just did some cooking and baking, a little laundry, and cleaned the house."

"Right! When we administered the anesthetic, you went out so fast we didn't even give you what we normally do. Thank goodness for that, or we probably would have killed you."

By now he had my full attention.

"But what did I do wrong?"

"Susanna, anesthesia is dangerous to administer. For a person to regain consciousness, they have to have an inner desire to live and be awake again. In your exhausted state, you almost slept yourself into a coma. I was so worried about you that I have been at your bedside all afternoon."

Feeling thoroughly chastised, I said, "I really am sorry. I guess I really *was* tired and to just let go and sleep sounded so good. I'm sorry I was such a worry for you." Again I tried to push back the covers and put my feet over the side of the bed. "But I'm feeling fine now. I need to be getting home. Poor DeNiece, she's probably wondering why I'm staying here so long."

"You aren't going anywhere tonight, Susanna. I have called Gertrude, and she has promised to take care of the cow—and the children. In fact, you won't be going anywhere tomorrow or the next day, either." I jerked my head up in disbelief, but from the look on Dr. Clark's face, I believed him. "I want to be sure that you are healthy before I release you. I don't want any more scares. Besides, Gertrude has called Morris, and he will be here on the train by tomorrow morning.

Through the bitter cold winter and awakening spring, Morris was able to come home about once a month on a Saturday. By midmorning on Sunday, he had to return to southern Utah. We were grateful for the visits, even though they were way too short. We were managing, but our long-distance marriage stretched the months into a *l-o-n-g* year.

The hot, dry summer of grasshopper infestation was past now too. It was September again, with shorter days and cooler nights. The drudgery of single parenting was becoming old—but routine. About one o'clock in the morning, I awoke to the noise of an intruder at the back door. While still in the process of getting out of bed and locating a wrapper, Morris burst into the bedroom. He had arrived home on the midnight train for a surprise visit and had walked home from the railroad yards.

"Susanna! Wake up, sweetheart! I have good news!" He was wide-awake and bubbling. "I have been offered an apprenticeship—in Pocatello—for the next three years. When I finish that, I will be a full-fledged machinist." As he tenderly enfolded me in his arms, we acknowledged our prayers had been answered. Our difficult separation was at an end.

Chapter 14

Morris and I had been married almost twenty *l-o-n-g* years, he teasingly reminded me, when child number five finally made an appearance. DeNiece and Elred were a mere nineteen months apart, but as the time had passed and we had no more children, we sold the crib and high chair. Six years later, Barth and Daryl were born, with only a year separating them in age. Now, ten years after Daryl's birth, with a house minus any baby furniture—because we had been sure we were finished with our family—we were expecting our fifth and sixth children.

No, I wasn't having twins—I didn't think so, at least—but if things progressed normally for us, this baby would only be a prelude to the one to follow. We were convinced this was the established routine in our household. We figured if we were expecting a new baby now, then in a year to a year and a half later another baby would undoubtedly be on the way. The "year-aparts" had prepared us for such eventualities. We didn't know, of course, how soon number six would present itself. In the meantime, we were excited about the prospect of baby number five.

Understandably, DeNiece wanted this baby to be the sister she had always wanted. The boys didn't really care if the baby was a girl or a boy. Truth be known, they were a little embarrassed to think I was expecting another baby. After all, Elred was almost seventeen, with Barth and Daryl almost eleven and ten, respectively. They all kind of thought I should have stopped while I was ahead. Whether they were excited or not, the baby was on the way, and there was nothing they could do about it.

Baby Karen entered the world early on a mellow June morning, as the first pastels of dawn were just beginning to paint the sky. She was a fragile little thing, weighing just over four and a half pounds. I had discovered several pregnancies before that my milk just didn't agree with my babies. They had consistently been too delicate to try and force the issue, so I didn't even try to nurse this tiny girl.

At age eighteen, pretty, vivacious DeNiece was in her element. This sister was like a baby doll, so petite she could actually dress her in doll clothes and lay her on a comfortable pillow in a soft, flannel-lined basket. Because I was not able to nurse Karen, DeNiece would pick her up at the least whimper to rock her while holding her bottle, to change her diaper, or to tickle her to get a wrinkled-up nose and baby smiles. It was good DeNiece had the chance to have this bonding time with Karen because within two short years she would be married to a handsome air force cadet and on her way to China for a honeymoon and to live there for a time.

Even if all the boys thought a baby was pretty much useless, it wasn't long until each brother was securely wrapped around Karen's baby finger. Each boy had his own special way of entertaining this dainty new marvel. When they thought no one was watching, each in turn would read to her, dance with her, sing to her, play with her, and generally make big-brother fools of themselves.

Amazingly, however, this child did not have a "twin" waiting in the wings. We would have loved to have another addition to our family, but this time it just didn't happen.

Child bearing can take a toll on parents. In marriage, what begins as a loving, two-way communion between husband and wife quickly changes in the advent of a baby to the full-time responsibility of diapering, feeding, washing, teaching, and raising a new, separate, demanding human being. One would think the birth of a child would pull parents together with a solid, unbreakable bond as they worked to care for the child and provide for it. However, being home all day, every day, can move the mother onto center stage in that child's life, while the father gets pushed into the wings without anyone even realizing it. That certainly could have happened to us, for each child had presented us with its own unique set of weighty concerns.

But somehow, even with all the worries and inconveniences of child rearing, the importance of each individual, and the constant loving and caring for each one—and I did love each of them dearly—my life was wrapped up in Morris. For being so unsure of my love for him before marriage, he was now my life and my inspiration. He was always there for me, supporting me when my self-confidence was low, sympathetic when my decisions were less than accurate, encouraging me to be the best I could be.

And so it was no wonder, then, that when Morris became very ill, I tried to carry the load so he could receive the help he needed. He was to undergo extensive exploratory surgery on his back to try and correct a painful problem he had endured for years. Even as a young missionary, and later a young husband, he had suffered constant, low-grade pain in his back. That problem had been escalated by the cold, raw winters in Idaho and the hard, unforgiving cement floors in the railroad machine shops where he worked. At the time of his training, being a machinist at the railroad yards had seemed like the perfect solution to our financial woes. Now we realized that kind of work was not in his best interest. We were again looking at him being in Utah for an undetermined amount of time. Salt Lake City was the closest city that provided the medical procedure he needed.

There was one bright star on the horizon. Upon graduating from high school, DeNiece had moved to Salt Lake to take a business course. (At this point, she hadn't met that tall, slim air force cadet yet.) Without her own set of wheels, but with reliable bus service running daily, she would be able to visit her dad at the hospital fairly often. She was well into her second year of school when Elred graduated from high school, whereupon he immediately moved to California to look for work. And then, after a summer of taking on odd jobs, Elred joined the navy.

Jobs were at a premium as World War II finally came to a grinding halt. World peace felt good. The nation was generally glad to have the conflict over. War, however, had provided jobs for many people, and with it at an end, many laborers were out of work. That meant that jobs for a woman with a family, even if the size had dwindled to two children and a baby, were almost non-existent. Pocatello was basically a city supported by the surrounding farming communities. The outlook was bleak, both outside with a blustery winter well upon us and inside our hearts, wondering how we would handle this new dilemma.

I knew the hospital stay for Morris would be a lengthy one, but more than anything I wanted him to get well. This surgery was not an option. It was a necessity, if Morris didn't want to be permanently crippled.

The weekly letters from me to Morris in Salt Lake were filled with lies, told lovingly for a purpose, but blatant in their untruthfulness. I just didn't want Morris to worry. I wanted him to use his strength to get well.

"We are well and happy. Gertrude is such a true friend. She is always offering me housework to help put groceries on the table. (Once a week, and then only because she could see our need.) Ruth is a stalwart too. She makes sure her children bring us meat for the freezer and fresh eggs almost daily (Ruth and her husband were very generous, but they were barely making ends meet for their family). You see, there is no reason to worry. We are getting along famously. Karen is growing bigger every day. (At ten months, she was still wearing her baby clothes, and they fit perfectly.) Barth and Daryl are such good helpers. (This, at least, was true.) They keep the coal bin full (there was hardly enough coal to keep the fire burning), and the house is warm and cozy (only if you sat right next to the stove, and only during the day)."

I don't know if Morris was really fooled by my letters, but there was little he could do about any of it. Incapacitated, he was flat on his back in the hospital, and after the surgery, he was slowly learning to walk all over again with painful, daily therapy.

As the days dragged on, I could see I needed to take the initiative and find some kind of work. To tell the truth, I never did check into going on government welfare, so I don't know if such an avenue was even possible, although one good friend suggested it. I hadn't been raised to accept handouts, from the government or from the Church, and I knew there must be something for a willing, able-bodied woman to do.

After much searching, I stumbled onto a dry cleaning business that was being sold in Lava Hot Springs, a pleasant little resort town about forty-five miles south of Pocatello. As I began to consider this possibility, I visited with one of Gertrude's sons who ran a dry cleaning establishment in Pocatello.

"What do you know about dry cleaning?" was Lionel's first inquiry.

"Not a thing," I told him and then hurried on, "but I can learn. I will work free for several weeks until I know what to do and can do a good job. Come on, Lionel, give me this chance. You know Morris would do the same for you."

That was the clincher. Lionel, Morris's nephew, knew Morris would do that for him and more if it were necessary. Everyone loved Morris because he was always so willing to help.

And so my letters and my lies continued to flow weekly to Morris's bedside. "Things are working out fine as I do housework for those living on the east bench of Pocatello. The war hasn't seemed to affect their livelihood at all. (I was much too shy to ever ask for such a job, even if one had been available.)"

What I did not tell him about was the dry cleaning possibility. If that worked out, and I prayed that it would, there would be plenty of time to inform him of those plans.

I mostly talked of the children. "Karen took her first steps alone today at ten months. She has been walking around the furniture, and holding Daryl's hands, but today we should have had a camera to capture the moment. There was definitely a look of defiance on her little face as she struck out on her own, and a look of total surprise as her petite fanny plopped down on the hard linoleum floor. Get well quickly, my darling, for we need you home, and she will be a delight for you to watch."

I was so afraid that if I told Morris the truth about our situation, he would insist on coming home on the first train, even though he could hardly walk a step himself.

I determined I would make a go of the dry cleaning business. I mean, how many opportunities were going to fall into my lap? There were three major problems in this dramatic solution to our financial worries. The first was that the old blue 1932 Chevy was barely holding together, and I had to drive to Lava each day from Pocatello and home again at night. I have no doubt in my mind that it was prayer and chewing gum that kept the car running.

And then there was the issue of my being able to stay awake when I drove. In the morning, I hurried around getting the boys off to school and then bundled Karen up and strapped her into the seat next to me with a tough old leather belt so she couldn't squirm around out of my reach. All I really needed to do was give that child a picture book, and she was content to look, carefully turning the pages, while she jabbered non-stop. My mind would be filled with the ins and outs of the business as I planned my day. But, on the way home, after a hard day of moving heavy bags of clothes and being on my feet constantly, Karen slept while I fought the urge to join her.

The third problem was almost the most serious of the three. I was *so* shy. When customers would enter the door of the shop, I would stand behind the racks of clothes, shaking and worrying myself almost into a frenzy before moving out into their vision to wait on them. By that time, they would have rung the bell several times for assistance. My willingness to work was constantly overshadowed by my shyness and lack of self-confidence. Gradually over the next several months my timorous nature receded as I came to know the people of Lava and feel more comfortable with them.

One day, out of the front shop window, I observed a giant lumberjack of a man with chestnut beard and hair sticking out in every direction. Red-faced, with arms pumping, he was striding across the street toward the shop. Frightening to look at even at a distance, almost before I knew it and had time to hide, he was ringing the bell on the counter with short, quick jabs. Frankly, I was afraid to wait on him but was equally afraid to ignore him! Finally I peeked out and inquired softly, "May I help you?"

"Well, actually, ma'am, I think we can help each other," he boomed in a voice as large as he was.

"Help each other?" I squeaked.

The gruffness softened and a huge smile lit up his whole face, altering his features and making him look almost pleasant. "Help each other! You see, Mrs. Teeples—you are Mrs. Teeples, aren't you?" and then he nodded as if he'd made up his own mind to that question, "I have a house in Lava that I haven't been able to sell. I work every day in Pocatello, and I'm finding the daily drive is just too far. Would you be interested?"

"Oh, a house would be lovely, Mr.—what did you say your name was?"

"Oh, it's Mr. Robinson. Sorry, I should have introduced myself first off, Mrs. Teeples."

"Well, Mr. Robinson, a house would be lovely, but I just couldn't afford to buy your house, as much as I do need to move to Lava to be closer to my work."

"Oh, Mrs. Teeples," chuckled Mr. Robinson, "I didn't mean you should buy my house, or even rent it. You must have a house in Pocatello where you are living with your family. How about if we trade houses? Straight across! Maybe not for good, but for a while until we can both work out a better arrangement for ourselves. That way I can be closer to my work, and you can be closer to yours. My house is only about four blocks from your shop here. It's not a bad little house, and it would be real convenient for you."

I don't know who was more surprised, me or Mr. Robinson, as I flew around the counter, stretched tall on my tiptoes, and threw my arms around his neck. And then, quickly collecting myself, I stammered, "Are you sure you mean it?"

"How could I go back on the bargain now?" he chortled. "I no more want to change my mind than I want to give up your hug."

At that I turned a delightful shade of pink.

"Well, Mr. Robinson, the idea sounds like just what I have been praying for, but you haven't even seen my house to see if you would like to live there."

Mr. Robinson laughed and shrugged. "You haven't seen my house to see if you would like to live there, either. But, I'll bet we can both get along fine with whatever the houses are like, at least for a while. What do you say, Mrs. Teeples?" and his huge hand shot out in my direction. As I put my smaller, softer hand in his, I knew it was the right decision and truly an answer to prayer.

Easy to say: "We're moving to Lava." But, how? I had no idea.

As I began checking into moving costs, I was appalled. It would cost seventy-five dollars to have our furniture and household goods moved from Pocatello to Lava Hot Springs. It might as well have been a thousand. There was no possible way I could afford that kind of money.

As I sat on a stool at the front counter of my shop, with not an idea in my head but a constant prayer in my heart, I became conscious of men going in and coming out of the local pool hall across the road. Something in my brain told me to watch more closely. It seemed each fellow parked a large farm truck along the street before entering the pool hall. Most of them were dressed like farmers, in well-worn jeans and jackets, and cowboy boots or rubber boots. Because I was the queen of shyness, I couldn't imagine approaching any of them about anything.

Imagine my surprise at my own resourcefulness, when I donned my brown woolen coat and slowly walked across the slushy street, my hands shoved low into my pockets. "What are you doing?" my brain was shouting at me. "Shhh," I whispered to my subconscious.

And then, there he was: a farmer who looked approachable, and there I was, standing outside the pool hall.

"Excuse me," I began. The man slid to a halt with a puzzled look on his face. "I own the dry cleaning place across the street and—" I hadn't thought about how I would present my case.

I cleared my throat and began again. "Hello, I'm Mrs. Teeples, and I need to ask a favor of you."

He nodded slightly, so I went on. "My husband is in the hospital in Salt Lake City. He's been there for several weeks now. I have three children at home. Uh, my home is in Pocatello, but every day I drive to work here in Lava. You see, I have the opportunity to move here so I don't have to do that anymore."

The farmer was beginning to look at me, like, "—and how does this concern me?"

I rushed on. "The only problem is that I don't have a truck to move my furniture and boxes to Lava. The only vehicle I have is that old blue Chev over there," I said as I pointed across the street where the car was parked. "I was just wondering—if there was any way—that—uh—"

Now that I needed to come out and ask the question, I was beginning to be tongue-tied and scared again.

"—You could use my truck to move your things?" The farmer finally came to my rescue.

"Yes," the tears were welling up in my eyes. "I hate to ask, but I just don't know what I am going to do."

"Tell you what, Mrs. Teeples, day after tomorrow I was planning on a trip to Pokey to pick up a machine part for my tractor. I try to repair my equipment during the winter while it's slow on the farm." And then a slow smile moved across his face. "If you could *not* come to work that day in Lava but stay home so I'd know what to load up, we could probably get that furniture and those boxes to Lava for you without too much trouble."

"Oh," I gulped, not believing my good fortune. "I'd pay for the gas," I quickly volunteered.

"Yup, my trip to Pokey would be paid for, and you'd get your things here safe and sound." Again he nodded his head with a look of self-satisfaction. "Sounds like a deal." And for the second time that week, a stranger stuck out his hand for me to shake, sealing the bargain.

When Morris was finally to be released from the hospital in Salt Lake, I wrote to him, "Don't take the train all the way to Pocatello. We live in Lava Hot Springs now." Luckily, the train passed through Lava.

Chapter 15

Morris was home! Home but certainly not well.

"Susanna, could you help me get out of bed? I really need to be at the shop helping you." Morris felt miserable. He couldn't work without being in tremendous pain, and he couldn't just sit at home and think about his suffering. That was driving him mad.

"Uh, Morris," I finished buttering the toast and setting it on the table, "why don't you stay here until Karen wakes up? She was sick again during the night, and I could get so much more done without her underfoot for a while."

It seemed that each night I went to bed overtired, slept poorly, and woke tired in the morning. Part of my fatigue was the long hours I was keeping. Part was the constant stress under which I labored. Even though Morris had endured the exploratory surgeon's knife in Salt Lake, he was far from well. He knew it, I knew it, and the doctors in Salt Lake knew it. Their recommendation: Morris needed to see a specialist at the famed Mayo Clinic in Rochester, Minnesota.

Founded by brothers Charlie and Will Mayo, the clinic was the best in education and research, best in diagnosis and treatment of difficult medical problems, and renowned in the medical field. Their search for excellence in medicine and consultation with other specialists had earned them a significant medical reputation. By 1919, the brothers had turned the Mayo Clinic into a charitable, not-for-profit organization that blessed the lives of many.

Oh, yes, we were willing to send Morris to the Mayo Clinic, but as usual, we had no money.

"Besides, last night Rulon called," I went on, "saying he was driving down from Pocatello. He wanted to talk with you this morning."

Rulon was Morris's younger brother. They looked a lot alike—Morris and Rulon—enough that they could have been the twins in the family, except Rulon was slighter in build. Because they had such a close relationship, the prospect of a visit from Rulon was like telling a kid he was receiving a treat that day.

"What does he want to talk to me about?" inquired Morris. "I'm poor company at best, right now."

"I really don't know. He sounded like it was fairly urgent, though. You eat some breakfast and listen for Karen. After Rulon leaves, you and Karen can come and tell me what the visit was all about." I smiled encouragingly, hoping Morris would agree to the plan. I had a lot of heavy, lifting-type work to do this morning, and I didn't want him there, trying to help, and being frustrated because he was too weak to do it.

Karen had been sick much of her first year of life and into her second. The doctor in Pocatello said she needed her tonsils and adenoids out sometime, but she was too small to go through such an operation at the present time. Constant infection seemed to rule her existence.

About noon, Rulon, Morris, and Karen all arrived at the shop. Rulon needed to be on his way home, but first he wanted to stop and say hello. Gertrude, their sister, had told the rest of the family about this new business venture, but all the siblings had been busy with their own lives, and no one had been there to see just what was happening with us.

"Hi, Susanna." Rulon greeted me with a brief hug. "Show me around. Hey, this looks great!"

"There isn't too much to show. The business is small at this point, although we have a lead on buying some more equipment that will help us expand." Even though I was shy about showing off what we had, I was justifiably proud of what I had accomplished during the past year.

"Well, it looks like you are doing fine."

Define "fine," I thought. Fine, as in keeping our heads above water? *Fine, as in barely making ends meet? Fine, as in feeding two adults, two fast-growing boys, and one tiny mite of a girl?* But then I quickly repented of that attitude. We *were* doing fine. Fine in helping each other; fine in loving and caring; fine in being surrounded by concerned Church members; fine in having a good extended family. Take, for instance, Rulon: he was a busy man too, with a family to care for, and yet here he was giving Morris a much-needed moral boost. Yes, we *were* doing fine.

"We are doing just fine, Rulon. How are Bernice and the kids?" I inquired.

"Everyone is keeping busy," stated Rulon. He looked over at Morris like he was expecting something; and then, ever so slightly, Morris nodded.

"Susanna, Rulon has offered to raffle off his 1939 lever-action Winchester shotgun to help raise money to send me to Rochester. The gun is a dream. The sights are perfect. It is sleek, reliable, and balanced. The walnut stock is polished to a sheen, and when you gently squeeze the trigger, ohhh—it's as smooth as silk. I've told him it's too much of a sacrifice, but he doesn't see it that way." The lump in his throat was getting in the way as Morris extolled the gun's merits and then Rulon's proposal.

"It's just a gun, Susanna. What is a gun compared with the health of someone you love? The gun can be replaced, eventually. Morris's health needs to be taken care of now. Some of the other family members have an item or two they are willing to sell. Between us, we should have enough for train tickets to Rochester. The railroad has agreed to give him tickets at a reduced rate, and the fees at the clinic are lower than you would think for such an impressive place."

Standing in stunned silence, I stared down at my durable

brown oxfords and the worn planking on the floor. "How can you all be so good to us?" I finally whispered. "We would be ever so grateful."

"Let me arrange everything," stated Rulon in his easy-going but efficient way. "We should be able to have this man on his way to a new life within a month or two—or three at the most."

"Give Bernice our love, Rulon. And thank you. Thank you for just being you and for thinking of us at this time."

By mid-November, appointments and arrangements had been made, and Morris was on a train to Rochester, Minnesota. Thanks to generous family and friends, the trip was all paid for ahead of time. It was nothing short of a miracle. Accommodations, train tickets, meals, taxi fare, doctors' fees—there was money for it all. Rulon was the one to finally accompany Morris. The family had said I should go, but that really wasn't feasible. With work and family responsibilities, I needed to be home.

And then the bombshell struck.

"Mr. Teeples, during your stay here this past week, we have examined you thoroughly. What kind of butchers do they have there in Salt Lake?" The middle-aged doctor, dressed in a blue hospital smock, with matching snug-fitting cap, balanced on the front edge of the desk in his office. "Your recent surgery came to within a fraction of an inch of paralyzing you for the rest of your life. Further surgery could be helpful to you, but under no circumstances would we consider such measures for at least two years. Your body must have time to heal and rebuild some resilience before you go under the knife again."

To say that Morris came home discouraged was a gross understatement. How could this possibly be? Family members had been so generous to dig deep into their pockets to offer the much-needed financial aid. We were trying to live the way we should. We were willing to do whatever it took. What about all the prayers and fasting? What about all the money spent?

What about the gun that had been sold and could not be replaced? What about the—hope? Now it seemed there was no hope on the horizon. Two years seemed like forever.

Strong, gusty wind rattled the front shop window. Hard, crusted snow lined the street outside. Dreariness everywhere. No money for Christmas, no money for school clothes, barely enough food for a growing family, little work coming in during the winter, and especially no relief for my beloved husband. What to do? What to do?

"This is just something I am going to have to learn to live with, Susanna. I can't go back to the railroad yards, even though I have some seniority there now. I feel the working conditions would just be too difficult for me to bear. The cement floors have no give, and the bending and twisting required would be impossible. But you, dear, sweet Susanna, have begun a business venture here that will work for us. Let me just work with you."

Sometimes Heavenly Father takes his own sweet time in showing us the light at the end of the tunnel. But he is always there. Isn't that a marvel? Just when we think we can't endure another moment, another meal of pinto beans, another walk to work through the battering cold with our threadbare winter coat pulled tightly around us, another crying child in the night, another look of pity, there it is, the tiny spark, like a pin-prick lighting the darkness of despair. Light! Even the most minute speck in a cavity of black seems bright and reassuring.

We reach out to grasp the tiniest of miracles, and hope again begins to smolder softly, giving off a touch of fragrance into the air for a new beginning. Sometimes the hope smolders almost unseen for a long time before it bursts into flame.

Time is such an enigma. We may say time flies, time drags, time heals, but whether we mismanage it or use it well, it marches on relentlessly. The trick is to take this mysterious component and mold it to our own use. In the meantime, we hold on, make do, and pray.

Walking to work was getting easier as the icy chill in the air softened. The lightest touch of spring was all around. The bare, spindly trees were blowing less ferociously than yesterday. A changing of seasons and a warming of the earth always seemed to encourage me. Warmth itself seemed like a ray of light or hope.

Lava stretched its early spring arms and groaned with pleasure as the grass turned an emerald green. The trees leafed out, and the summer months finally arrived, teeming with visitors: tourists ready to play, health seekers coming to soak in the soothing, healing water that bubbled freely out of the ground in Lava, families wanting to swim in the deliciously warm pools. Some of the hotels had health spas in their basements, and the state of Idaho owned not only a popular swimming pool but also some famed hot pools. It felt exhilarating to have the people return. And with their return, our dry cleaning business flourished.

That spring, a larger building across the street from our small shop came up for lease. During the winter, the opportunity to purchase more dry cleaning equipment had come to our attention. The owners wanted to sell it as a package, and as quickly as possible. Of course, we didn't have the cash.

As the months went by, though, with still no buyer, they dropped the price considerably and finally agreed to sell it for low monthly payments. We came to realize the seeming inconvenience of the Lord's timing had turned despairing moments into an amazing blessing, and the deal was closed.

"Morris, I have the greatest idea." Morris always shuddered a little whenever I said that. It inevitably meant more work.

"And what would that be, Susanna?" he questioned cautiously.

"Well, the building we are going to lease across the street is huge. It will easily hold the new dry cleaning equipment, plus a front desk and room for clothes racks for the clean clothes—*and* be large enough for us to live there as well."

At first Morris looked at me as if I had gone mad. And then he reconsidered. "What did you have in mind?"

Quickly, I pulled a blank piece of paper toward me. Dividing the paper into four areas, I labeled the back two compartments: dry cleaning equipment. In the left front portion of the paper, I sketched clothes racks and a front desk. Finally, I divided the last segment of the paper into a living room, two bedrooms and a kitchen, placed trailer style, one behind the other. The plumbing for the bathroom was already in the far back corner of the building. It could stay there.

"The ceilings over there are twelve or fourteen feet high. That would be quite a project," Morris stated as he considered the drawing.

"Oh, you wouldn't have to put the walls clear to the ceiling. If you just put up two-by-fours to stand the normal eight feet—that would be high enough. I know we don't have enough money for doors between rooms, but with a cafe rod across each doorway, I could hang curtains so no one could casually see inside the rooms of our living area. Gertrude gave me several yards of that heavy, forest green material last fall, and I haven't used it yet."

"Would you really be willing to live there?" My husband was staring at me—actually gazing at me with great love. "What I really mean is: how was I lucky enough to ever get you to marry me? You are the darnedest woman I know. You just keep thinking up ways to make things work out for us."

And then, "Have I told you lately that I love you?" Morris sang the words out, exactly on key, as he hugged me to him. "You are a wonder!"

Gradually, the project came together. As it did, we could see many benefits, not the least of which was the fact that I didn't have to walk outside in windy or stormy weather to get to work. The trading of houses had worked perfectly for a time for Mr. Robinson and us. By this time, though, he had found a house to buy in Pocatello and a buyer for his house in Lava. By living on site at our business in Lava, we would have a single lease payment. We even determined that we could rent out our Pocatello house to pay for the Lava lease! Of course, we would have to go to Pocatello and give the house a good cleaning before we tried to rent it to anyone, but Barth and Daryl were both getting old enough to be a tremendous help in that area. Also, DeNiece had just returned from school in Salt Lake and was eager to assist.

With the housing project well underway, I turned my ever-busy mind once more to the problem of Morris's health. Earlier in the spring, I had read an article in a magazine that had been left in the shop by a customer. Inside was an advertisement about two 'miracle' pills: Calcium Wafers and Iodine Ration. "Feeling rundown? No energy? Is life a drag? Here is the help you need!"

Morris was still suffering excruciating pain in his back. Because he was such a congenial person, many people really didn't understand the misery he was in as he visited with them, asking about their lives and not dwelling on his own problems. He didn't sing much, though, and hardly ever whistled, so I knew the pain still persisted.

Were the pills too expensive for us to afford? Not if they would do all the marvelous things they promised. As in most great deals, the pills were less expensive per pill the more pills you purchased. I was so convinced by reading the ad that this was just the thing for Morris that I sent away for the biggest bottle of Iodine Ration and the largest box of Calcium Wafers available. The advertisement said you had to stay on them for a while before you would really see a difference. There was no use just buying a few. If Morris was really going to put them to the test, he needed a good supply. We were living on a shoestring, but hopefully we could afford this extra expense. Every time I read the printed material I felt justified. I was sure Morris would reap huge benefits from these pills.

By the time the order came, we had moved into the larger building. The post office was just two doors away. Every morning, while I turned on the steam for the presses and spotting gun, Morris would meander over to the post office to see if we had any mail. The mail was really a sidelight. Ben, the white-haired, bespectacled postmaster had a lively sense of humor, and Morris loved to visit with him. It was the perfect way for each of them to start his day.

This morning, when Ben handed Morris the rather large box, he looked at it and shook his head. "That woman of mine! What in the world has she ordered now?"

"Now, Morris. Don't you worry about that little woman of yours. She's a worker if ever I saw one. This here package is probably something for your business, knowing her."

"Oh, you're probably right," muttered Morris.

"Besides, I have weightier things to talk to you about." Ben was looking a little grumpy as he made that last statement.

"What would that be?" Morris inquired as he set the box on the ledge by Ben's wicket.

"I heard somebody tell someone (this was Ben's way of chattering about other people without using names, which in his mind would have been gossiping) that your daughter DeNiece is thinking of going to China to be with her husband just as soon as the air force says it's okay."

"That's right. They have been married almost six months now, and she is anxious to go and be with Don. That's just natural. Heck, what newlyweds want to be oceans apart?"

"Yeah, well, that's all fine and good, Morris, but I think it's a crying shame that she is planning on leaving her little girl here while she goes. I mean, I know you guys love Karen and will take real good care of her, and China is a long ways off and maybe it's not too civilized, or something, but to leave Karen behind just don't seem right to me." Ben finally paused long enough to take a breath.

"What in the heck are you talking about, Ben Snow?" Morris was shaking his head, trying to understand the words he had just heard.

"Well, what kind of a family reunion is that if DeNiece flies off to be with Don, and their little girl Karen is left here?

No mommy would . . ."

"Karen is *not* DeNiece's little girl," Morris forced through clenched teeth. "Of course DeNiece would not leave her child behind. Karen is *my* daughter. Susanna is Karen's mother. And DeNiece sure as heck won't be flying off across no ocean with her little sister in tow! Karen will be staying right here with her parents. Good grief, man, DeNiece and Don haven't been married long enough to even have a child!" With that, Morris turned around and stomped out of the post office, the box clutched tightly to his chest.

As soon as Morris banged through the front door of the shop, I knew something was wrong. "Dang, I'll bet he's mad I bought all that vitamin stuff. Well, it's for his own good, so he just better not give me any hassle."

As the post office story poured out of Morris's lips, I began to smile, and then to laugh.

"C'mon, Morris. I guess when you have a twenty-year-old daughter constantly taking care of a little girl who is not yet two—and is so small she looks like she's barely a year old—the mistake is an honest one."

"If Karen was DeNiece's daughter, I would be her grandfather. I don't look that old," Morris growled, still not wanting to see the humor in the situation.

But, in the days—and years—to come, Morris told the post office story over and over again to many of our customers, enjoying it completely. I guess it had just caught him off guard. He loved both his girls immensely and always loved a good joke, even when it was on himself.

The pills were another matter. No matter how I cajoled him, he flatly refused to swallow even one. "What a waste of money," was all he would say.

"How can you help someone, if they won't help themselves?" My frustration level was at an all-time high. I knew that Morris felt that if the famed Mayo Clinic couldn't help him, surely a pill wasn't going to do it. *What about my investment, though?* I inwardly raged. *Well, I won't let that money be wasted. I spent good cash on those pills, and if Morris won't take them, then I will.*

The beautiful, warm summer was drawing to a close. We had finally waited on the last customer of the day. Morris sat by the kitchen table, watching me closely as I prepared supper. "What's different about you, Susanna?"

"What are you talking about? My hairdo's the same, my feet are tired, my apron's fairly clean—I haven't grown horns or anything, have I?" Even as I made light of the situation, I could feel my eyes sparkling, my sense of humor intact.

"That's just it," Morris mused. "You look the same and yet you don't. I don't know, it's like your energy level has moved from 'High'—with a drag to your feet—to 'Highest'—with a spring to your step. It's kind of hard to explain, but—there's—there's definitely something different."

"Well, Mr. Teeples, if you will remember, last spring I ordered a huge box of Calcium Wafers and a bottle of Iodine Ration. You flatly refused to take them, even though I had ordered them especially for you. What did you expect me to do with them? I wasn't about to throw them away—they cost good, hard-earned money, and I couldn't see sending them back when I had felt so strongly I should order them in the first place."

With a stunned look on his face, Morris realized what I was talking about. "Those white wafer things and those big gray pills? You have been taking them?"

"Two of each, every day, just like the instructions say."

Morris sat shaking his head in disbelief. "And they are really making you feel that much better?"

"Enough better that I believe in them," I said quietly, the mirth now gone from my voice.

"Well, maybe I'd better try them," stated Morris humbly. "I mean, what harm can they do? It might be worth a try."

Sickness! I was sick of it! But still, it sat on our doorstep like a lost, hungry puppy, not willing to leave. Various forms of penicillin constantly haunted our medicine cabinet as we tried to find some relief for Karen. If I hadn't been feeling a little better myself, I would never have been able to be up night after night with that girl and still work the next day. Finally, I couldn't take it any longer.

"Doctor, something has to be done. This little girl isn't growing any bigger. We pump her full of medicine and still she constantly has a sore throat and runs a fever."

"You are right, Mrs. Teeples. Karen needs her tonsils out, and until that happens, she will not ever get appreciably better. The swelling that she is experiencing right now must be reduced before we can operate." The doctor hesitated as if considering something. And then he went on, "I have recently been sent this new antibiotic. Let's try it out on her and then operate just as soon as she is well enough to undergo surgery."

I hated the thought of her going under the surgeon's knife when she was so small and helpless, but there seemed no other solution. We went ahead with the doctor's plan. After the surgery was completed, the cold and infections were greatly diminished, but Karen still did not grow very quickly. Medicine was given to improve her appetite. It helped some, when we could talk her into taking it.

One day Morris wanted to take a business associate over to the cafe just down the street. I was trying to finish pressing some draperies for a good customer. "Could Karen go with you?" I pleaded. "It would help so much to be able to work in silence for the next half hour."

That was the day we discovered the best medicine of all to get Karen to eat. She loved to "eat at the cafe." Her favorites were a hamburger, fries, and a milkshake. We tried to make the same diet at home, but that was not nearly as effective. She simply loved to eat out.

The two years we thought would never pass before Morris was to return to the Mayo Clinic were almost up, when an incident happened which changed the whole scenario.

One of the benefits of our new shop was that it boasted a large coal furnace in the basement. Coal burned a long time, gave off good heat, and produced the steam needed for our presses and spotting equipment. The tradition of a yearly spring cleaning probably came about because coal wasn't the cleanest fuel, but it was efficient. So, people put up with it.

When we heard a friend talking about an exceptional deal he had gotten on a load of coal, our ears perked up immediately. Within the week, we had ordered half a ton of coal to be dropped down our coal chute. Obviously we had no idea how much a thousand pounds of coal was until we saw the enormous pile it formed in the basement. We were stunned—but the price had been so good! Surely we had our year's supply.

The first Monday morning we fired up the furnace with the new coal, Barth dug his shovel into the black, shiny mass and quickly filled the guts of the furnace with large lumps of coal. Filling the furnace with coal was his assigned job before school—this week. Next week it would be Daryl's job.

This job sure goes a lot faster when there are big pieces of coal to put inside, he thought to himself. *When the pile is new like this—almost to the furnace door, it's easier too. You don't have to carry it so far. I'm glad this is my week to shovel.*

"Barth, get moving," Morris called down the basement stairs. "It's just about bus time." Barth had to catch the school bus at the corner a block away from the shop for his ride to Marsh Valley High School.

"I'm comin' Dad," Barth called back. *There,* he thought, *Nice and full. That should burn a long time today.*

But by eight thirty when I wanted to start spotting clothes (actually I was removing the spots from the clothes with a chemical and hot steam), the pressure still wasn't up in my spotter.

"Morris, didn't Barth fill the furnace before he left for school?" I inquired.

"I'm sure he did because he was bragging about how easy it was to shovel with the pieces so big again. As you know, we were scraping the floor before we received this load of coal."

By this time, I had moved over to the press, where it was

essential we have a good head of steam for the equipment to work properly. I pulled the handle on the press to close it and stepped on the foot pedal. Only the tiniest hiss of steam could be heard.

"This isn't good," I muttered as I moved to the industrial ironing board. The iron was plugged in and should have been steaming by that time without any persuasion. Nothing. The iron was just barely warm.

"Oh, Morris," I sighed, "I'll run downstairs and see what is wrong."

"No, you stay up here. I'll go and check out the furnace."

Discouraged, I let him go slowly down the stairs. Shaking my head in exasperation, I moved back into the small kitchen to finish doing the breakfast dishes.

Several minutes later, Morris was at my elbow. "The furnace is full of coal, but it's no wonder the steam isn't coming up as it should. Only small patches on each piece of coal even seem hot." We looked at each other in alarm. Slag! We had a basement full of slag coal. No wonder it had been such a good price! Slag coal was useless. It burned poorly, if at all. Slag coal and steam equipment just didn't belong in the same building with each other.

After removing the new coal from the furnace and searching around on the basement floor for some old coal, we finally got the steam building for the day's work. But how depressing to have a whole basement full of useless slag. And that wasn't the worst of it. Not only had we already spent the money, we had to somehow get the coal hauled out of the basement to make room for coal that would burn properly. Whereas a truck had backed up to the coal chute and dumped the coal into the basement, we now had to shovel the useless coal into large buckets and lift it back up to the top of the chute.

"Two of Barth's friends are coming over to shovel coal into buckets this afternoon," I announced the next Saturday. "I told them we would pay them to work for us."

When nine o'clock rolled around, the boys arrived, and

Morris went down into the basement with them to supervise. Although they began with the best of intentions, the back-breaking work dragged after a time. As muscles strained, the rest breaks became longer and the work became slower. Without thinking, Morris began to shovel a little coal to give the boys the idea it was time to get back to work. Karen sat on the basement steps and watched.

"Daddy, I didn't think you were supposed to be doing that kind of work," Karen stated innocently.

"Well, sweetheart, we really need to get this coal out of the basement. Do you think you could keep a secret?" Morris employed.

"Oh, sure, Daddy. What's the secret?" Karen loved the new game.

"Promise you won't tell Mommy?"

"I won't tell, I promise. What's the secret, Daddy?"

"The secret is that I am going to help the boys shovel a little more coal before we quit for today. Just a little, but I don't want Mommy to know because she would worry about my sore back. So, don't tell, okay? You promised."

"I know, Daddy. I won't tell."

Before the hour was out, Morris had sent his hired help home and Barth and Daryl upstairs to finish their Saturday chores. Only he and Karen remained in the basement.

Each day, Morris and Karen disappeared for longer and longer stretches of time. As busy as I was, it was like heaven to have Karen not underfoot, and I assumed that Morris was taking her with him as he visited up and down the block. What I didn't know at the time was that each day Morris was shoveling more and more coal and lifting it outside the coal chute.

"I expected to really pay for my impetuousness with a sore, aching back, but it just never happened," Morris admitted to me later. "I won't be going to Rochester next spring. My back feels fine—so fine it's unbelievable. I'm not sure if you prayed me healthy, or if it was those darned pills, but this feels wonderful."

Chapter 16

About five years passed. And then, just when we thought we finally had Morris's health under control and Karen growing at a more regular rate, the next challenge arrived. (No, it wasn't as wonderful as another baby.) For several years, Morris had been the bishop of the Lava Hot Springs Ward. Our dry cleaning business continued to provide only partially. We were okay, though, because we had expanded to selling LDS garments and LDS books and being custodians of the Lava meetinghouse. Morris also drove the Lava Hot Springs ambulance when one was needed. These years were busy but rewarding ones.

As bishop, Morris attended general conference in Salt Lake City every April and October. It was a wonderful time for him to receive instruction from the General Authorities and to rejuvenate himself for further Church service. He loved to go, and I loved to have him go because he would come home with such exciting reports of what he had heard. For weeks afterward, as we worked together in the shop, or sat at the supper table, or lay in bed at night, he would share with me every tidbit of information he had received. Morris seemed to have the uncanny ability to hear a talk once and then retain the details in his head. He would report them with flair, even to imitating the gestures and enunciation of the speakers. Though I could not actually be there myself, it became my opportunity to soak in the testimonies of the Apostles.

Morris arose early one overcast, April Saturday morning

to travel to Salt Lake. Rain was forecast for later in the day, with sunny patches for Sunday. I knew Morris would come home and tell me not only about the messages that he had received but also describe Temple Square with it's artful array of tulips, daffodils, pansies, and hyacinths in all their varieties. The flowerbeds would be laid out like a gardener's dream with the prettiest spring had to offer. Knowing how I loved both flowers and Temple Square, he made sure he paid particular attention to the beauty around him so he could share it with me.

Luckily, Morris had a younger brother, Donald, living in Salt Lake with whom he could stay, making the trip more affordable. By leaving early, Morris would have some rare visiting time with Donald before the meetings began. They both looked forward to this time together. So, Morris was on the road by six in the morning, and I was headed for the shower by six-thirty, knowing I needed to get an early start on my working day.

As I arose from the bed, I felt a pin prick me rather sharply on my right side, under my arm. I couldn't imagine having a pin in my nightgown or my undergarments but quickly checked both articles of clothing to see what had stuck me so harshly. By this time, it felt like the side of my right breast was being used as a pincushion. I quickly undressed. Feeling around for pins, I discovered that even though the clothes were off, the pain was constant.

As I stepped into the shower, my fingers applying pressure on the tender area, I realized I was feeling a fairly prominent lump in the side of my right breast. All sorts of emotions surged through my body. *A lump in the breast is a scary thing*, I thought. And then my defense reaction kicked in. *Maybe not! Maybe it was just a gland that was infected. Maybe I was bruised and swollen from bumping my side. Maybe, maybe*—I really didn't want to think what the possibilities were.

By the time I had showered and dressed, the pricking sensation was gone. Maybe I imagined the whole thing. Maybe—

No, I knew that wasn't true. It had been much too painful. Throughout the weekend, I reassured myself it was probably nothing. And then I fretted and stewed—because—what if it was something?

When Morris returned late Sunday evening, I told him about the lump. At first I had thought I would not tell him. The pinpricks had not returned. But when something is so constantly on your mind for two days, you have to tell someone. I was, in fact, like a small child in my telling, interrupting him in the middle of what I am sure was an interesting conference story to blurt out my news.

"Morris, after you left for conference, I discovered a lump on the side of my right breast. It's not huge, but it's definitely there." I paused, taking a long breath. "What could it be?"

After checking it over carefully, Morris responded, "Susanna, you need to have this checked out tomorrow. I don't know what it is, but it shouldn't be there, and you need to see the doctor."

"Oh, maybe it's not so important after all," I replied. Having received the attention and sympathy I had been yearning for since discovering the lump and feeling the initial scare, I was now vacillating on its importance. The lump was still there, but the pain had receded, making it seem not quite so urgent now.

"Susanna, I don't want you to wait on this. Just make the appointment and see the doctor. And then we can both be reassured that it's nothing to worry about. Okay?" he said as he nuzzled in, taking me softly into his arms.

"Okay, okay. You have quite a method of persuasion, I must say," I giggled. But even with the playfulness, we were both still anxious.

The appointment was arranged for Tuesday morning in Pocatello at Dr. Call's clinic. The good doctor took a biopsy right there in his office and asked me to return in a couple of days for the results.

"He didn't seem too worried," I told Morris when I

returned home. "I think we are reading more into this than we need to." But secretly, I continued to wonder. I could also sense the concern and questions in the eyes of my husband.

By Thursday afternoon, I was back in Pocatello to see the doctor again. On each trip to the city, we tried to run necessary errands to keep down maintenance costs. I had left work late, but needed to pick up a furnace part before actually going to the doctor's office. At the store, I ran into Vernon, Morris's nephew.

"Oh, hi, Susanna. What are you doing here?"

"Hello, Vernon. I'm just picking up a furnace part. You know that old furnace of ours, it needs more care than a preemie baby."

"Um," Vernon mused, "I thought Annie said she had seen you here in Pokey on Tuesday too."

"Oh, right, I did run into your wife on Tuesday, when I was at Dr. Call's office. It was good to see Annie again."

"Susanna, is everything okay?" Vernon's tone sounded a little urgent. "Are you feeling all right? I mean, you are looking good and all—" He trailed the sentence off for a few seconds. "But, uh—but I just wondered how you are feeling these days?" he finished in a rush.

"Oh, I'm feeling fine, Vernon. But—I am late for an appointment. Good to see you again," I breezed.

Annie was head nurse at Pocatello General Hospital. Did Vernon know something I didn't? He sure sounded like I shouldn't be feeling so well.

As I headed up the hill to my doctor's office, my head was full of Vernon's concern. What was wrong with me? The dreaded word—cancer—came forcefully into my mind. Try as I might, I could not seem to shove that word out, as I had rudely done many times before during the week. Now it stuck there, like the painful pinlike pricks I had first felt when discovering the lump.

As I hurried into Dr. Call's office, his receptionist, Julie, interrupted my forward flow of motion by quickly stating, "Oh,

Susanna, it's good to see you. How are you feeling today?" She was very solicitous. "Dr. Call was called up to the hospital on an emergency, but he phoned just a few minutes ago and said he would only be about fifteen or twenty minutes late. Have a seat."

Is Julie acting strange or overanxious? I wondered.

"Can I get you anything?" she offered as she saw my darting glance around the waiting room.

My mind was whirling! In my distraught condition, I could hear the concern in her voice.

"Actually Julie, I have another errand to run and if the doctor is going to be late, I think I'll go do it quickly." And with that, I left.

Outside the office door again, I just couldn't seem to get control of my racing thoughts. My feet moved across the parking lot, past my car, and down the uneven sidewalk into a residential neighborhood. I had no errand to run. I had nowhere to go and no one to talk to about the fears that were quickly building to gigantic proportions in my mind.

The weekend of promised rain had waited until Wednesday to materialize. Now, along with the cold drizzle of rain, a cutting wind had picked up from the north. My unbuttoned coat flapped open and shut as my feet hurried along on a path of their own. I tried to pray, but my mind couldn't settle on any word except—cancer—cancer—*CANCER!*

I just couldn't have cancer. People died of cancer! Or if they didn't die, their bodies were cut and maimed trying to save them from it. Barth had joined the army. Daryl was attending college, but Karen was still at home and needing mothering. The business in Lava required constant, hard work. Besides, my brain screamed, *CANCER* is for old people, or sick people, or—my thoughts continued to tumble across themselves, never stopping to consider their lack of reasoning.

Finally, blocks away from the doctor's office, my teeth began to clatter from the shock and the cold. A jutting piece of sidewalk caused me to stumble. As I staggered to regain my balance without falling, it seemed to shake me into lucidness again. Reluctantly I turned around, slowly pulling my long brown coat around my thoroughly chilled body and began to retrace my steps, my teeth chattering.

In the meantime, Dr. Call had arrived at his office and inquired after me. He had seen my car in the parking lot on his way in.

"Susanna isn't here. She slipped out to run an errand," Julie reported.

Realizing something was wrong but not knowing where to look, he paced the floor until the office door finally opened, and I shakily staggered back into the waiting room. Immediately he recognized that I was in a severe state of shock.

"Oh, Susanna, I didn't want you to find out something was wrong in this manner," he soothed as he gently wrapped me in a warm, cozy blanket and sat me in his own soft leather chair. Not releasing my frozen hands, but tenderly massaging the circulation back into them, he continued, "Who have you been talking to today?"

"It doesn't matter." My teeth were still chattering as I tried to get my wits about me. "It's true, isn't it, Doctor? I have cancer, don't I?"

"Julie, bring Mrs. Teeples a drink of hot chocolate to help her warm up." And then, turning to me, he said softly, "Yes, Susanna, you have breast cancer. The biopsy was malignant. We need to operate very soon."

"Yes, I know you do. Will I die?"

"No, Susanna, no! You will not die. The operation should be effective in removing all the cancer cells. We will perform a radical mastectomy, where your right breast will be removed and also the glands under your right arm to make sure we get all the cancer cells. With some radiation treatments and a good therapy program, you will regain the strength in your arm, and you will be as good as new." The picture he painted sounded reassuring, but I wasn't buying it.

"Not as good as new, Doctor," I muttered as I began to sob.

"My breasts are so large. I'll be so unbalanced with one gone. I won't be attractive to my husband anymore, and, Doctor, *that* will kill me more than anything! I may not die, but I will be dead inside. In fact, I feel that way already. What man would want a wife with only one breast?"

"Oh, Susanna, do you think Morris cares whether you have one breast or two? He only wants you alive and at his side for many years to come. You mean everything to him. Think about it! You know what I'm saying is true!"

After feeding so many negative thoughts into my brain, I didn't know if I was ready to hear that, and yet, I did know it was true. I could not deny it. I was secure in Morris's love for me. Too many times he had succored me in my time of need for me not to know that what Dr. Call said was absolutely true. Morris would love me and stick with me through it all. In fact, his love for me would make it possible for me to survive.

Still, the shock of hearing you have something as scary as cancer—that big, bad C word no one ever talks about—was enough to set every nerve questioning what would happen to me.

"When will I need to come for the operation?" I questioned reluctantly.

"You need to be in the hospital this coming Sunday evening, so we can operate on Monday morning. I have already made arrangements at the hospital." (No wonder Annie and Vernon knew that I wasn't well!) "Now, I want you to drink this hot chocolate to warm your insides and sit here a while longer." Dr. Call stood up and moved toward his jacket hanging on the coat tree to locate his keys. "I can drive you home, and Julie will follow so I will have a way to return to Pocatello. It is all arranged."

The cozy blanket and warm chocolate drink were doing their work in calming my spirit and getting my emotions under control.

"No, Doctor. I can drive myself home."

"But, Susanna—" he began, turning to look back at me.

"No, Doctor," I said again, meeting his eyes with my own steady gaze. "I need the time to myself to get a handle on this before I arrive home and have to tell my family. The forty-five minute drive will be good for me. It will give me the time I need. I'm okay now. Really! Please?" My voice broke slightly as I pleaded for understanding. "Please let me do this my way."

What could he say? I could see the concern in his eyes as he struggled to listen to what I was saying and to respect my feelings. Finally he agreed to let me go.

As this wonderfully compassionate doctor tucked me into my car, the gray flannel blanket wrapped loosely around my legs, the storm whipping around the car outside, I could still feel his anxiety.

"I need to talk to my Heavenly Father, Dr. Call. This will be the perfect time for it." He nodded and firmly shut the door.

And that is exactly what I did. Even before I reached the city limits of Pocatello, heading home, I was pouring out my soul to the Lord. What had been locked securely inside during my mad dash in the cold wind now came gushing out in torrents, as I laid all my fears, my desires, and my concerns before the Lord. I had always trusted him before. Surely he could help me attain some understanding now.

On the road between Pocatello and Lava Hot Springs, about two-thirds of the way home, is a large, steel bridge. The cars drive on the bridge and the train winds its way beneath it through the valley. This bridge is unique in its design. Great steel girders go up each side in giant V's, forming a boxed-in effect of steel, and yet the landscape and sky are still visible through the latticed steel beams.

The black of night was descending as I distinctly remember entering the north end of the bridge. When I came out of my trance, I was safely on the other side, my headlights cutting a slash of light through the darkness, while I drove on down the road. I do not remember actually crossing the bridge. What I do remember, very clearly, is the roof of the car opening up in a smooth, liquid motion like a feather duvet being folded back on the bed of my childhood. Strong, tender arms reached down into my car and gently embraced my shoulders. Peace, warmth, and love filled my body, and I knew without a doubt that my Heavenly Father loved me and was watching over me. I still wasn't happy about having cancer, but I knew I was literally in the Lord's hands and would be sustained by him.

At home, Morris and Ray, a bishopric counselor, were working on the furnace. Calmly, I took the furnace part I had picked up in Pocatello downstairs to them, reminding them that they had a bishopric meeting that was supposed to begin in less than half an hour. The reminder sent them up the stairs, Ray to his home and Morris into the bedroom to change clothes. In a few short minutes, Morris pecked me on the cheek, saying, "This meeting is going to be a fairly long one. Don't wait up. Love you!" and he was out the door.

After calling Karen into the kitchen from her bedroom, where she had been reading, we discussed what we would like for supper. I had no sooner placed the toasted cheese sandwiches on the grill when Karen asked, "What did the doctor say, Mommy?"

I knew the questions would come. I had just hoped not quite so soon. "Well, sis, I am going to have an operation."

"An operation? When?" she asked, her green eyes big and round.

"Next Monday morning. You and Daddy will take me to the hospital in Pocatello after stake conference on Sunday.

"What are they going to do in the operation?" Karen persisted, her almost eight-year-old mind groping for facts.

"I have cancer, sweetheart," I said, trying to hold my voice steady. "But you know Dr. Call. He is a good doctor, and he is going to remove it from my body."

"Remove it? Like—cut it out?" Karen was trying to understand what I was talking about.

"Yes, cut it out. But, you know what?" I said with more conviction than I realized was possible, "Everything is going to be all right. I'm sure of it."

By then she was around the side of the table, her little arms wrapped securely around my neck. "Oh, I'm glad everything will be okay, Mommy, 'cause—'cause I love you." And then without a pause, "And Daddy and Heavenly Father love you too."

That sweet, pure reassurance of my child helped immeasurably.

Gratefully, Karen turned into bed after only one story and prayers (in which she admonished Heavenly Father to please "make my mommy all better, real soon").

I wandered back into the kitchen and cleaned up the supper dishes. My hands moved in slow motion, not with their normal decisiveness. There was a newspaper lying on the table. Picking it up, I tried to make sense of what was going on in the world. Finding I could not concentrate, I moved down the hall into the living room. Forcing myself to sit down on the sofa, I picked up my scriptures. Maybe there was a message of hope in them for me to read. My mind just couldn't seem to focus on the words. Instead, I closed my eyes, reliving my bridge experience. My Heavenly Father was *so* good to me. Turning around and dropping to my knees by the chair, I again poured out my thanks to him. After my prayers were said, I moved to the bedroom, changed into my nightgown, and lay down to try and sleep. The day had been a hectic, emotional one.

Just as I was about to slip into netherland, Morris returned home from his bishopric meeting. It was well after midnight. Assuming I was already asleep, he slipped quietly into his side of the bed. He was asleep in an instant. Nerves taut once more, I turned over carefully, trying to find a comfortable spot. Within thirty minutes, and just as I was slipping into unconsciousness again, Morris sat straight up in bed, wide awake.

"Oh, Susanna!" he said as he groped for me in the dark.

"It's okay, Morris. I'm right here."

"Susanna, what did the doctor say?" We were both fully awake now.

"First, I want to tell you about this wonderful experience I had on the way home from Pocatello, Morris." He moved his arm under his head and turned on his side, drawing me over next to him, as he listened. "I am going to need an operation, but I know that everything is going to work out okay. You know that steel bridge about twelve miles out of town? Well, when I drove over it tonight, I kind of had a manifestation, or something. It's hard to explain, but it was like the roof of the car was folded back and someone's gentle arms embraced my shoulders. I felt like I was wrapped in the arms of my Savior's love." As the tears leaked out of my eyes and onto my pillowcase, I again felt the peace and calm wash over me that I had experienced earlier in the evening.

Morris had not moved or spoken. His silence allowed me to tell it my way. I was grateful to him for that.

"I have breast cancer, Morris. Dr. Call needs to operate on me next Monday morning. We are to be at the Pocatello General Hospital on Sunday afternoon." By this time, Morris's strong arms were wrapped securely around me.

I went on to tell my husband what had happened that afternoon. Running into Vernon, walking wildly away from the doctor's office in the mounting storm, Dr. Call's concern, my doubts and fears, all came pouring out, as my best friend held me and reassured me of his love.

We talked on. I told him of Karen's comment at the kitchen table and her prayer for my recovery. We spoke of the other children, pondering the best way to tell them. We knew I needed an interest in their faith and prayers. I also knew, beyond a shadow of a doubt that my eternal companion was there for me. He loved me, unconditionally, and would stand by me.

After discussing all that had happened and much of what was to come, I asked hesitantly, "Do you think President Criddle would give me a priesthood blessing on Sunday after the first session of stake conference?"

The following Sunday, between sessions of stake conference in Arimo, our beloved stake president, President Criddle, gave me a special priesthood blessing. In the blessing, President Criddle reiterated what I already knew: my Father in Heaven loved me and was aware of what I was going through. He promised me I would not experience pain at any time: not during the operation, not after the operation, and not during the healing process. That blessing was literally fulfilled. The nurses could not understand why I would not take any painkillers, saying that I must surely need them. But I did not.

Cancer—that dreaded word! There are so many varieties and forms. It attacks young and old, strong and weak, active and sedentary. I hated the word when they removed my right breast, hated the fact that my body could be invaded by such an uncaring monster, hated the physical changes it wrought on my body, as well as draining my energy and self-esteem. But as much as I hated the word cancer when it struck me with total disregard, I absolutely loathed the word twenty-five years later when it was discovered in my beloved Morris.

I did survive the breast cancer operation, the radiation treatments afterward, the fear of a reoccurrence, the years of apprehension, the uncertainty that cancer can thrust on the body. I also survived the cancerous brain tumor that later took the life of my eternal sweetheart. I didn't survive either of the cancers easily, but I did survive.

On the first visit made by Dr. Call to my bedside after my operation, I questioned him closely about whether all the cancer had been removed.

"Dr. Call, *is* the cancer all gone? You just seemed kind of vague to me when I asked the question right after the operation. Did you say, 'I think so'? What kind of answer is that?"

Now he elaborated. "Susanna, during the operation, when we were preparing to remove the lump on the side of your breast, actually, just as we touched it, the lump burst open. As quickly and efficiently as possible, we gathered up those cancerous cells and removed them from your body. The only problem is that we have no way of knowing if we captured every cell. We hope we did. We tried. But if even one cancer cell escaped into your blood stream, there is a possibility of another outbreak of cancer at a later date. Even now I hate to tell you that, but you need to be aware of the risk."

"Now I understand," I stated, my heart heavy.

"We may have gotten it all. The radiation treatments will certainly help. But, it is a wait-and-see game, at best."

Between the time I was released from the hospital several days after the operation and the start of my radiation treatments, our oldest son, Elred, and his wife, Audrey, wanted me to visit them in California so I could rest and recuperate. I don't know all the telephone calls that were made during that time, but I have a notion that the doctor suggested I should not be able to return to work too quickly. A California vacation seemed the most logical plan to curb those tendencies. With Karen in elementary school and Morris handling work at the shop, it seemed to be the perfect arrangement.

Under normal circumstances, I would have loved to visit California. Elred and Audrey loved me and pampered me thoroughly. That was the problem. I wasn't used to being pampered. Through necessity, it had never been my lifestyle. Finally, to prevent myself from going entirely stir-crazy, I got up one morning, prepared a bucket of soapy water, and proceeded to wash down every kitchen wall. That was after Elred and Audrey had both left for work, of course. Audrey was one upset daughter-in-law when she returned and found out what I had done.

So, it was with some reluctance that I returned to Pocatello to take cancer radiation treatments and live in Daryl's apartment. What would I do with myself all day? Dr. Call knew my nature and could see my dilemma. I wasn't sick now; my right arm was just weak. I needed to be of assistance somewhere. Before long, he acquired me a job at the hospital cafeteria as a cashier, for which I was grateful.

Chapter 17

In the years after the first cancer scare, both Morris and I began to change our priorities. All we were accustomed to doing, day after long-working day, was labor for the necessities of life. It wasn't that we didn't find joy in our lives: our love for each other and our being together supplied much satisfaction.

But, as we evaluated where we were going and where we had been, the tally sheet was extremely heavy on the responsibility side and almost non-existent on the just-for-fun side. For instance, each fall during Daryl's high school years, he played football on Friday afternoons. They were lovely autumn afternoons: the trees magnificent in their final blaze of glory, the air currents moving slowly as if to warn the leaves of shaky days ahead, the field still green from a good summer of watering, a barely discernable nip in the air. All were tailor-made for high school football.

Friday was our busiest day of the week at the shop. Every time we planned to slip away to attend one of Daryl's football games, we would have an unusually large order to have ready for a customer, or a piece of equipment would inconveniently break down. Four years of high school went by quickly, and before we knew it, Barth and then Daryl were graduating, and we still hadn't seen Daryl play a game. "We'll do better when Karen gets there," we vowed.

Before we knew it, Karen had completed her ninth grade year at Marsh Valley High School and was begging to try out for the drill team. This varsity team wore matching uniforms and did precision marching at the football and basketball games at half time. After years of dance training, Karen was anxious to be part of this high school activity. We simply did not have the money for that venture. The day of tryouts, she called home from McCammon, pleading again to at least be able to try out for the team.

"How will you pay for your uniforms? And it's not just one uniform, is it? There are several uniforms—right?" Because Karen had been talking nonstop about the high school drill team for weeks, I was aware of some of the restrictions.

As soon as I answered the phone, I knew what this was about.

"Mom—how about—" she paused, afraid to say what was on her mind. The pause wasn't long though, and I could tell she had thought out her petition beforehand. "How about if I wash all the football uniforms and towels on Saturdays?" she suggested quickly.

"I don't know, Karen. I thought we had already talked through all this." After a longer hesitation where Karen was absolutely silent, I tried to think of an answer that would appease her. It wasn't that I didn't want her to be on a high school team. She associated with good girls. We liked her friends. "Let me talk to Dad," I finally said. "You call me back in ten minutes."

"We do have the contract to wash those grungy old uniforms and filthy towels every week," Morris said when I asked him what we should do.

"I thought that money was earmarked for Karen's college fund. We have had this conversation before." Why did I have to be the voice of reason? I was only trying to stay focused on practicality.

"Maybe this will teach her something about time and money management. We could have her pay for the soap out of the profit. We'd pay for the water she used, of course. She will have to arrange her time carefully to attend drill team practices, get her homework done, practice the piano regularly, and wash uniforms. It might be a worthwhile lesson." With thoughtful love, Morris tried to address the strong emotions of both his careful wife and his strong-willed teenaged daughter.

In the end, the bottom line was that we did not have the heart to say no. As Morris and I talked about Karen's request, we both knew we would allow this privilege of trying out. The high school drill team coach only needed four girls to replace the graduating seniors, and there were well over thirty girls hoping for spots on the team. Psychologically tightening our belts and truly desiring to be good parents, the answer was yes when she called again in exactly ten minutes.

An hour and a half later, before her ride left Marsh Valley, Karen called and was crying.

"It's okay, sweetheart. Maybe next year you'll make it."

"No, Mom. I'm calling to tell you I made the team *this* year," she said as her voice broke with emotion. "Thank you! Thank you so much for letting me do this! I love you! I'll be home in about an hour."

This was obviously something Karen wanted very much. Every Saturday morning by nine o'clock, she was filling the wringer washer with hot, soapy water, to keep her part of the agreement. We soon discovered, though, that marching boots, short military outfits, hats with plumes, gauntlets, etc. were only the start of the expenses. When the team traveled to games away from their home field, there were fast food, treats, and bus fare. Karen was semiaware of the extra expense and what it did to our budget, but not totally. Instead of complaining and taking away her pleasure, we cut back in other areas and worked longer hours.

It wasn't just the money. It was a time factor. There just didn't seem to be enough time to enjoy our children and their successes. When Karen modeled the 4-H dress she had sewn, winning a first-place ribbon, we heard of it and were proud of her as the word filtered back to Lava Hot Springs from others who had attended the event. When Daryl played the piano at a talent show at Idaho State College, we enjoyed hearing about his triumph from neighbors who had gone. But we weren't there! We realized we were short-changing ourselves. Life was too short to be missing out on so many family achievements.

The problem was it took all our time and energy to sustain life—not lifestyle—with the jobs in which we were currently engaged. And so we began talking quietly between ourselves about other possibilities. Where could we go? What could we do to lessen the load and still survive?

One of our many business ventures was selling LDS garments. Brother Harmon, the manager of Beehive Clothing Mills in Salt Lake City where the garments were sewn, had often told me I could have a job with them anytime. Morris thought Salt Lake would be a wonderful place to move to. Utah winters were considerably milder than the bitterly cold Idaho winters, AND the Salt Lake Temple was there.

DeNiece and Elred were both married with families. Barth was married and serving in the army. Daryl was attending school at BYU after returning from his mission in Switzerland. Our baby, Karen, was moving through high school and would soon be looking for a university to attend. Salt Lake City seemed like the golden Mecca we had been searching for.

Early in February, Morris drove to Salt Lake to look for a job as a railroad machinist. Although he hadn't worked at that job for many years, that was where he had his training. If he could just land a job in Salt Lake, maybe I could work for Beehive Clothing. With the two jobs, we could make ends meet.

To his dismay, he discovered that the railroad did not want to hire a man who was within five years of the mandatory retirement age of sixty-five. Discouraged, but proceeding with undaunted faith, he attended church the following Sunday.

"We have a visitor in high priests quorum today, Donald. Why don't you introduce your friend?"

"My friend," and Donald motioned in Morris's direction, "is

my friend, but he is also my brother. My older, bossy brother." That got a laugh from everyone. "He has been his own boss with his own business, but now he and his wife would like to move to the Salt Lake area and work here. I think he wants to keep a closer eye on Hazel and me. That's what older brothers do, you know." Everyone laughed again.

However, after class was over, one of the high priests struck up a conversation with Morris. "I don't know what you would think about janitorial work, but I've heard there are some jobs available at church buildings around Salt Lake. It might be worth looking into, if you're interested."

"Thanks, I appreciate the suggestion."

Bright and early Monday morning, Morris drove to downtown Salt Lake to the Church Office Building. After several inquiries, he found someone who could help him.

"Hi, I'm Bishop Morris Teeples. I heard yesterday at church that there are some janitorial jobs available with the Church here in Salt Lake City."

"There are, Bishop. As a matter of fact, there is a church house presently being built up in the Monument Park area on the east side of Salt Lake. The bishop of the ward there, Bishop Egbert, is working on site. He is a pleasant man, easy to spot because he's about six foot four, with fiery red hair. He could tell you what is available at that particular chapel."

Morris enjoyed the tangy morning air as he immediately drove to the building site. Bishop Egbert, a standout, was soon visiting with Morris amicably.

"Hans," Bishop Egbert motioned to the big, Swedish construction foreman, "come and meet Morris Teeples." In five long strides, Hans was standing next to the two bishops. "Hans, Morris is looking for a janitorial job. You were talking just this morning of needing someone to clean up the building site as we go along. Have you hired anyone yet?"

Han's smile was as big as he was. "Morris Teeples, pleased to meet you." His large hand shot out in front of him. As he shook Morris's hand enthusiastically, he silently observed the striped bib overalls, warm jacket, and sturdy work boots. "I am looking for another worker, but I really need him to start work today—right now, in fact."

"I'm your man, Hans. I can begin immediately."

Morris called back to Lava that night. "I've found a possible job, Susanna," he said, "but I don't know if I should take it."

"Already? You've found a job already? Why wouldn't you take it?" I inquired. "What is it?"

"Well, I wasn't sure if you would want to be married to a janitor." The voice was serious, with just a hint of humor.

"Well," I responded, picking up on the humor immediately, "you might as well know that I am already married to a janitor. Right now he thinks he is also a businessman, a bishop, a salesman, and an ambulance driver, but I've heard rumors he's being fired from all those jobs. A janitor with one good, solid job, rather than a janitor with a plethora of jobs sounds fine to me."

When the Lava Hot Springs Ward heard about the new job, they absolutely refused to release Morris as bishop. "We will wait and see if this new job opportunity really pans out" was the prevailing attitude of the ward—and the stake president.

So, Morris worked in Salt Lake all week, while I tried to hold things together at the dry cleaning shop. Early Friday evenings found him traveling the road to Idaho, where he would attend meetings and speak with members until late Sunday afternoon. After sharing an often-hurried Sunday dinner, he would be on the road again headed for Utah. Our reason for staying on in Lava: we were trying to let Karen complete her tenth grade school year at Marsh Valley High School.

Finally, the exact week we began loading our furnishings onto an old borrowed truck, the new stake president gave Morris his release. It was a sad and happy time for us. We were sad to be leaving the many stalwart friends we had made over the years in Lava Hot Springs. Eleven years and two months is a long time to be a bishop (or a bishop's wife). Karen couldn't remember ever living anywhere else. She would be moving from a high school of about two hundred and fifty students to a high school of 2500 students in Salt Lake. If she hadn't missed her dad so fiercely during his absence that spring, she probably would not have wanted to go with us. But, like me, she felt the need for us to be a "living together" family once again. The happy part came with the anticipation of a new adventure. It all seemed a bit scary, but also rather exciting.

The best part of the move was the part we had contemplated. We did have more time for ourselves, our children, our love of attending the temple—our spiritual, emotional, and social lives. And because we had more time for these important things, our children seemed to make more time for us.

Several years later, each of our children got a call from their dad. "In three years time, Mom and I will have been married for fifty years. Fifty *l-o-n-g* years!" he reiterated in his lilting, teasing voice. "Can you believe it?"

Each of the children responded with such comments as: "Fifty years married? Wow! That means you are really getting old." Or, "Come on, Dad, you can't kid us. You mean Mom's still with you?" Or, "Hey, Dad, what are you going to do on the big day?"

And that gave him the lead-in he wanted. "Fifty years married to the same woman calls for a celebration, don't you think?"

"Sure, Dad. What did you have in mind?"

"A party! An anniversary bash! A celebration of the grandest kind! That means, of course, that all our family would be here. I would like to invite our old friends from Lava Hot Springs and our new friends from Salt Lake. Our anniversary is December 2, and that's probably an inconvenient time for everyone to come, but maybe right after Christmas would work. I don't care if it's on the exact date. I just want the celebration. What do you think?"

Each of his adult married children responded, "That

sounds fantastic—except—what about Mom?"

"Well, actually, that is why I am calling you well in advance. I think she will come around if she has time to get her mind into it. I know that ol' shy bug of hers is getting in the way right now, but with time and good planning, she'll be okay. I'm sure of it!"

When he called Karen at her home in Canada, he pled his cause with extra intensity. "I know you would be carrying the brunt of such a party, but I have subconsciously been planning this for years." DeNiece had been battling multiple sclerosis for several years, and Morris's sons, well, they were men. They would help all they could, but a party of this magnitude would need a woman's touch.

Karen, with her usual energy, said, "Let me handle this, Dad. You will need to keep working on Mom, but I will get everyone else on line for you."

It wasn't that I didn't want to please Morris. Being in the limelight was just not my idea of pleasure. But for the love of Morris, who talked of nothing else, I succumbed. Morris and I were given the job of making out the guest list. I never realized we knew so many people—or that Morris would want them all there at this special time.

Fifty years earlier, Morris and I had a picture taken of us together. I remember that day so well. My brother John had set an old wooden pickle barrel on a wood slat in our yard. We were afraid the top of the barrel would give way and fall inside if I sat on it. There was much laughing and joking about such a possibility. So, John covered the barrel with a tin washtub, turned upside down. In the picture, Morris looked dapper in a striped suit and bowler hat. He stood just to the side and behind me slightly. I sat on the large wooden barrel, decked out in my nicest dress and heels, wearing a floppy brimmed hat with pom-poms hanging down around it. My hat was special because Morris had won it for me at the Idaho State Fair. We were young and happily in love, and it showed on our faces.

Daryl was the photographer in the family, and he had

always loved that picture. In designing the invitation, Daryl combined that family heirloom with a current picture of Morris and I that he had taken just for the occasion. In that picture, Morris was his handsome, distinguished self in a dark suit and striped tie. With a full head of pure white hair, tanned face, and dignified bearing, my, that man of mine was handsome! He had stayed slim and trim over the years. But for all of that, his crooked little grin was still his best feature. I felt good about my presentation as well. I had sewn the dress myself, and the rosy fabric complemented me in both color and design. As we stood together, our eyes alight with the love that had grown over the years, we were a handsome couple.

The family all came for Christmas, which was a delight in itself.

For the anniversary party, our children collaborated to make the evening a grand success. Our daughters- and sons-in-law manned the kitchen, taking care of the refreshments, while Morris and I and each of our five children formed a receiving line. It was a delightful triumph for Morris! For me, I wasn't sure I would quell the quaking inside my body even by evening's end. Although no one could fault my cream lace dress over the burnt gold lining, which enhanced my dark brown hair and made me feel optimistic and attractive, the thought of receiving so much attention was overwhelming. Morris, dressed in his dark suit, white shirt, and dark tie, looked like a patriarch. When someone would come through the line that he knew might intimidate me, he would slip his left arm easily around my waist, while greeting the person with a handshake and a smile. Because Morris was right there by my side, supporting me, I felt doubly cherished, and when the evening was concluded, I found that I too had enjoyed the celebration.

During the years that followed, we found the time to spend together in pleasures we hadn't known were possible. During these years, we visited Germany, Canada, and much of the United States, including Hawaii, as we traveled around to see our children in their moves. This also allowed us to get to know our grandchildren and be part of their lives.

"Susanna, I have just heard about an exciting adventure! I think we should be part of it! Brother Johnson was talking in high priests quorum today about a tour group of senior citizens who are traveling to the eastern United States to visit Church history sites." My good husband's face was alight with excitement. "What do you think? Should we go on it?"

"Would we have the funds available? When does it leave? Is there still time to sign up? Are you sure?" The questions tumbled out of my mouth as my brain tried to comprehend such a thrilling possibility. This was something we had always talked of doing together.

"I'll call Brother Johnson right now and get the details."

Within the week, arrangements were made for us to join the tour group for what sounded like a delightful adventure. Morris was in his element. He liked nothing better than being around people, visiting, exchanging stories, listening to their anecdotes, sharing good, wholesome fun. As for me, well it was a delight to follow along, watching and listening, absorbing the goodwill that ebbed and flowed around us. I loved being Morris's silent, but steady, partner.

It was August—glorious, warm, beautiful, relaxing August! Everywhere we looked was a bright mix of emerald green, wheat-ripened gold, or a riot of brilliant color. We rode on an enormous touring bus with high, open windows, marvelous temperature control, and lively associates. All young seniors, we were in the prime of our seniority, with vitality and good cheer. Many had pictures of grandchildren to show off and brag about. One man brought an article he had written that had been published in a magazine. Another gentleman had a song he had composed especially for us to learn. Morris didn't fall behind. He took his latest string-art to show to the others. It was a horse's head made of shiny bronzed copper wire strung on brass nails, which were pounded into a board. The picture was his own design and was truly a work of art.

The beginning of the trip was all we had anticipated.

Stories, jokes, singing, and whistling were all enjoyed as the wheels of the bus took us toward our destinations. Everyone had been listening to stories of how some of the couples had met their companions. Some were hilarious. Others were down right embarrassing, but all were told in good fun.

As the storytelling activity waned, Morris reached into his pocket, his fingers closing around his harmonica. When Morris had served his mission in the Southern States, he had learned to play the mouth organ. He owned several sizes of harmonicas and had tucked a small one into his shirt pocket—just in case such an instrument was needed on the trip. As he pulled it out, he tapped the open-holed side gently on his other hand, the way he had done countless times before. And then putting it to his mouth, he blew into it, moving the instrument back and forth, playing a quick scale up and down. That seemed to be the routine of all harmonica players. Another quick tap on his hand, and he was ready to take requests. "Oh, Johnny Oh," someone called out. Songs ranging in variety from "Nobody Knows the Trouble I've Seen," to "Goodnight, Irene," to "I've Been Workin' on the Railroad," sweetened the air. Every suggested song title was met with a slight pause, a soft grin, and then lively music. While Morris was in his element, my heart smiled.

"Morris, the group is going to the Sizzler tonight for supper. Should we join them?"

"Tonight—not—I think—" he stuttered. "Oh, Susanna, I'm feeling tired. You mind if I stay and rest?"

"Of course not. I was thinking a sandwich would taste just right after a day of sitting. I'll make you a small one too." But Morris was already asleep. I couldn't understand where his vitality of ten days before had gone. Suddenly he didn't try to visit with the others because his words would come out garbled and strange, causing him frustration and embarrassment.

"Would you like to walk with the Johnsons down by the river tonight? It's such a lovely, warm, calm evening."

"You go my love. I think bed maybe I'll go. Just a bit tired, okay?" Morris looked at me with sad, troubled eyes.

"Oh, Susanna, I ruining you lovely trip. I don't mean be tired all the time."

"You are ruining nothing. I am here with you, aren't I?" I said almost ferociously. "That is what makes the trip worthwhile and fun. Seeing all the sights are just added reason to come. But being with you is the true reason for my being here."

At first, many who knew Morris invited us to enjoy the evening activities with them because the bus would stop each suppertime at predetermined spots. Evenings were a time for socializing, window-shopping, or taking in the local tourist attractions. As time went on, the group in general began to realize that something was wrong with Morris, something he couldn't control, and something we certainly had not anticipated. He wasn't sick, really. There was no fever, no headache, no flu symptoms, nothing hurting—just a constant tiredness, garbled speech, a listlessness that was totally foreign to my normally effervescent companion.

We had visited Sharon, Vermont, Palmyra, the Hill Cumorah, the Sacred Grove, Kirtland, Nauvoo, Carthage, Liberty Jail, Independence, Adam-ondi-Ahman, Far West, and were now on our way to Chimney Rock. Our companions were not oblivious to what was happening with Morris. They knew him well and sensed something was terribly wrong. Another two or three days of sightseeing were still on the agenda, when a delegation of fellow travelers approached the bus driver.

"Take us back to Salt Lake without any more stops. Morris Teeples needs to see a doctor, and we don't think we should prolong this trip any longer," said the spokesman.

"Are you sure?" the driver asked in dismay. "You have paid for a longer tour."

"But what good is a longer tour when our hearts and minds are filled with the needs of one we love? Just drive on through to Salt Lake so Morris can receive the medical attention he needs. We are all in agreement, every last person on the bus. Please take us home."

I never thought I would be so happy to see Salt Lake City

again. With anxious trepidation, I called Dr. Call (same name but different doctor as our beloved doctor in Pocatello), our family doctor, and asked him what to do.

"Bring Morris right in, Susanna."

"I can't really help you on this after all, Susanna, but I can recommend a good specialist. In fact, I will stress the urgency of the matter and recommend that he examine Morris as soon as possible. As I have been checking Morris over, he keeps pulling at this small growth on his ear. I can remove that so it will not continue to bother him."

Dr. Call was as good as his word, and Dr. Morrison's nurse called early the following morning with an appointment time for a brain scan the next day.

"I can't believe we have sat here since eight o'clock this morning, and they still haven't called you, Morris. Let me go and inquire what is going on."

"Mrs. Teeples, we can't take your husband in for this brain scan until the proper paperwork arrives from the clinic. That is what gives us the authorization to go ahead with the scan. It should be here any time," the nurse explained apologetically.

"Okay, but he must be getting hungry. Maybe we should just slip out for a short time and get something to eat."

"That would be fine, Mrs. Teeples."

But Morris denied being hungry, and I was afraid we would lose our place in the waiting room, as the office continued to fill with people.

Finally, at about two-thirty, the paperwork was found, but by then, several people were ahead of us on the schedule. At five o'clock, a technician announced they were closing for the day and that work not finished would have to be done the following day.

"Wait! Hold it! That just can't happen." I was on my feet moving rapidly toward the man who spoke. "We have been here since early this morning. We came when we were told to come and have waited as patiently as possible, with nothing being accomplished: no lunch, no scan—this just isn't possible.

You cannot send us home without the doctor seeing my husband. He needs your help!" The anger in my voice suddenly broke with a sob. "Don't you understand? He needs your help today!"

"Okay, Mrs.—"

"Teeples, Mrs. Teeples. My husband is Morris Teeples."

"Okay, Mrs. Teeples, we will do the brain scan now, but the EKG that was requested will have to wait until tomorrow. That is the best I can do."

"Morris, I know the day has been a long, tiring one, but we just need to make a quick stop at Dr. Call's office. He was supposed to remove those stitches from your ear today. Should we just do that on the way home?"

Morris nodded slightly as I headed for the Sugar House area and Dr. Call's office. But, after having the ear checked, Dr. Call just said, "Bring Morris back in two or three days, and I'll take them out."

"Oh, I'm so sorry, Morris. That was such a futile trip. I should have just taken you home. I'll help you into the bedroom to lie down while I fix us some supper, my love."

I could tell Morris was exhausted, so I offered to take supper to him on a tray, but he preferred to be with me in the kitchen. Just as I turned briefly away to dish our plates, I heard a strange noise, and turning quickly around again, I saw Morris holding tightly to the table, staring straight ahead, shaking violently.

"Oh, Morris, something is wrong! Let me help you into bed."

With Morris leaning heavily on me, we staggered toward the bedroom. At one point, he suddenly fell to the side, knocking me into the wall.

"Just a few more steps—" I reassured him.

Morris did his best, just managing to reach the bed before he collapsed again, this time unconscious.

And then began a nightmare of telephone calls. Dr. Call could not admit Morris to the hospital because he had been turned over to another doctor. The new doctor was out of town, so I called the doctor who was supposed to be taking the doctor's patients while he was gone. That doctor was also out of town. Feeling nearly hysterical, I asked if there was anyone else I could call and was given another doctor's name. This time the doctor was in.

In the meantime, I had called Donald, Morris's brother, and he came to the house immediately, where he helped me get Morris into the car for the drive to the hospital. Having never dealt with such an emergency before, it never occurred to me to call an ambulance.

Upon arriving at the hospital, we were met by three people in medical attire with a stretcher.

"Dr. Smith has been detained by an emergency, but he has asked us to examine Mr. Teeples and inform him what is going on. Now, Mrs. Teeples, if you could just answer a few questions while we do our examination."

The first intern asked dozens of questions, and upon completing his examination, he said, "Mrs. Teeples, I can't find anything wrong with this man."

I looked at him in dismay. "You can't find anything wrong? My husband is in a coma. There is obviously something terribly wrong."

Another one of the interns began a second examination, asking many of the same questions again. Finally, he turned, "Mrs. Teeples, this is the healthiest sick man I've ever seen."

"You know, a brain scan was taken on Morris just today. Have you examined his head?"

"Well, we really aren't authorized to look at the results of that scan. We would need a doctor's authorization for that."

"Then get it! What good are you as doctors if you can't get the information you need?" I felt so alone in this highly educated medical field where they had all the answers, yet no answer at all.

By this time, the first intern had Dr. Smith on the phone. Upon hearing what had happened so far, he quickly authorized the interns to get the results of the brain scan.

"May I see the scan?" I was becoming rather intimidating in my frustration.

As the four of us looked together at the film on the lighted board, several gasped, and the female intern interjected softly, "Even a child can look at this and see that something is very wrong."

So, Morris was admitted into the hospital, with a Dr. Ericson as his doctor. The female intern, her heart softened to our need, had suggested he was the best in the valley.

Several hours later, Dr. Ericson came to the hospital to see Morris and me. What a caring, compassionate doctor he was! He had spent the previous several hours in surgery with the victim of a motorcycle accident, and yet he was not the least cross or short with me.

"Susanna," explained Dr. Ericson after talking to me for a long time, "it is possible that Morris is not in a coma. Your husband has a growth inside his head, and the day has been a long and tiring one. It is possible that the growth is swollen—like your ankles might swell when you are on your feet all day. The swelling could cause extra pressure in the brain and produce extreme sleepiness. If this is so, when the swelling has a chance to go down, Morris will wake up again."

"But is he in pain, Doctor?"

"No, Susanna, he is just resting. He is not in pain. Now, what you need to do is to go home and get some rest yourself. You can come back early tomorrow morning."

"No, Dr. Ericson. Just let me stay here. I need to be here."

In the wee hours of the morning, I was so grateful I had stayed, for Morris did wake up and slowly laid back the covers of his bed. I understood exactly what he wanted me to do and climbed into bed with him, snuggling close to his warmth for the rest of the night. I spoke softly of the surgery he was going to have to determine if the growth was malignant. Morris understood and held me tightly.

The sagacity of science and medicine is a wondrous thing.

Life expectancy has increased many-fold since my grandparents' day. Time and money are expended in huge amounts to increase man's knowledge of the things only God really knows for sure.

Morris had his operation. The tumor was both malignant and widespread. It could not be removed without extensive damage to the brain. During that morning's surgery, a small portion of the tumor was cut from the top, simply to ease the pressure and make Morris a little more comfortable. There were several options open to the family to consider: radiation, chemotherapy, or possibly more surgery. Each process would extend his life briefly. None would save it.

Each family member expressed his or her opinion, but ultimately, I had the final say. Morris was unable to speak for himself. Believe me, I wanted what was best for my sweetheart! As I sat in the cold, sterile hospital room alone with Morris, I talked through each option even though Morris could not express himself at all, his power of speech permanently withdrawn.

And I prayed. Oh, how I prayed! I needed spiritual guidance as at no other time in my life. Finally the answer came, one that would give me peace, and one I felt was what Morris would choose for himself.

When I informed our children, some were totally supportive, while others were angry, feeling I had erred in judgment. But the decision was made. I would not be swayed.

There was much for me to accomplish before they released Morris from the hospital. First of all, I needed to get our financial affairs in order and be appointed by the court to be Morris's legal guardian. And then I needed to learn how to care for him properly because I was determined I was going to take him home instead of putting him in a nursing home. A lawyer in my ward helped me take care of the legal aspects, but I told no one about my determination to care for Morris myself because I knew I would have a fight on every hand.

Chapter 18

I barely came to Morris's shoulder, a fact I had loved over the years because it made me feel protected by an impressive guardian. Morris was a big man. I was a small woman. I had never received any training in nursing. Of course, I had nursed my family when they were ill with common childhood ailments, but other than desire and tenderness, I was ill prepared to care for this man I loved. I did have a warm home, an extensive food supply, washing facilities, and a vehicle to use when needed. I did not have a hospital bed that could be moved up and down, a wheelchair, or any help. As much as my family loved their dad, they each had families of their own and lives of their own. Morris was my responsibility and my life.

What I did have, most of all, was tenacity. No one realized at first just how far that one trait would carry me. Besides, they referred to it as being stubborn.

Roxaline, a buxom brunette who was quite outspoken, was the head nurse at the hospital. She was the first one to run into this brick wall of determination, and she didn't like the encounter one bit.

"Mrs. Teeples, I cannot let you stay in the room when the nurses are caring for Morris. You just need to step out for a few minutes while they do their job, and then you can go in again."

"All I want to do is see what they are doing. What can be so wrong in that? I won't get in the way, Roxaline."

"I don't have the authority to grant your request. Please

just cooperate on this, Mrs. Teeples."

So the answer to my desire was a resounding no—until I spoke to Dr. Ericson.

In my heart, I was smiling, thinking I had gotten my way fairly easily because Dr. Ericson gave his permission for me to watch all that was done to care for Morris. I should have known it was much too simple.

For some reason, the nurses acted like I was trying to interfere in their work. So even though they did allow me to watch, they would not talk to me or explain simple procedures or answer questions that would have been easy for them to discuss with me. As time went on, they even did little things to irritate me. I guess they felt that somehow they would discourage me from—whatever it was I was trying to prove by being in the room.

One crisp, crimson and gold autumn morning in early October, I arrived at the hospital to find that Morris had been given a laxative. It had worked! But no one had come to clean up the resulting mess.

Even after reporting the need for assistance to the nurse's station, no one came. We waited for almost two hours. The next thing I knew, the nurses were talking of going to lunch. I knew help was *not* on its way.

Speaking gently to Morris, I explained what I was going to do. "Sweetheart, I hope I don't hurt you, but I am going to clean you up again so you smell fresh and sweet. I need to find some clean sheets, another hospital gown, and some disposable wipes. Don't worry, I will be right back."

Pulling the top sheet from the bed, I spread it on the floor to hold all the soiled items. I washed Morris thoroughly with soap and water, all the while talking to him, and then dressed him in a clean hospital gown. Carefully, while still explaining to him what I was doing, I rolled him over on his side and began changing the sheets on the bed. By rolling him from one side to the other, I was able to accomplish that formidable task. When I was finally finished, Morris fell asleep immediately with a slight smile on his face. He had lived with me for a long time, and besides being grateful for what I had done, he understood. He understood my pleasure in caring for him, and he understood my triumph in being able to do so. He had always understood me perfectly.

Because I certainly didn't want to retain the smelly package in Morris's room, I tied the corners of the sheet together and left it right in front of the nurse's station in the hall.

After a while, I could hear the nurses coming back from lunch. They were talking and laughing among themselves. When they spotted the stinky bundle in the middle of the hall, there was some whispering and then it went completely quiet.

Finally, the male nurse tapped at the door and asked, "Mrs. Teeples, may I come in?"

Imagine that, a nurse asking if he could come in. "Of course," I stated calmly. He came in and looked around.

"Is his blood pressure all right?" I inquired.

"He's fine," was the answer after a quick check of vitals. "When did he go to sleep?"

"As soon as I got him clean and on his back again."

Almost immediately, there seemed to be a change of attitude among the nursing staff. Whereas before they had been belligerent and uncooperative, now they spoke freely to me, explaining equipment and procedures in detail. And I soaked it all in like a hungry sponge.

The time was nearing, according to the doctors, for me to choose a suitable nursing home in which to place Morris where he would be well cared for and comfortable. Roxaline, the head nurse, described each possibility to me in detail, explaining their merits. I think even Roxaline had come, with some reluctance, to like and respect me. But that regard was fragile, at best.

"Mrs. Teeples, have you decided which nursing home to line up for Morris? Dr. Ericson is going to be out of town for a few days, but by Monday, when he returns, you need to have made a decision so he can sign the referral papers."

"Well, Roxaline, I'm glad you brought that up." (Actually, I had been dreading this encounter.) "I have decided not to put Morris into any nursing home. I have a warm, comfortable home, and I plan on taking him home with me and caring for him myself."

"Caring for him yourself?" Roxaline's face was contorted with her indignation. "Are you mad? You can't do that!" she spat out angrily.

"And why not?" I had known this was going to be an uncomfortable standoff. Roxaline didn't really know me nearly as well as she thought she did, but I felt I knew her pretty well by now. I knew she was going to be not only unhappy about my decision but on the fight. I wasn't disappointed.

"I know I haven't received formal nurses' training, but I have been observing everything that is done for Morris. I know I can do it."

"Is that why you have been watching the nurses so carefully?" Her voice was now full of sarcasm. "You can't put in an IV, and that is how Morris is being fed. I went through years of schooling to know how to do these things," announced Roxaline triumphantly. "And even if you *could* learn to do that, a registered nurse is required to supervise that procedure."

"There has got to be a way," I stated softly. "There just has to be because I *am* taking my husband home."

I hadn't meant for it to happen this way, but the battle lines were drawn. I knew Roxaline would try to convince Dr. Ericson that "Mrs. Teeples was a stubborn, delirious woman who was incapable of accomplishing what she wanted to do."

That evening, I met the doctor who was on call in Dr. Ericson's absence. When he made his rounds to Morris's room, we visited together for a few minutes about inconsequential matters. And then the conversation turned to Morris's need to soon be out of the hospital. In an amazingly short period of time, I felt a special rapport with this doctor. Finally I screwed up my courage and asked, "Doctor, do you think I could take care of Morris at home?"

His eyes perused me up and down. "You're pretty small, Mrs. Teeples, and Morris is a big man."

Now if Roxaline had said that to me, I probably would have given her some kind of an argument about Morris losing weight since being sick, etc. Instead, I replied, "Doctor, in my day we took care of our own sick. I have been watching everything the nurses do for Morris." With direct eye contact I pled my case. "I really feel I can do this. I want him to receive good attention. I love this man dearly, and I wouldn't suggest I should take him home unless I felt I could give him adequate care."

The doctor looked at me again, as if taking my true measure, and then he said, "Yes, I believe you could care for your husband."

Shocked and pleased with his answer, I replied, "Oh, will you tell Dr. Ericson that when he comes back?"

"Well, we'll talk," he said as he left the room, a slight smile crossing his lips.

No one awaited Dr. Ericson's return with more trepidation or anxiety than me. So, when I heard him talking to Roxaline by the nurses' station on Monday afternoon, I entered the hallway slowly and carefully.

"Mrs. Teeples is being totally obstinate, Dr. Ericson. She refuses to consider any nursing home for Morris. She won't even go look at one to see what the facility is like." Tightly wound up, Roxaline was expressing all her frustration in a rush.

Out of the corner of his eye, Dr. Ericson could see me approaching. He waited with his reply until I was even with them, and Roxaline was aware of my presence. Looking me straight in the eye, Dr. Ericson answered, "Yes, Mrs. Teeples, I believe we will let you take Morris home to care for him."

Simultaneously, I responded, "Oh, thank you, Doctor," while Roxaline exclaimed in a shocked voice, "Doctor, you must be out of your mind!"

As Dr. Ericson leveled a look at Roxaline, she knew she

was out of order. "We will have to talk about several things, but we will let Mrs. Teeples try."

As I returned to Morris's room, I gave a slight squeal of delight. "Morris, you can come home! The doctor has given his permission. Back home to our house. Oh, I'm so grateful!" As I held Morris's hand, he gently squeezed mine to show that he understood and was also pleased.

Never before had I wanted things to work out as much as I did this time. I had no idea how long Morris would live. But I so wanted him to live in comfort and with dignity. For weeks, my total energy had been focused on being given permission to take Morris home. Now I needed to make sure our home was ready so I could care for him there. On the top of my priority list was an electric hospital bed I had already chosen that needed to be delivered to the house. Because I was planning for the long term, I purchased the bed instead of renting it.

The following day, Roxaline arranged a time for Dr. Ericson to meet with me. I quickly realized this was no small adventure. The doctor explained several things. We discussed the problem of the IV for feeding. I would not be able to use that method at home. Roxaline had been correct when she said that procedure had to be supervised by a nurse. Dr. Ericson suggested we use a gavage, a method of feeding that involved passing a tube through one nostril into the stomach. Liquids could be administered through the tube.

"Ensure is a complete food in liquid form, sometimes used for babies when they are struggling, to give them a start. It is quite rich, but after a short spell of diarrhea while Morris's body adjusts to the richness, that will stop. In the meantime, I will prescribe some pills that can be mashed and mixed with the formula so the diarrhea doesn't become too aggravated."

"Do the babies have diarrhea too?" I inquired.

"Oh, no, we dilute the Ensure with lots of water so the babies' systems can absorb the richness of the food slowly," explained Dr. Ericson.

Morris would not have diarrhea, nor would he need to be

given the pills. I was determined to do what was best for him and in a way that would cause him the least distress. Already I could see better ways of doing things for his best good.

Roxaline was still aghast to think she would be filling boxes with supplies for me to take home. With real reluctance, she explained how to use the gavage tube. "Several other problems might arise," she said, as she methodically and professionally talked through those with me.

I wasn't to learn until several months later that Dr. Ericson never expected me to be able to keep Morris at home. Roxaline was also unaware of the reverse psychology he was employing. The good doctor actually figured that letting me try was the surest way to end the discussion and get Morris to a nursing home.

As when I was sixteen and abruptly called upon to care for my birth family, I really had no idea of the commitment I was making. But, I was still a fast learner! My determination to succeed and my love for my eternal companion spurred me on to be the best nurse he could possibly have. A community nurse was assigned to check by the house daily to bathe Morris and answer any questions I had concerning Morris's care.

When the nurse arrived the first day, I invited her in. She seemed pleasant, and it was good to visit with someone. After looking around at our clean, orderly home and talking for a few minutes, she was ready to get to work.

"If you could just get me a large bowl of water and a wash cloth, I will give Morris his bath," she said with a smile.

"Oh, I've already bathed him this morning and changed his sheets. Would you like to see him?" I asked, motioning her toward the bedroom.

Morris lay comfortably in bed. His face was shaved, his hair was combed, and his body looked and smelled clean.

"Well, Mrs. Teeples, I will check his vital signs while I am here, but you have him clean and fresh and have done a beautiful job. There really isn't anything else for me to do."

After three consecutive days of checking by the commu-

nity nurse, the health care board decided to discontinue the nurse's daily visits unless I called with a specific problem, because each day I had the sheets changed and Morris washed and fed when the health care worker arrived.

In my determination to care for Morris the very best that I could, I purchased a sheepskin for him to lie on so he wouldn't develop bedsores. The sheepskin was the recommended prevention. In the hospital, I had been concerned because they left him sitting or lying in one position for such a long period of time. By projecting how tired I became after sitting still or lying on one side for an extended interval, I was more aware of Morris's need to have his body weight shifted regularly. Early on in my care for him, I resolved to keep his body free of sores.

Much of the care I gave my husband was trial and error. Fortunately, he didn't have a choice except to be extremely patient with me because he could not move himself. He could not speak to me. He could not laugh with me, although often I felt he must have been laughing inside at my feeble attempts.

Even with all his weight loss, Morris was still a large man. The first time I stood him on his feet just about overwhelmed us both. I had been thinking constantly about how to help Morris stand up for a few minutes each day so the circulation in his legs would be more normal. A push of a button on the hospital bed sat him upright. The sidebars on the bed were easy to lower so I could move his legs over the side. Leaning across his chest and taking a firm grip on the sheepskin behind his shoulders, with a—one—two—three—PULL, I stood him up against me. He was definitely heavier than I had anticipated. Rocking back and forth slightly, I spread my legs and established a balance for us. While I stood there holding him, I rubbed his back and talked to him. As always, he understood what I was trying to accomplish. Five minutes is a long time to hold this position, but my, it was good for him. I could see his feet were pinker. The blood was flowing freely.

Not wanting to overtire him, I knew it was time to put

him back in bed. I was able to sit him back down on the bed, laying him back gently, and lift his legs up onto the bed. The only problem was, for some reason his feet now hung far over the end.

"I'm thinking, my love," I said rather out of breath, as I put some pillows under his legs against the footboard. Even in his exhaustion, I could see the smile play on his face. "I can do this. Let me see." After a short rest, up I stood with a plan. Moving toward the head of the bed, I grasped the sheepskin, which had shifted over to one side. "If I pull this hard and fast enough, I think it will work. One—two—three—PULL." It worked all right. The sheepskin came sliding out from beneath Morris like a magician's tablecloth. Morris had not moved.

Carefully rolling Morris from side to side, I returned the sheepskin to the bed, this time positioning it more uniformly underneath him. Again I tried, but instead of pulling with one large jerk, I pulled slowly, stopping to rest frequently. By small degrees, Morris moved back up into the middle of the bed where he needed to be. For the next seven months, I changed Morris's position every two hours, day and night.

Nursing is a skill and an art. By watching a substitute nurse change the gavage tube in his nose, I realized I needed to learn how to do that without hurting him. I could see she had hurt him, as the tears ran down his cheeks during the procedure. It should not have to hurt that way! I was afraid to try. The next time I called, needing the gavage tube changed, a more experienced male nurse came, and while he worked, he explained the principle behind the procedure. "When putting a gavage down someone's nose, you need to gently push it in while they breathe in and stop pushing when they exhale."

"I'm glad you do that so well, without hurting my husband." This was the way it should work, I could tell. "Thank you."

"Now you try it." Justin, the male nurse, indicated I should take the tube from him and carefully finish the process.

"Oh, no! I couldn't! What if I do it wrong?" I was shaking

my head as my eyes misted up.

"How else are you going to learn? I will help you so you get it right, and it will not hurt Morris. I promise! C'mon, Susanna, you can do this." Hearing Justin verbalize what I had told myself so often before, I smiled thinly and gave it a try. And it worked, slowly but surely, it worked.

Over the intervening months, my diet was pretty boring because I cooked what was easiest and fastest for me to eat. I needed to conserve my strength for my nursing duties. I did have a good food supply on hand in my food storage. Other than fresh produce and dairy products, I pretty well had what I needed. I was concerned for Morris though. If I thought my homemade stew day after day was boring, what must he think of his dull diet? Whatever food I fed him had to be liquid so it could go directly into his stomach through the gavage tube. From happier, more normal days, I remembered that Morris liked fruit juice. I had several kinds in my storage and purchased others, particularly cranberry juice, at the store when I would slip away for a half hour of food shopping. And so, every day, I gave Morris some fruit juice, as a snack, between his feedings of Ensure.

One snowy morning, not long before Christmas, the doorbell rang. It was Justin, my favorite nurse.

"Hi, Susanna. Merry Christmas!" And he thrust a basket full of fruit and nuts into my hands.

"You are so darn sweet. All I have to share back is some snickerdoodles that are just coming out of the oven. Some of my grandkids are coming for Christmas," I replied as I ushered him through the door.

"Snickerdoodles are my all-time favorite cookies. Got any milk to go with them?" Justin chuckled as he entered the house. "Umm, it smells delicious in here."

After enjoying his cookies and milk, Justin headed for the bedroom. "Let's get that catheter changed, Morris." (One of the reasons I loved Justin was because he talked to Morris like he could hear and respond, just like I did.)

"What have you been feeding this man of yours, Susanna?" Justin inquired as he removed the used catheter to replace it with a new one. "Have you been feeding him something besides what the doctor gave you?" His voice asked the question, while sounding like he already knew the answer.

"Why, is something wrong, Justin?" I honestly had not thought to get permission about the juice.

"Just answer the question." Justin continued with his job, his back turned in my direction.

"Well, yes—just some juice. I still feed him the Ensure at every feeding. But you know, Justin, that diet must get awfully boring after a while." Defending my reasoning, I rushed on. "How would you like to drink only Ensure every meal?"

"Morris can't taste it, you know." I could see Justin's shoulders shaking with laughter.

"He can't?" I hadn't thought about that.

"No, he can't. However, I thought you were giving him cranberry juice. It is one of the best things you can give him. It clears the kidneys and keeps the catheter from corroding as quickly." Justin turned with a smile. "You know, Susanna, you are a darned good nurse. Even when you don't know what you are doing, you do things right."

High praise from Justin! That statement had been better than the Christmas basket of goodies.

"Oh, Justin, you really know how to make a person's day." And I gave him an appreciative hug.

For Christmas that year, some of the grandchildren came for a week to Grandma's house. It was a different Christmas, to say the least. They loved their grandfather, but they didn't know how to act around him. This was the man who had always met them in the driveway as the car pulled up. He had homemade root beer in the basement and homemade ice cream in the freezer. Because Morris was always working on some kind of a wood project, the grandchildren were used to working alongside him, not seeing him just lie there, not moving. I asked them to talk to him and hold his hand. "He might even squeeze it," I told them. But the children were young. They really didn't understand. Besides, Morris's hand squeeze was getting pretty weak. I could still feel it faintly—sometimes.

And so the winter passed.

One lovely spring morning in late March, with my internal alarm clock working perfectly, I awoke to the sounds of birds chirping outside and felt a slight, refreshing breeze coming through the open window into the bedroom. I stretched and arose quickly to check on Morris. I had gotten into the habit of singing hymns and ditties as I worked with him so he could hear the sound of my voice. We had developed a system of him squeezing my hand after I had cared for him. It was such a reassuring form of communication, and we both treasured his ability to ever so gently acknowledge his love for me in this subtle way. I was pleased with the way my own body had adjusted to the schedule we had perfected together. We always had been a great team.

With clean linens, Morris washed, shaved, and fed, and my bath and breakfast accomplished as well, imagine my surprise when the doorbell rang. There, paying us an unexpected but not unwelcome visit, was Roxaline. I invited her into Morris's room and we visited for quite some time.

"Mrs. Teeples—"

"It's Susanna."

"Susanna, you are doing a wonderful job here. I know I didn't think you could do this, but you are and you have, and I take my nurse's hat off to you. It is such a big job, though, and so constant. Why don't you let us take Morris back to the hospital for just a week or two so you can have a rest? And then you could bring him back home again."

"No, Roxaline. Morris will never go back to the hospital again. He is home, where he wants to be, and where I want him to be."

"Honestly, Susanna, I'm not trying to undermine the work you have been doing here. I just thought I could give you a small break—"

And then, while giving me a slight hug on the doorstep, "I want to tell you, you're doing a marvelous job. And I want to tell you something else. If you ever need work, give us a call. People frequently leave the hospital who need someone to stay with them for a little while, and we could put you in touch with them." The thought made me a bit tired, but it was difficult to know what would happen next or when.

One short week later, I realized that Morris was no longer responding to the massaging of limbs. Nor was he able to squeeze my hand in thanks—not even slightly. He seemed whiter and stiller. What to do? I called a cousin who was a registered nurse and asked her to come and check Morris's vital signs. After the checkup, Jesse was quiet and guarded in her comments. When I asked her if I should call Daryl, my son living in Bountiful, she said yes.

My love, my only love! The one I had lived for, cared for, and would have gladly died for, quietly and peacefully slipped from this mortal life on March 29, 1978. Daryl, Jesse, and I were in the room with him. I was not sorry for his release from a body that no longer functioned properly. But I found in the days that followed how much I missed him. I did not care that he had been in a subdued state for the past several months. My heart longed for his presence once again. I looked forward to eternity.

Chapter 19

I am living in Canada—a foreign country. Isn't that strange? I never expected to live so far away from the Salt Lake home Morris and I purchased together. There, in our little bungalow, we enjoyed a fine degree of peace and joy. But Morris was gone. And I was lonesome!

My youngest daughter, Karen, lives here. She suggested that I come and live closer to her family. That was a major decision to make: to sell my home where I had been so happy with Morris, to give away many of my earthly possessions, and to say good-bye to long-time neighbors and friends. It was with considerable reluctance that I decided to uproot myself after being established in Salt Lake City for so many years.

What would I do with myself in Canada? But then, what was I doing in Salt Lake? I attended the temple. I could do that in Cardston. Sometimes I played my piano. I drove my van. I read my scriptures, watched old movies, and crocheted. I could do all of those things in Canada. Some of my grandchildren would be able to visit me every day. We could laugh and talk together. We could enjoy our association. What were families for, if we didn't love and care for one another? Over the years, Morris and I had visited Cardston many times. Often we had remarked to one another that it was a pleasant place. Morris's spirit could be with me there just as easily as in Salt Lake. And so I made the move.

My oldest daughter, DeNiece, passed away about a year after Morris's passing. After suffering for over a decade with

multiple sclerosis, she was released from this earth life. Thank goodness for her faithful husband who took such tender care of her in her illness, and thank goodness for a merciful Heavenly Father who called her home. And to think that Morris could be there to greet her!

My oldest son, Elred, still lives in California. My middle son, Barth, lives in Tooele. Daryl, my youngest son, lives in Bountiful. Living in closest proximity to me, Daryl visits me as often as he can, but of course, he is busy with his own job and family responsibilities. All are married with families, good jobs, and busy lives.

My living conditions are good. I live in a government housing unit, which allows me to pay a percentage of my income for rent, still leaving me enough to live comfortably. I feel I have the best apartment in the building because the view is toward the Lord's temple.

Back in Salt Lake, after Morris passed away, I worked at several jobs to provide a living for myself. At age seventy, jobs weren't all that easy to come by, but the Lord blessed me abundantly to find the work and provided the energy I needed to carry it through.

During that time, I cared for an elderly, handicapped woman in my home. Thankfully, I found I could get up and attend the Salt Lake Temple on a weekly basis if I attended the five a.m. session. By going early, I could be back in my home by seven-thirty when Isabel would be waking up for the day. Somehow I felt closer to Morris in the temple than anywhere else, so the sacrifice of early morning attendance didn't seem too great.

On one particular winter's morning, the darkness and chill were compounded by a heavy rain and a stiff wind. I awoke early, as was my routine. After checking the weather outside, I debated whether to go to the temple that day. I wandered into the bathroom, back into the living room to survey the storm through the window, and then back into my bedroom. It would be so easy to climb back into bed and snuggle deep into my comforter for a little more sleep! But even as I contemplated this possibility, some special presence seemed to push me into getting dressed and ready to go.

When the decision had been made, and once I was outside sitting in the cold car, I again contemplated the advisability of a twenty-minute drive through that type of weather. The one good thing about it, I reasoned, was there wouldn't be much traffic at that time in the morning; so I finally decided to brave the elements and go. The bare-branched trees, whipped into a frenzy of activity, seemed like they would attack my car with their long skinny fingers as I carefully backed out of the driveway and into a water-laden street.

I think I must have misread my clock when I arose, for even with all my indecision about going, I arrived in downtown Salt Lake at the temple parking lot long before any temple workers. Sitting in my car, I watched until a lone man dressed in white came to unlock the temple gate. Hurrying across the street and through the gate, I was glad to go inside the warm temple annex. The short, white-haired brother standing at the recommend desk greeted me with, "My, Sister, you are very early this morning. After you have changed into your temple clothing, you are welcome to go directly to the creation room to wait for the first session to begin."

As I sat down in that lovely room—the clouds and sky painted on the ceiling overhead, the lush green vegetation on the walls—I was enveloped with a feeling of amazing sweetness. I don't know if I prayed or meditated or just absorbed the peacefulness of my surroundings, but when the feeling lifted, I realized the room was filling with people. Listening to the soothing instructional words of the temple ceremony, I pondered the spiritual manifestation I had experienced, wondering just what it meant.

As usual, I thoroughly enjoyed being in the house of the Lord. There is always such a calmness of spirit there. Outside cares seem to recede as eternal possibilities fill the mind. This day, I seemed more alert and attentive than ever before. My mind seemed clearer and more perceptive. What a wonderful way to begin the day!

After dressing back into street clothes covered by my warm winter coat and upon leaving the temple, I realized the rain had stopped. Looking up, I saw sun dogs—Morris's favorite celestial display—breaking through the clouds and sending down rays of sparkling light through the receding mist onto the shiny wet pavement. My heart felt full to bursting in my knowledge of my Heavenly Father's love and goodness to me. What a beautiful winter day he had created to gladden my spirit and delight my soul!

This profound spiritual feeling, on top of the hallowed experience I had just enjoyed inside the temple, caused my eyes to fill with unexplained tears as a feeling of warmth enveloped me. And then a voice spoke, saying, "Morris needs your help at the temple." With a rush of understanding, I marveled how my morning activity had helped Morris complete his missionary work on the other side of the veil. I had prayed that the sister whose endowment I was doing in the temple would be receptive to the work being done in her behalf. Now I knew for a surety that not only had the covenants been accepted, but that Morris was the missionary who had helped teach her the gospel of Jesus Christ. We were still being allowed to be a marvelous team.

My apartment in Cardston was designed for a handicapped person. Therefore, it is larger than the other apartments in this building. Because a handicapped person has never applied to live here, they rented it to me. Because of a little more room, I was able to bring several of my possessions with me: my upright spinet piano (a gift from Morris), my electric hospital bed (I need only to press a button at bedtime when I am tired of reading, and I am lowered into a reclining position for sleep), my cedar chest (filled with my most prized possessions—letters and pictures of family and friends), my typewriter (I am teaching myself to type), and my sewing machine (a long-time friend which has produced many homemade items over the years). I was also able to bring my Volkswagen van! It is parked right outside my living room window. Having my own set of wheels makes me feel I still have some degree of independence, and that is important to me.

The thing I do not have, and which I miss terribly, is my beloved Morris. I often sit and contemplate how he could have left me so many years ago to live by myself without his constant physical love. Others have been good to me. My family visits and carts me around with them. Frequently they write or call on the phone. In fact, Karen, or a member of her family, brings my supper every evening. It's a part of the day I genuinely enjoy because it means a visit from one of them, as well.

But Morris has truly been my life. How could I ever have wondered, even for a second, if I loved him enough to marry him? I thank my Heavenly Father daily for my inspired bishop who advised me to marry Morris and my training from stalwart parents that I should always follow a bishop's advice. Even as the children grew up, as much as I cared for them and tried in every way to anticipate their needs, my driving force in everything I accomplished was Morris. I was a better person because I wanted him to be proud of me. To see his love shining in his eyes for me—shy, ungifted, backward Susanna—was a treat I never tired of.

I have prayed for years for Morris to come and take me home, to our heavenly home, to be with him. I try to be patient, knowing the Lord will answer me in his own good time. Last night as I said my prayers and went to bed, I had a persistent thought. Acting upon it, I got up and pinned my diamond brooch from Morris onto my clothes.

When Morris took me to the Logan Temple those many years ago, he gave me a beautiful ruby solitaire with white gold etching on the sides of a slender gold band. After we had been married many years, I lost the ruby stone from the ring as I sat in the hot baths at Lava Hot Springs, relaxing at the end of a full day's work. The pool bottom was covered with a thick layer of small smooth stones to allow the natural hot mineral water to bubble freely out of the ground and into the pool. We would sit on the cedar benches in the pool, the hot water coming up to our shoulders. There were always people to visit with, as the warm water did its work of soothing and relaxing sore muscles. Of course, when we discovered the ruby was missing, there was not a chance of finding it between the rocks. What a disappointment! The loss was a hard one for me because I knew we did not have the money to buy another ring.

One winter evening in late November, I still remember Morris saying, "Susanna, on Monday it will be our fortieth wedding anniversary. What would you think if I invited our family to come and celebrate it with us at the Sizzler in Sugar House? I think everyone likes their food."

Pleasantly surprised, I agreed. "That would be great! I'd love it!" Morris wasn't one to eat out at restaurants very often, always claiming he liked my menu best. Because I loved to eat out, both the thought and the gesture were especially appreciated.

On Monday, when we were all seated in a private corner of the room, Morris stood up and declared, "Thank you all for coming. This is a very special evening for Mom and me. We have been married for forty years. You might think that is a long time for this good woman to put up with a man like me, but thankfully she has done that. This evening, I have a special presentation to make to her to reward her fortitude." And then, pulling out my chair, he motioned for me to stand up next to him. "Stand up here by me, Mother. I'm going to tell a story about you!"

He grinned down at me and then went on, "You see, many years ago when we lived in Lava Hot Springs, this good woman took care of our family in a way I was unable to at the time. She knew you had to be cared for, so she did all in her power to provide what you needed. In the meantime, I was kind of a sickly guy." He grinned and went on, "One of the real pleasures she derived at the end of a long, hard-working day was to go to the public hot baths and soak out her aches and pains. I knew she really liked the hot water, and I really liked being with her, so I would usually go too. Actually, I quite enjoyed it as well," he reminisced, a far-away look in his eye. "Remember those days, sweetheart?" he said as he pulled me firmly into his side.

"Well, one evening, after we had gone back to our dressing rooms to change out of our swimming suits, she noticed that the ruby was gone from her wedding ring." Here he pulled me in even closer to him. "She was pretty sad about that. We went to the ticket sales office and reported the loss, hoping someone might find it, but of course, it was never found. We knew at the time that was pretty unlikely."

Everyone had been caught up in the tale. Morris loved to tell a good story. "So this evening, I thought maybe it was about time I replaced that tiny ruby with a real diamond. You see, I couldn't afford a diamond when we first got married." My eyes got big as Morris held up my left hand which he had been holding and slipped my original wedding band onto my finger. The gaping hole of so many years was filled with a large, twinkling diamond.

What a surprise! What a grand surprise! My Morris loved surprises!

Some years later, I developed an allergy, which would not allow me to wear my rings. The gold made my fingers itch and swell. But I certainly didn't want to stop wearing the diamond—this elegant reminder of Morris's eternal love—so I had the gem reset in a lovely gold filigree pin.

How pleasant to reminisce in my mind about that lovely memory. Sometimes I forget to wear my significant diamond pin, but tonight night I feel Morris is reminding me to pin it on my clothes, so he will be close to my heart.

Putting memories aside for the night, and after saying my evening prayers, a softly lingering but persistent thought remains: tomorrow is the day I should return home. I assume that means home to Salt Lake. I am still driving my little, white Volkswagen van, and I'm sure I can find my way home, if I drive carefully. I will eat a good breakfast and be on my way before noon. I could ask Karen the way to Salt Lake, but of course, she wouldn't let me go alone. Actually, we are scheduled to drive to Salt Lake in about four days' time. Her family is going to vacation there, and they have asked me to accompany them. It's strange. I have been so reluctant to go with them, wishing to stay at home. But now, I want to go home tomorrow—tomorrow is the day I am to go. I'm not quite sure about "home" lately—except that tomorrow I know it is time to *go home.*

Tomorrow is today! After several days of wet spring drizzle and cooler weather, this day is so beautiful! The lingering snow is gone and the pale blue sky has only a smattering of leftover clouds. The sun feels warm and good as it seeps into my old bones. As I think back about it, it's a day much like the one when I first met Morris: a lovely spring day—my favorite time of year.

Sixteen years ago—exactly to the day—Morris left me to return to his heavenly home. He had such a peaceful look on his face, I'm sure he was greeting Lodisa and Ransford with fond hugs and tender kisses and shaking hands with my dad. Mama would have been there, meeting Morris for the first time. I know she would have given him a huge hug, thanking him for taking such good care of her little Susanna, and he would have loved her instantly.

I am feeling a little uncertain as to the road I am to take to travel to Salt Lake. It seems I should travel out of town a little way and then turn off on another road, to be correct. Where should I turn? Where should I turn? There, I am sure that is the road. I'll just drive down it for a bit and see if I am right.

Oh, this road is not the main road. I can plainly see that. I will have to turn around and go back. Or, maybe not, if I turn here, I can see a main road just up there a ways.

Oh, Susanna, now you've done it. I should have turned around while I had the chance. The van is stuck in the mud. It's okay, though. I just need to walk through that field. There is an opening in the fence just back there, and I can find someone to help me get unstuck.

This field is rather rough going, and somehow I left my cane in the van. I never go anywhere without my cane—not so much as to the door of my apartment. But it's okay. I'm amazed at how easy it is to walk on this uneven soil. What is ahead in the field? It's lighter and brighter than the rest of the ground.

Morris, my beloved Morris is walking toward me! He remembered! He remembered to come and get me. He must still love me, after all these years! Love me enough to finally come and get me!

"Oh, Susanna, my darling Susanna! It is time for you to come home. I hoped you had received my message last night. I have been waiting for this time to come and get you. You won't believe the beautiful place I have ready for you. Oh, Susanna, it is so good to be with you again!"

Epilogue

Late March 1994

Karen took Susanna's supper to her about six o'clock in the evening of March 29, 1994. Standing in the entryway, pushing the buzzer, Karen waited a little impatiently. The family was leaving for Utah in just a couple of days, and there was much she needed to get accomplished before they would be ready to go. She was so glad her mom had finally consented to go with them. After the second ring, when Susanna didn't respond over the intercom with her usual cheery voice, Karen buzzed a neighbor's apartment to ask for admittance. Susanna's next-door neighbor and friend let her in immediately.

Karen set the covered plate on the floor by Susanna's apartment door, feeling a slight bit frustrated that her mom had never given her a key to her apartment. She couldn't go inside to see if something was wrong. Looking out the hallway window, Karen realized the Volkswagen van was gone.

"She's probably down getting her mail at the post office," Karen reasoned. "She'll give me a call when she returns because she loves to visit with me at the end of the day."

Finally Karen's phone did ring. But when she answered it, it was the neighbor saying that Susanna's dinner was still sitting by her door, and Susanna had not returned.

Karen immediately got into her car and began looking for Susanna's van. The community of Cardston was small, and it didn't take long for her to realize that her mom was in none of the familiar places where she often drove. Beginning to feel alarmed, Karen stopped an RCMP officer and asked him to help her look for a white Volkswagen van. She then returned home, asking her husband and several others who were at the house if they would help her look for her mother. They all quickly complied. Susanna's van was not to be found.

Wondering if her mom had tried to drive back to Salt Lake by herself, Karen drove to the United States-Canadian border to ask if a white Volkswagen minivan had gone through that crossing that evening. She was assured one had not.

Now feeling desperate, Karen and her husband, Leroy, drove to another small community to see if Susanna had become confused in her driving and had gone the opposite direction. The longer they drove, searching, the heavier Karen's heart felt. She was frightened! It was well after dark. She knew her mother felt the cold easily and would be prone to hypothermia in the chill of the evening.

As the darkness deepened, and still with no success, Leroy suggested he line up a small plane for morning, to continue the search via air. Through a long, restless night, they worried. Leroy was up and moving early to meet the pilot. Karen stayed home to answer the phone, if needed.

A couple of hours passed, with neighbors and friends arriving to offer their comfort and support. About midmorning, Karen saw an RCMP officer getting out of his vehicle in front of the house. Obviously there was news of some kind!

"Where is she? Is she alive?" Karen questioned as she rushed out the front door, meeting him in the middle of the driveway.

"Let's go into the living room and sit down, Mrs. Walker." Immediately she knew her mom was dead. She had been found, and she was dead.

After first searching further afield, the small biplane had spotted the minivan not far from town. It was parked on a soggy, rutted country road. But Susanna was not there. Her cane was inside, but she was gone. More hunting and then they spotted her: she was face down in a field, about one and one-half miles from the van, her gray-brown hair and tan clothing blending in with the dry stubble covering the field.

She had been walking away from the existing farmhouses in the vicinity. Although the field was rough and uneven, she was not bruised from falling; only the bottoms of her feet showed evidence of the rugged terrain she had crossed. Stretched out on the ground, not curled up as if cold or distressed, her hand was clutched over the lovely diamond pin she wore inside her blouse.

About the Author

Karen T. Walker was born in Pocatello, Idaho, and raised in Lava Hot Springs, Idaho, and Salt Lake City. She now lives in Cardston, Alberta, Canada. She received her bachelor's degree in homemaking education from Brigham Young University in the summer of 1967.

Teaching school took a backseat to enjoying a satisfying team effort with her husband, Leroy, in raising a family of six children. Now that all of the children are married with families of their own, she is involved in the joy of being a grandmother.

Karen has always loved to read. She believes that avid readers should have a choice of uplifting, inspirational novels. Just as members of other cultures and religions write freely and extensively about their lives, so too, Karen believes, LDS culture should be shared and enjoyed.

Oh Susanna is Karen's first published novel. As a writer, she is self-taught, and she finds that the more she writes, the more she enjoys writing. Her public teaching background, leadership responsibilities in the LDS Church, and speaking opportunities have all supplemented her ability to tell a good story.